DIFFICULT BUT NOT IMPOSSIBLE

With the wipe of a dish towel, the last pan is dry. The dishes was the last chore momma gave him. Now the boy can go in the living room and play with his army men.

He jumps off his step stool and puts it in the closet by the hallway door. He runs over to the toy chest, where he gets his army men out. Counts them. Forty-nine. Wait. He sees two army men legs sticking out from underneath the jack-in-the-box. He pulls the army man out. Fifty!

He sets the army men up in battle formation.

"This is your commander," the boy says in a voice so official it's almost robotic, "We have the enemy surrounded. Prepare to attack."

Momma is at the door. Three fast knocks and two slow knocks. That's how he knows it's Momma. She must be back from the five-and-dime early. She doesn't like taking her key when she leaves him alone. In case something happens to her, no stranger would get her house key.

The boy goes to the hallway door. He always checks the peephole just in case. He drags his step stool to the door and stands on it. He looks out the peephole and sees momma waiting there. Momma doesn't look right though. She's scared. She glances over her shoulder, behind her.

"Andy!" she yells from the other side of the door, "Let me in right away please. There's something-"

Another even louder knock comes from the kitchen door at the back of the house. Three fast knocks two slow also... what?

The boy looks over at the kitchen door. It's got a window and curtains, but the boy can see someone peering in between the curtains. It's... also Momma! "Andy!!" her voice is shaking with terror, "Do not open that door! Get over here as fast as you can and let me in!"

What the devil?

He looks out the living room door peephole again. There's First Momma pounding on the door looking just as scared. "Andy for the love of God do not let that monster in here! It wants to kill you!"

Pounding now from the kitchen door. "Don't listen to it, son, it's not even human!" That Momma sounds downright desperate. "Please let me in!"

He looks from peephole to window. Peephole. Window. Peephole. Window. The faces are identical. Both Mommas wear the same scarf in the same brown hair. Both wear the exact same plaid shirt.

One's Momma. The other a stranger. And strangers are bad. The boy knows what to do. He runs to the closet between the two doors and takes out grandpa's rifle. It's a little unwieldy but Momma taught him how to use it in case of just such an emergency. He can shoot a tin can off the back fence from twenty paces away now.

The knocking stops. The boy hears Momma's voices again, only this time they are both in stereo. "Stay away from him!" he can hear them both yell. The boy carries the rifle toward the window in the dining room, the one that faces the back yard.

There he sees Momma and Momma face off against each other. One Momma's got a pitchfork. The other a shovel. They attack each with their respective weapons. Neither gets in an effective blow though. It's like each already knows what the other is going to do.

"I don't know what's going on or who you are," he hears one Momma say, "But you are in for one hell of a fight."

"You touch my sweet baby," the other Momma says, "I will skin you alive, cook you and feed you to the pigs!"

The boy slides the window open, getting their attention. He steadies the rifle on the ledge and gets aim on one... then the other. The Momma with the pitchfork stares up at the boy a second too long. Momma with the shovel slams that shovel right over pitchfork Momma's head. She drops her pitchfork and falls to the ground. Shovel Momma raises the shovel again but Pitchfork Momma kicks her in the gut laying her out. She climbs on shovel Momma and begins choking her- then looks up and grins at him in triumph, "She's right where we want her baby! Go ahead right between the eyes just like Momma taught you!"

The boy aims the rifle at the one Momma presently being choked. That Momma turns to the boy and talks between gritted teeth, "Andrew Taylor Smith... That is not... your mother..."

Whoa. That Momma knows his full name. And she sounds mad.

"Your birthday is November Ninth," the Momma doing the choking says, tightening her hands around the other Momma's neck.

"Your favorite color is purple," rasps the Momma being choked.

"You've got a birthmark under your right arm..."

The Momma being choked suddenly bites the other's wrist, sending her rolling off in pain.

The two Mommas brawl on the ground until the boy loses track of which Momma's which. Shucks! This is turning into quite the pickle.

Now one Momma has the other Momma in a headlock.

"Son, please listen," Momma-who-has-the-other-in-a-headlock says, "There something awful happening. I went to the store today and I saw two Mr. Danielsons behind the register. One was holding a bloody knife. The other was on the floor stabbed to death! I drove home and I saw Mrs. Run over Kinnitson's body in the road. Then I saw her again pulling her car into her driveway, there was blood on her hood! Then this thing came out of the woods on highway nine pretending to me..." She starts to cry.

"You're the one that came out of the woods!" Momma in the headlock chokes out, tears rolling down her cheeks too. "It's telling you what just happened to me! It stole my memories! Please, Andy, shoot it now!"

The boy switches his aim from one Momma to the other. Both have the same desperate look on their face. Then... out of nowhere... the Momma in the headlock gives him a sad smile. Wait. Why is head-locked Momma smiling... but also sad?

"Kill us both," head-locked Momma says with that sad smile.

Momma who's doing the head-locking looks confused now. She tries to speak but words aren't coming.

"It's the only way to be sure, honey," head-locked Momma says with the sad smile, "If you let one of us live you have a fifty percent chance of being wrong and you'll die."

Momma doing the head-locking is speechless and getting more scared by the second. All she can do is act like she wants to say something. Her lips quiver uselessly. Finally, she tries to cover Sad Smiling Momma's mouth but Sad Smiling Momma bites the other Momma's hand, making her pull her hand away again.

4

So strange. Sad Smiling Momma seems to be at peace now. She gives the boy a confident nod. "You've got this son. Shoot us both. And remember your Momma always loved you with all her-" She is suddenly silenced by the rifle's fire and the bullet passing right between her eyes.

The dead Momma slides out of the other Momma's headlock, collapsing dead to the ground. The boy trains his rifle on the Momma left alive. She looks up at the boy. She smiles awkwardly like she has no idea what she is supposed to do. "G-good job uh... son," she stammers. "You killed the impostor. You..."

The boy holds his aim on Alive Momma. He says nothing.

Alive Momma raises her arms in surrender. She gulps audibly awaiting certain death. Then...

The boy blinks... revealing dark reptilian eyes. He speaks in a deep, guttural language not known on this planet. "At ease soldier."

"Commander!" Alive Momma answers in the same unearthly language and blinks, revealing a pair of her own reptile eyes. "You arrived ahead of me."

"You arrived late, lieutenant" interrupts the boy. He directs her attention to Dead Momma, "We will discuss your demerit later. For now, we bury the reproducer next to its larva."

Moments later in the backyard lay two telltale mounds of dirt, side-by-side. A long mound and a short mound.

Lizard-Eyed Momma pads the long mound with the shovel.

"You're lucky I killed the larva first," the Lizard Eyed boy says. "It would have seen right through your fear and figured out who its real parent was."

"The mother took me by surprise," Lizard Momma explained, "How was I to know it would be willing to sacrifice itself for a mere offspring?"

"Learn to act exactly as they do," Lizard Boy asserts, "These assimilation husks are exact. Speech, movement. We are even given memories. It shouldn't be too much work to act like one."

"Commander, what kind of creature would do that?" she says more than just a little concern in her voice, "Give its own life for a single larva? Something that can be replaced so easily?"

"Stop shaking, soldier. These aren't selfless beings who automatically sacrifice themselves for their genetic copies," the boy reaches down and picks up the old rifle now. "Look at these death machines they've already invented to use on one another. This weapon was here long before we were." The boy's lizard eyes stare down the barrel of the rifle, aiming it at random things... "Yes. Assimilation will be difficult. Difficult but not impossible."

...

(a love story)

Jane and Tanya walked hand in hand through the island village. They didn't have to talk. Colorful locals stood outside the eateries, shops, and taverns sending them salutations and invitations in a language they could barely understand. Jane and Tanya just smiled as they passed. Jane and Tanya weren't interested in what was inside those places anyway, quaint as it all seemed. They just loved walking outside together.

Like most days in this village, it was a great day to be outside. The locals said it was the time of year when the island was warm but not too hot. And a slight breeze kept things cool but not cold.

"Perfect," Jane said.

"Exactly," said Tanya.

They smiled at each other. These were the way most conversations happened between Jane and Tanya now. Decades of being together will do that to a couple. It will either do that or make them want to commit a murder-suicide. But Jane and Tanya were always happy together, even when they weren't altogether happy. After all these years, still happy. Fifty years to be exact. Fifty to the day.

That's why they had started this trip around the world. Both now in their seventies, they'd worked hard, lived sensibly. They scrimped and saved their pennies at meager careers. The years turned the pennies into dollars. Retirement came yet they still insisted on simplicity and frugality. By the time their forty-ninth anniversary rolled around they noticed they'd accrued a small fortune- literally reached their "golden years". No frugal retirement could put a dent in the mountain of money they were sitting on.

"Let's just do it," Tanya had said.

"You read my mind," Jane smiled knowing Tanya was referring to the trip they'd always talked about. They started planning the extensive trip that night.

This island whose name they couldn't even pronounce was their first stop. The so-called "Worldwind Tour" was going to last a year or until the money ran out. Or until...

But they weren't going to even think about that let alone say it out loud. Nevertheless, age had done to them what age does to a body. Limbs, bodily functions, mental acuity... mortality was catching up to them. Every once in a while, though neither knew the other was doing it, they would say a silent prayer to die together somehow. That way both would be spared the loss of the other.

The long walks Jane and Tanya took over the years had created a kind of fatigue synchronization. They both needed to rest their joints about the same time and found a stone bench at the end of the street.

The bench faced the ocean and a distant lofty cliff. The view was a majestic canvas, the crashing waves a whispering symphony. Jane leaned her head on Tanya's shoulder. Tanya rested her head on Jane's head. Their hands were clutched together right where their thighs touched. This is always how they rested, since day one. Fifty years ago.

The two old women almost went down for one of their epic naps right there and then. If it weren't for a scribbling noise and an offensive odor, which brought them back to the here and now.

A filthy, smelly man with gnarled hair and one leg was now seated on a rock in front of them, drawing with charcoal on crumbling sketchpad. He squinted one eye and stuck his tongue out sideways as he tried to draw. The one leg protruded from his torn pants and a crutch sat on the ground before him.

"Excuse me," Tanya said to the man.

"Shhh," the filthy man said. "Almost done." He smiled exposing hideous green teeth and bleeding gums.

"Sir," Jane began "You can't just walk up on people and..."

"It's an invasion of privacy!" Tanya finished.

"Here here!" the filthy man said, "All done!"

He turned the sketchpad around.

Jane and Tanya peered at the picture. It wasn't very good. To call it amateurish would be a compliment.

"Please take it," the filthy man said, "All I ask is a small donation for my work. Please, anything you can spare. If not, take the drawing anyway and I won't bother you again."

Jane and Tanya looked at each other. Then Jane took the paper like it was a dirty napkin.

The filthy man held out an empty cup and bowed his head. "Anything you can spare..."

Tanya and Jane studied the picture again. It was slanted, had way too many lines. It wasn't even ironically charming. They could make out their forms on the paper though. Jane's head on Tanya's shoulder. Tanya's head on Jane's head. Their interlocking fingers. They looked at each other now.

Figuring they weren't interested, the filthy man shrugged, withdrew his empty cup and grabbed his crutch, hoisting his one-legged self up on it. "I understand. Sorry to intrude. Enjoy your day..."

"Wait a moment sir," Tanya said. "Don't go anywhere."

The filthy man leaned against his crutch and watched as the ladies spoke in hush tones. The conversation must have taken less than thirty seconds but both nodded excitedly at the end of it as if they stumbled upon the idea of the century.

"Sir we are going to give you a donation," Tanya said.

"And it is all we can spare," Jane chimed in with a huge smile.

Then the two ladies huddled for a moment. Jane handed Tanya a pen and the checkbook. Tanya scribbled for a few seconds then handed the check over to the man.

"What's this?" the filthy man said looking at the check, jaw agape.

"You can cash it at the nearest bank," Tanya said.

Astonished, the filthy man took the check. "Ladies... I don't understand... what are you...?"

Jane smiled, "We have no children. No legacy. All we have is each other and..."

Tanya finished, "And it would make our love complete if we knew we made a difference in just one person's life."

The man processed all this then... to their shock, the filthy man laughed. It was the most joyous laugh. The women started chuckling along with him though they weren't sure why. He winked at them now. "Fact. The ancients believed that gods dressed up as beggars to test humankind. Now that belief is called a myth. Well, we gods beg to differ."

The filthy man let his walking stick drop and the women gasped... as his missing leg emerged from his torn pant leg. It was strong and sinewy.

His face was no longer the face of a filthy man but of a tanned distinguished gentleman. Now he smiled broadly but instead of green teeth and bleeding gums they saw perfect rows white healthy, pearly whites. His hair was no longer gnarly but rich and thick. Even the offensive smell was gone!

"Every thousand years I visit the children of mother earth. Once someone shows me that human kindness and generosity still exist, I am free to go home. Free to go home!" He breathed a long breath.

The women were astonished beyond words as he gave them back their check.

"You have already given me all I need, I have no use for this," the once filthy man said. "Now it's my turn. I can give you something before I go. Anything. Make a wish. Any wish at all."

Jane and Tanya couldn't have been caught more off guard.

"Take your time," the man continued, "I know you'll make a good one."

The two women stared at each other now. Each knew what the other was thinking.

"You do everything together. And right now you're both thinking the same thought," the man said, "Just say it."

"We want to live…" Tanya started.

"Forever…" Jane finished. "Together."

The man nodded. "Joint immortality it is." He pointed to the lofty cliff overlooking the ocean. "At the very top of that cliff is a pool. It's in a clearing you cannot miss it. Jump into it. When you come out of it, you will be alive… to love… together forever."

The two women gave each other the exact same look of disbelief.

Then they turned back to the filthy man… but he was gone. There was literally no sign of him anywhere. Both felt the hairs on the back of their neck go up. Was this really happening? Was it a dream?

Now they looked up at the lofty cliff.

"We are really going to do this aren't we?" Jane asked, a newly found energy in her voice. She casually folded the beggar's drawing and put it in her back pocket.

"Think about it. Either we become immortal," Tanya said, "Or we have one hell of a vacation story!"

They laughed like children. Then took each other's hand as they walked toward the cliff.

There was a switchback trail at the base of the cliff's incline. Jane and Tanya began the upward trudge and soon lapsed into their decades-old hiking routine. Tanya would take the lead at those points too narrow for two people. Jane would always put her hand on Tanya's shoulder half for balance, half to remind Tanya she was still behind her.

The halfway point is where they would ordinarily sit for a few minutes before tackling the rest of the hike. But they were too full of adrenaline to rest. Neither of them noticed they weren't even tired. And neither noticed when a gust of wind caught the drawing in Jane's back pocket and blew it toward the ocean...

The top of the cliff afforded a breathtaking view in three hundred and sixty degrees. In front of them, endless ocean and sky. Behind them, the island village was like a painting from a bygone era.

They walked a little further toward the cliff and stopped when they saw it.

At first, the pool looked like an illusion. A heat mirage that was slowly going to disappear as they closed in on it.

But it was real all right. They stopped at the pool's edge.

"My heart is pounding right now," Jane said. "And not from the hike!"

"Mine too," chimed Tanya. "I can't believe we're about to do this. It's crazy!"

They giggled again like children and began to disrobe.

Jane's fingers paused on one of her shirt buttons. "Hang on," she said, "Let's say this really is what we want to do…"

"You mean be together and live forever?" Tanya laughed. "Sounds like a no-brainer to me, sweetie."

"But forever is… infinite," Jane went on, "The universe is billions of years old and probably will go on for trillions. The world might get hurled into the sun what will we do then?"

Tanya put her hand on Jane's cheek. "Then we float in the vacuum of space to the end of the cosmos, our bodies intertwined," she took her hand away, "Come on it'll be fun…"

Jane thought about this and paused again, "You always were the poet. What about this pool? How do we know this water doesn't have parasites in it? Suppose that wasn't a god and just some mean man who's playing a mean trick on us?"

"Honey, we watched his leg grow back," Tanya said getting exasperated.

"It could have been a magic trick," Jane mused. "Suppose there's like poisonous snakes in there?"

Tanya gave Jane one more smile. "Then we had a very good run and we'll die together today. Come on, get naked, bitch!" Tanya was completely undressed now. The sun felt so warm on her skin. She touched the water with her toe. "Ooh, it's just a little chilly baby. Just the way we like it!"

Jane took her underwear off. She toe'd the water now. "Oh, it is cold." Jane was so preoccupied with the temperature of the water she hadn't noticed the mischievous look in Tanya's eye or she would have been ready when…

... without warning, Tanya got behind Jane and pushed her into the pool full force! Jane shrieked as she splashed in the water. Tanya laughed heartily as Jane went under.

She was only under a half second then burst back to the surface. "Why you little...!" Jane yelled. Only...

It wasn't Jane. Or it was, but not the seventy-one year old Jane that Tanya just pushed in. It was now the twenty-one-year-old girl Tanya met fifty years ago. She had gone from an old lady to a young woman in a split second! "I'm going to get you back for that!" Twenty-one year old Jane shouted.

Tanya gasped so hard she couldn't even catch her breath!

Sensing something was different Jane looked down at her own body now, then saw her reflection in the water, "Oh my God, it worked. I can feel it too. In my bones. Infinity, Tanya! We're going to live forever! Tanya get in here! Tanya...?"

Jane looked up at Tanya but she was no longer standing. She was on the ground now eyes rolled up in her head. Dead from the heart attack she had just suffered.

Somewhere down below the drawing of Jane and Tanya landed in the ocean, disappearing forever beneath the churning waves.

SKIN DEEP

11 February 2133

I was quite the big deal when they buried me back in 2033. On every screen in the world. For the two and a half weeks leading up to my burial mine was the most recognized face on planet earth. Pop stars, pro athletes, and politicians wanted my autograph. They wanted pictures with little old me! 2033. A hundred years ago. Seemed like it was only yesterday. Mainly because to me- my body, mind, and spirit- it was only yesterday.

Yes to me "yesterday" was a hundred years ago. February 11th, 2033. Today I was dug up and de-paused. Not a very poetic term I know but the Temponaut Team aren't... well, weren't the most eloquent bunch of scientists.

See I was the first Temponaut- a human being who undergoes PAUSE. Paralyze Atomically Until Stasis Ends. Every molecule in my body was stopped by a newly discovered gas- they named it Pausium- which can contain energy down to the subatomic level. In other words, it freezes something without lowering temperatures. And just like in freezing, the PAUSEd subject becomes solid through and through. A living thing that's been PAUSEd is like a marble statue of itself. I still don't know why they didn't just call it petrification. And by the way how clunky "Temponaut"? I tried to sell them on "Centurion" but apparently, that moniker was taken thousands of years ago. Ironic.

But naming things isn't my job anyway. Being the guinea pig is my job. Traveling through the eons a hundred years at a time is my job. Keeping a journal is... actually, do this for fun.

Day One AG (above ground) was a huge success. The medical staff who de-PAUSEd me were robots. No surprise there. I was kind of expecting that considering half of them were robots a hundred years ago. I wasn't fatigued at all didn't feel anything out of the ordinary. All vital signs and functions completely normal. My body hadn't aged even a fraction of a second. Pretty amazing stuff.

There's a mandatory twenty four hour quarantine here inside the lab but I have spoken on hologram with actual people on the outside who can't wait to meet me. Top scientists, the president, other celebrities.

I am thinking about this one reporter from 2133's premier news agency. It's called Pan or Span or something like that. Anyway, her name is Yvon. Judging from her holo she is breathtaking. Back in 2033, people could sculpt their 3-D holos to make themselves look more attractive. You know make the eyes bigger, noses smaller, jawlines more pronounced. But even if she does holo-sculpt, who cares? I found a connection with her on a level I never could with women in my own time. And the best friend I ever had back in my day was a woman (a story for another time). Talking to Yvon wasn't just the most exciting part of the day. It was the most exciting part of my entire 28 years of living.

As I get ready for bed I am excited. I hope I can sleep. I just need to shut the blinds to my room. There is an enormous billboard at the top of an adjacent building, so bright it's blinding. It's for something called "The Goop". I do hope that's not 22nd century speak for something edible. Over and out.

12 February 2133

Day Two AG. The sun hit my face at oh-nine-hundred. That's when I walked out of the lab and into a mob of fans I could never have dreamed of. The world is as stoked about digging me up as it was to put me in the ground. Just like when I went into the time capsule, everybody wants my autograph. Kids half my age holding out dermatographic pens so I could "tat" autographs on their skin. Old folks filming me. Very old, like ancient. I wonder if any of them had even been conceived when I was buried. Heck, the average human lifespan in 2133 is a hundred and three years.

I smiled at them all, waved, let them take their pictures, signed what they wanted me to sign. And when the bodyguards told me it was time to go I gave everyone a polite wave. The crowd let out a collective sigh of disappointment. The publicity guy spoke into his jaw-mike which was wired to the PA system. "It's all right folks he's not going anywhere for a while you'll get another chance before he goes hits the dirt again."

The crowd cheered as my entourage and I hopped aboard the Skytrain to see the president. Of all the new inventions I witnessed today this was the most impressive. A train that defies gravity and needs no tracks. Amazing. It snaked through the air, around buildings, over rooftops- we even dipped into a tunnel to avoid some thick sky traffic. Best part: the centrifugal force was autocorrected, so no air sickness! Unless you looked out one of the windows that is.

We finally arrived at the President's house and oh how The World Capitol has changed since 2033.

The President's house is no longer an ornate mansion. It is a humble home big enough for a small family but no more. It is the smallest building in Presidents Circle and is simply called The Abode.

President Alice Singer was a great host. Her wife Janet and sons Tom and Dave had all the charm, intelligence, and decorum you'd expect from a first family. President Singer gave me the tour of her house. It took all of two minutes. Something about the un-impressiveness of the president's house made it even more impressive.

Side note: at one point I had to use the restroom and I was amazed at its spartan design. I couldn't help notice a familiar jar on the sink though. "The Goop". There it was again. Jeez, I thought, this must be something else if even the president uses it! I studied the jar and still couldn't figure out what it was exactly. Pretty sure it's not edible so that question got answered. But then I have a lot more important questions to ask the year 2133. The mystery of The Goop will have to wait.

After the Abode, Singer showed me around Presidents Circle. I visited Unity Hall where the World Servants meet and The Alliance Quarters where mediators constantly negotiate peace among the Territories. Then it was time for the annual Capital Dinner, a huge feast held in the Globe- an inner-spherical banquet hall. From the outside, it's an enormous dome. But once inside simul-gravity pulls you to dome's inner surface. Everywhere you look- up, down, all around- there are tables with guests, rushing food servers bearing trays of drinks and hors-d'oeuvres, traveling violinists.

I was seated at a table with members from the press and found myself sitting right across from her. Yvon. The reporter I had holo'd with the night before. Now I was blown away. She is even more beautiful than her holo! Angelic is the word. Large hazel eyes, high cheekbones, the sweetest dimple on her chin, all framed by a mane of fiery red hair. She smiled the most radiant smile. Her face was so captivating I couldn't even tell you what she was wearing at that moment...

She finally called out to me and waved. I nodded back. I'm shy around the ladies, especially the ones I like. Over dinner, we kept sneaking looks at each other, smiling, nodding. I spoke politely with the reporters on either side of me. But my eyes belonged to Yvon.

After dinner, the tables were cleared away and a rock band took the stage. I was the only one who wasn't amazed at the sight of this quartet- singer, guitar, bass drums- performing some good old fashioned rock and roll. In 2133 a single singer/songwriter/musician record all their own music with their own instruments in their own studio. Live ensemble bands have long gone the way of the alternating current. People were amazed at how well the four musicians synchronized with each other. It was nothing new to me though. I'm a fan of "rock and roll" from way back.

What's new to me is this feeling I get around Yvon. When the band started playing I got over my shyness and held out my hand. "Let's dance!" I heard myself yell to her over the blare of Four On The Floor (a name that was even dated to me. I grew up with electric cars and only a true car historian would know what that meant.)

We danced for a few fast songs then a slow one came on. I took her hand and found it was just as sweaty as mine. We started slow dancing, cheek to cheek.

"So," she whispered, "When can I interview you?" Her breath was warm and dewy in my ear.

"For you, I'm free all day any day any time…" I answered, "As long as I get to interview you back."

She laughed and we looked at each other for a lingering moment. If we were alone I'm sure we would have kissed.

She did blow me a kiss on her way out of the globe. I have a date with her tomorrow night. To be interviewed of course.

Before the band's final number the lead singer said, "We've only got time for one more folks! Got to get home before The Goop wears off!" Eliciting a surge of laughter from the crowd.

Before the Goop wears off? Well, that's it. It's late now but first thing tomorrow morning I'm going to study up on what this Goop is. Over and out.

13 February 2133

Day Three AG.

"Be all the you that you can be." That's the tagline of the very vague "Goop" ad campaign. There's a jar of The Goop in the foreground of the ad, happy people enjoying themselves and one another in the background.

Once I started reading further into it I had to laugh.

The Goop is a viscous substance one applies to his or her skin. Once the goop makes contact with your pores "a certain scientific magic occurs". The Goop causes cells in the body to rearrange themselves until, quoth the ad, "an end result of pure magnetic beauty."

Overweight people apply the goop to fatty areas and fat cells are rearranged to appear as muscle cells. Unattractive people apply the goop to their face and classic symmetry is achieved. If one feels they are too short, enough goop on the legs and spine causes cells to stretch in a way that can add of up four inches to his height. If someone wants a washboard stomach they can apply it to their abdomen. On the flipside, if someone is flat in places they would rather not be flat, the Goop can add curves there too. It's also good for oily skin, dry skin, hair loss, back hair, crows feet, laugh lines, male pattern baldness, weak chins, pigeon toes, overbites, under-bites, crossed eyes, hawk noses, unwanted dimples, pimples, birthmarks... ad nauseum.

After reading all the hype I was tempted to try some myself. Then I looked at the price. Good grief! In its cheapest form the price is astronomical (and I am figuring for inflation). The most expensive kind, well, clearly the wealthiest people on earth could only afford that.

But then... the wealthiest people on earth would have to be the people who own The Goop's patent. Because the Goop is in nearly every home on the planet.

I should back up a second. When I talk about The Goop "in its cheapest form" I mean there are different levels in a tier system. At the bottom, there's the Goop that takes care of cosmetic issues. Then there's the Goop that can do that plus transform shapes and sizes of certain parts of the anatomy. Then there's the kind that can transform your entire body.

On top of that, there is the length of time you want your Goop to last. You have the Goop that lasts for minutes (about 90 or so). Good for a job interview, a cup of coffee with an old friend you want to impress, or maybe a leisurely stroll on the beach. Then there's the Goop that lasts for hours (about 8 maximum). Terrific for a first date, high school reunion, or a day at the beach. Then there's the Goop that lasts for days (up to 7 I've heard). Great for a business trip, a romantic getaway, or a stay at that old timeshare on the beach.

I did the math. The Goop that can transform your entire body and lasts for seven days would cost the average working person an entire year's income.

"Before the Goop wears off." I chuckled as I pictured Goop-addicts rushing to get home, their beautiful bodies literally dropping out of shape as they ran through the door. Like Cinderellas racing home from the ball as their exquisite carriages turn back into pumpkins.

There is a difference between the way people look now and the way they did a hundred years ago. Generally speaking, they are very attractive I have to say that. At the moment I can't remember meeting a single person with any kind of external imperfection of any kind. The crowd outside the lab, the Skytrain ride, the globe dinner… Every person I met so far has what we used to call movie-star good looks. You know, before all movie characters were computer animated. I wondered why I hadn't noticed this Goop Effect before. I guess when everyone looks beautiful, then beautiful becomes average looking. Everyone except Yvon. Because her beauty is not skin deep.

At about twelve hundred I started getting ready for my interview with her. Yes, that's what we called it, an interview. But she never got around to interviewing me. Get your mind out of the gutter I'm a gentleman and she's a lady so there was no hanky-panky.

We met at a food court located at the center of this enormous entertainment complex. To the right of us a massive "thrill ride"… I guess you could say a combination of a movie and a roller coaster. It takes two hours to rollercoast and tells a story as you go. To the left of us Museum City, an art exhibit so huge it could give the Smithsonian a run for its money. In front, The Arena, a sports haven where you can play, watch or gamble on every sport imaginable. You can even come up with your own sport and play it. And behind us, The Pleasure Portal, a network of interconnected nightclubs and restaurants. From what I hear the perfect place for a first date.

"So why did they call you Rip Van Winkle back in 2033?" Yvon asked, her writing tablet in the crook of her arm.

"Oh, it was a folktale from even before my time," I answered. "You could look it up."

"I did," she said laughing, "And all I could find were articles about you."

I considered this fact. My celebrity eclipsed a once beloved children's story to the point where any trace of the original story had been obliterated.

"It's about a man who falls asleep for twenty years and when he wakes up he finds the world a very different place..." I felt myself trailing off, staring into her hazel eyes.

"Okay you are going to tell me the whole story sometime," said Yvon, "But I want to hear all about you first."

I sat back and waited for the first question. She looked back at her writing tablet, trying to focus and doing a bad job of it.

"What was war like?" She asked.

I was surprised.

"Sorry is that a sensitive subject?"

"No," I answered, "I just wasn't expecting you to go there right away. I thought you'd ask where I was when World Peace was announced and the first World President was inaugurated."

"We have all kinds of videos from that time, I heard the first inaugural speech when I was in second grade..." she sighed.

"What about videos of war?"

"Silly!" she laughed, "They don't exist anymore. Part of the Second World Treaty amended. People who watched those videos were more likely to display violent tendencies."

"Oh... I guess that makes sense... monkey see monkey do."

"So tell me what was it like?" she prodded. "War?"

I shrugged, "All I can say is there is no feeling like the one where your life is in constant danger. Even when the gunfire ends. I guess you get numb to it but you also can't wait for it to be over." I looked straight at her, "Only another soldier can understand. And when it is over? The mind has a way of pushing out the bad and remembering the good. The consequence of that is the bad gets forced out before you can get closure with it."

"So what was... good about war?"

I didn't need time to think about this one. "I found people that I would have died for. Brothers and sisters in arms."

Yvon seemed entranced, "Someone died for you didn't they?"

I was shocked, "How did you...?"

"I'm a reporter," Yvon said. "I do my homework."

In my mind's eye, I saw her face as I spoke her name. "Corporal Shandra Toomey. Yes, she saved my life by giving her own."

"Did you and her... were you and her...?" Yvon lost her characteristic interview cool for a moment.

"We shared a bunk once..." I confessed. "But we were both just lonely and seeking comfort. When morning came we decided friendship was more important than romance. Especially in that bloody circus. I had plenty of acquaintances but she was the one true friend I made back in my time."

I must have been vibing anxiety because Yvon changed the subject. "Your parents? Your sister?"

"I have a picture of them. Other than that I don't remember too much about them. They died when our bomb shelter collapsed," I answered, "I was small enough to fit through the fallen debris. Mom told me to go and get help. My dad and my sister weren't saying anything. Off I went for help. By the time I found it, it was way too late."

"How old were you?" she asked now, eyes wide. There was a quiver in her voice too. She was losing that journalistic edge.

"Six," I responded.

"You grew up in a war. Lost your family in a war..."

I shrugged and nodded.

"Fell in love in a war."

I shook my head no.

"She loved you though..."

"We were soldiers. I would have jumped on that grenade if I was closer to it."

Yvon looked skeptical.

I decided to get assertive: "I'd love to ask you some questions too you know," I said.

"Such as…?"

"How would you like to take a two-hour rollercoaster ride with a hundred and twenty-eight-year-old man?"

Yvon scrunched her nose in the cutest way and smiled. She nodded.

Thus began a night I had only dreamed of a hundred years back. Funniest part? Yvon and I never wound up on that thrill ride. Nor did we muse, sport or dance. We walked through the maze of entertainment complexes. And did not stop talking the whole time. I got to know so much about her. Her childhood, her mom, and dad, what she did for laughs. At the end of it, I guess I'm the one who got the better interview! It went by too fast though and Yvon noticed it was getting late. So we shared a unicab back to her place- just to say goodnight. Like I said I am a gentleman and she a lady.

However. We did kiss. For a long time. It felt like seconds but we made out like a couple of teenagers in the back of that unicab.

She checked her watch again and she realized she had to go. She raced out of the cab and into her apartment.

The holo rang the minute I got home. It was her. But she had herself blanked so I just heard her voice. "Just wanted to say goodnight to the most dashing, handsome hundred and twenty-eight-year-old a girl could ask to spend an evening with…"

Her voice sounded so luscious. I won't stop thinking about her until I fall asleep. And when I fall asleep I won't stop dreaming about her.

Over and out.

18 February 2133

Day Eight AG

How lucky am I? What a life. What a day.

It started with the opening of the first inner-city cerebrary- a virtual library of books, videos, and music accumulated from around the world. We're talking trilibytes upon trilibytes of information in one location. The Summit Cerebrary opened its doors for the first time today and I was there with President Singer. The Capitol City cerebrary is located in a blue-collar neighborhood. Working class families showed up in droves, excited to have a learning advantage usually reserved for the upper class. The working families would have continued to go without were it not for a hundredth of a cent increase in world taxes and private donations. As I surveyed the cerebrary's first customers I noticed something that separated them from the rest of the people I've met in 2133. They didn't all look perfect. Some were bony, some obese, some had acne scars, some were bald, some had eyes that were too far apart, some had crooked teeth. I noticed all those imperfections. However, I was not repulsed by the imperfections. It was refreshing to meet people who looked real. Normal. Human.

I then realized I had not seen one ad for The Goop either. Not one billboard, not one Megabus ad, not one wall commercial.

A little later I was at lunch again with President Singer. I have no idea where she finds the time to sit down and eat let alone eat with me, a mere Temponaut. She insisted I was a "global treasure". There's a label I am still not comfortable with. I prefer "science project" but I can see where that would sound self-deprecating.

"So we've got the short list of things we'd like to bury with you again," the President stated out of nowhere, startling me. "Is there anything you personally would like to take with you into the next hundred years?"

Then it occurred to me. I looked at the date. I was set to be buried on March 11th. Damn this job I signed up for.

Yvon sprang into my mind. Everything else was momentarily shut out.

"Did you hear me?" the President said.

"I'm sorry," I said finally, "I just… you caught me by surprise…"

"It's okay you can think about it," President Singer said and went back to her lunch. "It can be anything really. But try to make it something you associate with us here in 2133."

"President Singer, I would like to ask you about the contract I have with the World Science Board…"

Now it was the President's turn to be surprised.

"I don't know how else to say this. I'm in love," I confessed. "And I want to grow old with this person."

The President's face went from shock to sternness to understanding in a matter of seconds. She smiled now. "Well, I certainly am happy for the two of you. I will have my people look at your contract."

In that instant, it hit me I was having a conversation with the President of the World. And I could understand how she got that job.

I raced back to my hotel room to meet with Yvon. She was going to do some more of my interview. At least that was the plan. But being in such a private place was a bad idea from the onset because our chemistry can no longer tolerate mere words. We both kept glancing at the bed until we went one glance too far.

Moments later I was no longer a gentleman and her no longer a lady. At least for the rest of the afternoon.

Afterward, I told her of my conversation with the president. Yvon was quiet, contemplating what I had said to the president and why I said it. She looked so happy she might cry.

After several minutes of blissful silence in each other's arms, she finally spoke. "It's going to be a book..."

"What?" I asked.

"My interview," she said. "I'm going to talk to my editor. I'm going to write your story in its entirety. I refuse to be constrained by the parameters of a mere human interest piece."

A book. Well. Rip Van Winkle strikes yet again.

And you thought I was exaggerating when I said I felt lucky? I have to admit if this is what the future holds I must have died and gone to heaven. Over and out.

19 February 2133

I thought I would be writing something much different today. But what a difference the last 24 hours has made. More- way more- than the last 100 years that's for sure.

Day Nine AG started out well enough. The President called. She said she was able to get me out of the contract I had with the World Science Board and that they would begin the search for my replacement, planet earth's next Temponaut.

I was overjoyed. I couldn't believe how easy that was. It certainly didn't prepare me for what the rest of the day was to bring.

Yvon and I got together in the early evening. Dinner was fantastic. We went to a World Diner, a place where you could eat cuisine from the culture of your choosing. I had Indian. Yvon, Thai. We went for a long walk in the city. Went up to the top of the Gravity Loop bridge and stared at the earth above us. You would think to be upside down "looking up at the ground" isn't the type of thing you would want to do right after dinner but I found it exhilarating, even on a full stomach.

Then we went back to her place.

We sat on her couch. We had tea. We played footsie. We kissed. We stared at each other for a long moment that went by in a nanosecond.

I wish I could bottle that moment. It really was the last pure moment we experienced. The last moment of pure innocent love.

"Listen, Rip", yes she decided my nickname was Rip, "It's only been eight days but we've been through so much. Emotionally. I just want to say is we haven't been together that long but… we're ready to share all of ourselves with each other don't you think?"

All of ourselves?

She laughed, "I'm ready for you to see the real me."

What?

"The me I don't let anybody else see," she continued.

It should have occurred to me by then but it didn't.

"And I want to see the real you too," she smiled. "You know what I mean?"

Again, Mr. Dense over here had no idea what she was talking about. "Yvon, this is the type of thing somebody says when they want to make love to you. And that ship's already sailed-more than once."

Yvon laughed harder this time, "Oh you're so silly of course I want to make love to you but... after the Goop wears off."

I was speechless.

"You use the Goop?" I asked.

"Of course," she laughed some more, "You think I was born like this?"

"But-"

She got nervous now. "Oh... it's all right if you'd rather not. Unless... do you have the kind that takes a long time to wear off? I get that too. We can postpone this until when we can synchronize. I just assumed you used one-day Goop. But... anyway, when does yours wear off?"

"It doesn't," I started tongue-tied, "I mean... I don't use the Goop. I'm before the Goop's time."

Now Yvon looked horrified. "Oh my God. You didn't have Goop in your time... you don't use- you never used the Goop? I thought the first thing you did when they woke you up was put on Goop."

I squinted at her. Then I did something I probably shouldn't have but I couldn't help myself. Something about hearing that word "goop" over and over. I let out a little chuckle.

This set her off. Tears started welling up in her eyes and she suddenly leaped out of my arms and ran into her bathroom. She slammed the door shut.

I called after her and ran up to the bathroom door. I could hear her crying. "Oh no!"

"What's gotten into you?" I asked. She didn't answer.

"Listen," she said from the other side of the door. But it didn't sound like her. Her voice was so different. "I need you to go to my bedroom. I left my Goop in there. I need you to go get it so I can put on a fresh coat."

"Yvon what's wrong talk to me."

"You don't understand," she said through the door, "You wouldn't ever understand."

"If you're worried that seeing the real you is going to change the way I feel-"

"Don't patronize me. You're a very good looking man and you don't even use the Goop! Naturally beautiful people never understand what the rest of the world goes through when the Goop wears off", she was very upset now, "Just go get that jar in my bedroom!"

God, she sounded so different. Nothing like the Yvon I had gotten to know and love the past week. Without saying another word I went to her bedroom and found the Goop jar.

I got back to the bathroom door.

"I have the Goop," I said. Again something about the word "goop" gave the whole conversation an absurdity it probably shouldn't have had.

"Leave it at the door and walk back into the living room," she said. "I can't let you look at me."

"Yvon I really don't care what you look like," I said, "If our love is strong it can handle anything."

"What do you know? You're beautiful and you don't even use the Goop!" she cried.

I had one last strategy. "Listen you've been looking at the real me this whole time and I've never seen the real you. Don't you think you owe me just one look?"

It was silent for a long time. So long that by the time the door opened it caught me off guard. She stood there staring at the ground. Tears streamed from her eyes.

"There," she said in a small sob, "The real me."

I took in the sight of her. I took her chin and tilted it up to me. She couldn't look at me.

"Yvon," I said, "You look exactly the same as you did when you went into the bathroom. Are you sure the Goop wore off?"

"Of course it did! Are you trying to be funny?"

I had no idea what to say. She did look exactly the same.

"You don't see them?" she sobbed. "All my flaws? How one corner of my mouth is lower than the other? The mole on my left ear? You don't notice the flab on my upper arms?"

I looked again. Even after she mentioned these things I couldn't see any difference from the way she looked before the Goop wore off. Even her eyes were the same mesmerizing hazel as when I first met her. Too bad they could no longer meet my gaze.

"I guess you're right. You are a lot different without the Goop," I finally managed. Then I leaned in and kissed her. She did not return the kiss. As I pulled away she grabbed the jar out of my hands and went back into the bathroom slamming the door in my face without another word.

I went back into the living room but I didn't stop there. I walked out of her apartment altogether.

When I got back to my hotel I had some holo-mails from Yvon. Quite a few in fact. Maybe she wondered why left. Maybe she tried to apologize. I'll never know. I deleted them all without even listening to them. Then I blocked her holo address so she couldn't call me again.

President Singer sounded groggy when she answered the phone. I realized the hour and apologized for waking her. I wanted to let her know I would not be breaking my contract after all and wanted to make sure it wasn't too late. She was a little surprised but mostly relieved that I would continue being civilization's "global treasure." And thankfully she didn't press me for a reason I went back on my decision. I also told her the item I would like to pack in the time capsule with me when I get buried again. She let out a confused laugh. "Are you sure?" she asked. I told her I was.

Over and out.

11 March 2133

Well, here it is Day 30 AG. Finally.

The rest of my visit to the year 2133 went without incident. I was a guest on a ton of popular talk videos. I explored the ruins of Manhattan, visited the Rain Desert where the Amazon River once flowed, got submerged in a deep sea air bubble and explored the Marianas Trench.

Every once in a while my mind would drift to Yvon. But it got better as the days went on.

From what I understand she wrote an amazing article about yours truly. I never read it. Maybe I'll look at it in a future eon. I'll just have search "Rip Van Winkle" to find it.

The last time I saw her was out the corner of my eye at the last public event I attended. There was an unveiling of a Peace Memorial in Central Square and President Singer said it would be criminal (her word, not mine) if I wasn't in attendance. It was a memorial commemorating the signing of the first World Peace Treaty. I remember seeing this moment on the old Tube. It was signed on the very spot where the memorial stood now. I felt chills. I both detested and accepted war. I don't know if being a veteran had anything to do with it. I met plenty of civilians in my time who felt that way too. War just seemed to be a part of the human condition back then. When that Peace Treaty was signed all I could say was we'll see. By the time I was entombed five years later in 2033, world peace was accepted as part of the human condition.

Now here it is a hundred years later. Who would have thought? Certainly not me. The unveiling was both inspiring and humbling. It was an abstract holo sculpture of a thousand doves bursting into flight.

I could see Yvon in the crowd with the other reporters... in my periphery like I said. I couldn't tell if she was staring at me or the statue. Maybe I wanted her to be staring at me. Maybe I wanted her to be staring at the statue. Whatever. In my heart, I wished her the best. As for me. Perhaps my one true love is waiting for me in the millennia ahead. Maybe she'll be born in the next hundred years who knows? As the HG Wells' Time Traveller once said I've got "all the time in the world."

So that's a wrap on the year 2133. A time without war, a time of world peace. And that's an achievement for sure. But an improvement? I fear 2133's occupants may have only traded vices. Mars is dead. Long live Narcissus. Oh well. At least nobody's getting killed.

I don't believe the Goop won't be around in the next hundred years. It is merely a symptom of the pursuit of physical beauty in this age. One day, the Goop will go the way of the internal combustion engine. That's why I insisted an empty jar of the Goop got buried in the time capsule with me.

Until 2233.

Over and out.

BAG OF HANDS

The salesman understood now what truckers meant by white line fever.   Been driving all night. On what had to be the emptiest stretch of highway in North America. Canada didn't even have roads this deserted, he was sure of it. Maybe there were trees out there. Maybe a cornfield. The salesman didn't know anything besides those white lines running under his headlights.

What was the name of the next town anyway? Boxton? Ballingham? Some kind of Midwestern B-name. That last place was all but forgotten as well. Nobody was buying there, that's all he knew. So sick of driving. But he couldn't stop either. Brixington, or whatever it was, was still two hours away. He rubbed his eyes. Blinked. And like magic...

The hitchhiker appeared in the high beams just up ahead. Trudging backward, thumb outstretched.

The salesman tapped on his brake. It was very late. Or very early depending on what time a body was used to waking. Either way, a very dangerous time to be hitching a ride. Or picking up hitchhikers depending on the circumstances.

In a different world, the salesman would have blown right by the hitcher. If either of them were a different color for instance.

But the hitchhiker was black. Just like the salesman, who's memory fast-forwarded through the restless days of his own youth. When he set out to change the world. Before he gave up and became a part of it. Nothing but a pocket full of loose change, a bus ticket across the country and not one shred of common sense. But crazy as he was, he was lucky too... some of the places he'd been, and who with. The salesman sighed...relieved those days were gone.

Still, this hitchhiker needed a ride. Maybe an ear to listen to him rant. Get some of that spit and vinegar out. He could also keep the salesman awake until he got to- what was it- Boxtown? The salesman braked in earnest just as he passed the young man...

... who's face seemed to light up within when he saw the salesman stopping. Or maybe it was just the sudden red glow from the car's brake lights. "It's your lucky night," the salesman said to the hitcher's reflection in his rearview.

A few seconds later Redge- that was the young man's name- was in the passenger seat staring out the side window. Redge was content to go as far as the next town, whatever it was.

He took an open bag of sour cream and onion potato chips from his pocket and dipped a grimy hand into it. Taking a mouthful, Redge munched, holding the bag out to the salesman, who took a second look at Redge's grimy fingernails and patted his stomach. "Big dinner," the salesman said.

They sat in silence for the moment it took for the car to get back up to sixty. Then the salesman simply had to ask: "What in God's name are you doing hitchhiking in the middle of nowhere in the middle of the night?"

Redge tried not to smile. "Oh you know," he finally answered, putting a foot up on the immaculate dashboard. "Things don't work out somewhere and you've got to move on. However, you can."

The salesman said nothing. But he could relate.

"How about you?" Redge asked.

"I sell swag," the salesman said.

"That what they call it out here?" Redge said, "Man am I a long way from home."

"Sorry," the salesman chuckled, rubbing his tired eyes, "It's an industry nickname for promotional merchandise... Like, you work for a company and you do a good job, but they don't want to give you a raise. So they give you a pen set with the company logo on it. Or you open a bank account and..."

"They give you a coffee mug, I get it," Redge nodded, licking the potato chip grease from his dirty fingers. The salesman promised himself that'd be the last time he'd look at Redge's hands.

"Been on the road long, Redge?"

"No. Maybe. I don't know, depends on your concept of time."

"Days? Weeks? Months?"

Redge smiled again. "I kind of lost track."

"Mind if I ask what set you off in the first place?"

Thinking, Redge played with his thumbnail a bit. Then he took another pinch of potato chips. Munch, munch, munch... And just when the salesman was beginning to think Redge hadn't heard him, the hitchhiker finally answered, his mouth full: "Yeah... yeah, I mind."

"Just curious," the salesman said, sure he had somehow upset the young man.

But Redge was calm. "I'm not an interesting subject, you know? I get bored talking about myself."

"Too bad, I was hoping for a nice story to keep me awake."

The two of them shared a courtesy laugh. The salesman heard himself laugh at least.

"Well, you definitely don't want to hear my story. You'll nod right out after two minutes..." Redge trailed off. He lifted the potato chip bag to his mouth and poured what was left into his gaping mouth: sour cream and onion grit. Licking his chops, he crumpled the empty bag and shoved it back into his pocket. Then he took to staring out that passenger window again. As if there was something out there besides the pitch dark.

The soothing hum of the car's engine began to grind on the salesman after a moment. The salesman was beginning to think Redge enjoyed awkward pauses. And beginning to question his own judgment- picking up a total stranger on account of something as superficial as skin color. It was way too quiet way too long now. The salesman thought about pulling over and asking Redge to get out. But what if the young man refused? The salesman remembered the knife in the driver door bucket. A hunting knife he'd bought as an afterthought once he learned he'd be driving around the country alone. Just in case. He reached down and touched the handle, reassuring himself it was still there. With one quick move, he could grab it, open it and scare Redge the hell out. If need be. Which could be soon if-

"I got a story for you!" Redge suddenly announced, startling the salesman. "It's really good too. Gooood ending!" Redge grinned that last phrase out, baring two rows of yellowy, potato-chipped teeth.

"Well then," the salesman said, maybe a little relieved, "Let's hear it, Redge."

The hitchhiker may have hated talking about himself. But he geared up to tell this story like a master raconteur, rubbing excess chip residue off his hands, shaking his head in expectant zeal. Apparently, the salesman was going to enjoy this story very very much. Redge cleared his throat. If he were an orchestra conductor this would be the baton-tap.

45

"You ever hear about... Bag of Hands?" Redge asked.

The salesman shrugged and shook his head no.

"Oh. You're gonna love this!" Redge said, rubbing his hands together again. "It started in a little town called Vinton, Louisiana. You familiar with that neck of the woods?"

"Sure," the salesman nodded, "Right near the Texas border. Louisiana used to be in my territory..."

"You've been to Louisiana and you never heard of Bag of Hands?"

"Hey, I only stick around long enough to see if anybody's buying swag."

"No time for small talk," Redge said, "All business."

The salesman shrugged and nodded. Pretty much, yeah...

Redge continued, "All right. These Louisiana state troopers are tailing a car heading into Vinton. It's got Texas plates. And five brothers in it. You imagine? Five brothers from Texas?"

The salesman laughed. "If they were in a hurry to get out I believe it..."

"Needless to say, the cops pull this Texas car over. They say these dudes had all kinds of things hanging from the rearview, chains and whatnot. The cops claimed there was an obstruction of the view out the windshield. Hence they were driving hazardously, and hence they needed to get pulled over. Otherwise, the cops didn't have a damn thing to pull them over for, you see?"

The salesman nodded. Enough said. Chalk it up to life in White America.

"So the cops get out, and they start walking up. And, my friend, they no idea what they just stumbled on. First thing the cops notice is everybody in the car's trying to look cool

46

and doing a bad job of it. Like, pissing-themselves bad. And the brother who was driving? He's trying to stuff something under the seat. Right away the cops take their guns out, thinking it's drugs or worse. They tell the driver to show them what he's got. At first, the driver's just staring at them. They keep asking him what he's got under the seat and he won't show it to them. Everybody else in the car is dropping a brick. The cops just about have to shove their guns up the driver's nose... and that's when he pulls it out..." Redge took his foot off the dash- leaving a muddy boot print- then angled himself toward the salesman. He finished a little softer now. In case somebody else was listening. "It was this bag... with four hands in it."

The salesman suddenly felt a chill. "Hands..." he echoed.

"Human hands," Redge went on, "Two left ones. Two right ones. One pair was definitely female. All manicured and be-jeweled. The others were probably a guy's from what they could tell. The Louisiana troopers nearly faint. They've never come close to seeing anything like this, not even in their little corner of voodoo country. At first, they figure this car is coming from what's got to be one of the messiest double homicide in recent memory. But right off the bat one of the brothers in the back seat flips out. I mean, coo-coo for Cocoa Puffs. It was the first time he'd seen the bag of hands too! Now the cops start asking questions. And from what they can piece together, the driver of this car picked up his friends and happened to have this bag of hands he had to get rid of. And they had just picked up Cocoa Puffs but never got the chance to bring him up to speed on a, uh..."

"The situation at hand?" the salesman interjected.

"Yeah. So. The cops get everybody out of the car, search'm and cuff'm. During this, the only other funny thing they find is the driver's got scratches all over him. I mean scratched up bad like he lost a fight with a pack of alley cats. Now, since Mr. Bag of Hands didn't have a license they run the plates on the car. It's registered to a John Nawls. So Louisiana calls the Texas police who head to the Nawls residence- some rundown apartment complex in a border town named Beaumont. What they find is a crime scene for the history books.

"It was this tiny little apartment, walls used to be white but just got a fresh coat of red, know what I mean? Give you more of an idea how bad it was, homicide didn't even know how many people'd been killed. Body parts all over the place. Forensics finally put all the pieces together and it turns out to be two victims. John and Sara Nawls. Every organ and limb is accounted for. Except for- you guessed it- the hands. They were sawed off what was left of the arms and taken away. The Beaumont PD makes a call to Louisiana and about twenty minutes later a little Igloo cooler is flown into the crime scene. The hands recovered from that car belong to the victims without a shadow of a doubt.

"Police start questioning the Nawls's neighbors. Just about everybody talks about this homeless dude who started showing up a few weeks prior. Description of this guy matches the driver of the Bag of Hands car to a tee. Apparently, Bag of Hands had a thing for Mrs. Nawls, who was creeped out enough to tell her husband to give ol' Bag of Hands a talking to. Nawls did. With a baseball bat. Put a hurting on his ass like the wrath of judgment day. The night Bag of Hands got out of East Texas General, he stole some rubber gloves and a bunch of surgical tools - including a bone saw- and paid a visit to the Nawls's. Coincidentally they were making it in the bedroom when he broke in. In the split second he shocked them he managed to plunge a knife into their chests. Then he really went to work on them... over and over again. They fought like hell but he was good with that knife. Like he was some kind of Ginsu master.

"Once they were finally dead, he busied himself dismembering them for the next few hours. My guess is for the sheer pleasure of it. When he was done he washed up in the Nawls's bathroom. Then he put their hands in a freezer bag and took off in their car."

"And exactly why did he take the hands?" the salesman had to ask.

"Like I said the Nawls's fought like hell. Scratched the daylights out of Bag of Hands. And he knew a thing or two about the DNA evidence they scrape out from under a corpse's fingernails."

"And the other guys in the car?"

"Just some small time dealers Bag of Hands became acquainted with during his short visit. The long way around the barn goes like this. Mr. Nawls didn't trust banks. So he had a buttload of money stashed in his dresser. Right next to his gun, which he was going for when Bag of Hands showed up. Nawls got the drawer open when he got stabbed. Bag of Hands saw that money- had to be about fifty grand, cash- and I think that's when he came up with his little plan. He stole the Nawls' hands, their cash and their car and picked up the other four, promised them he'd split the cash five ways if they could help him dispose of the evidence. Least that was the theory the Texas police came up with. The Nawls' money was never actually recovered."

Redge stopped here. The salesman was thankful for the second he actually thought this gruesome story had come to an end. He was definitely awake, that was for sure. Then Redge went on...

"So by all accounts, this should have been an open and shut case right?"

The salesman nodded wearily.

"Well, first of all, the traffic stop was thrown out of court in Louisiana. Racial profiling, the DA said. The cops pulled that car over because all the guys in it had dark skin and Afros.

"The Louisiana DA's case was so strong, Texas jumped on the bandwagon. So because that traffic stop was ruled as bogus in both Louisiana and Texas, the bag of hands was inadmissible as evidence. Like it never existed."

Redge snickered to himself.

The salesman clenched his jaw. Caressed the handle of that hunting knife. Redge's unhealthy fascination for true crime was growing worrisome.

"During all this, Bag of Hands and his carpool buddies came up with the plan. Or rather Bag of Hands did and he talked the rest of these guys into it. How he talked them into doing something like this, I'll never know. Just have to accept the fact that Bag of Hands was one scary bastard..." Redge let this idea sit in the for a moment, then went on: "Anyway, all of the other brothers come forward and confess to the crime, one by one. 'I did it'- 'No, I did it'- 'No, it was me'. Why, the cops asked? Every one of them had a reason. Temporary insanity type stuff. 'John and Sara Nawls were minions of the Satan' - 'My poodle told me to do it' – 'I had too many Twinkies'. And it was working too. Nobody knew which end was up on the double-murder.

"Until Bag of Hands himself showed up. He was the last one to go in for questioning. And he had the whole thing figured out. He even got himself this slick, high-priced attorney, who tells everyone what really happened. The other four did the murders. Together. See John and Sara Nawls' owed those four scumbags money for drugs. A lot of money. The others saw Bag of Hands on the street, picked him up and told him to drive. Said they had to drop off something but they needed somebody to watch the car. At first, his client refused to get in. Then the other four show him the bag. 'You don't do this for us,' they said, 'we're gonna do this to you too.' The bottom line: attorney general's office not only bought Bag of Hands' story hook line and sinker... they figured justice was served. No matter who did the crime or how they got four convictions. Yeah, everybody came out of that one looking real pretty. Except for the four chumps who got the death penalty for no reason."

The salesman looked stunned.

Redge wrapped it up: "And that's how those poor innocent bastards are sitting on death row today. And the psycho who did do it? He's free to kill again..." He laughed this last bit out and clapped the salesman on the shoulder.

50

"Isn't that the best story you ever heard?" Redge said, beaming proudly.

"Not exactly," the salesman said, "It sure kept me awake though..."

"You know what the coolest part of this story is my friend?"

The salesman shook his head again, tension building.

"It's one hundred percent true..." he whispered. Then burst into hearty laughter.

The salesman was breaking a sweat now, his heart hammering in his chest. "So... you know Bag of Hands?"

Redge nodded slowly.

The salesman gulped louder than he wanted to. He was ready to go for that hunting knife any second now... "Where is he today?"

"Somewhere on the highways and byways of this great land," Redge said cryptically, "You can bet on that. Any other questions?"

"Yeah. You wouldn't happen to know what Bag of Hands looks like?" the salesman asked.

"Sure I do," Redge said, smile turning wicked, "He's my height, my weight... and got my face!"

The salesman slammed on the brake. He got a grip on the hunting knife in his door bucket. But Redge was howling with benign laughter, slapping his thigh in delight. All right. The salesman was really confused now. But he wasn't letting go of that knife either.

"Oh come on, relax!" Redge said, "I'm just playing with you! It's a campfire story you know? Got to give your audience that big scare at the end! It's theatrics!"

The salesman studied Redge's face... then felt his own foolishness flooding in. He chuckled nervously. "You scared me pretty good, Redge."

"I just love telling that story, especially to nice folks who give me rides!" Redge wiped the tears from his eyes and finally stopped laughing. "Uh... Hey, can we get going again?"

Realizing they were stopped in the middle of the road, the salesman threw the car into drive. God was he an idiot! "So far as you know Bag of Hands is just an urban legend right?"

"No. It's true," Redge said, "Trust me on that. I had some experience with the Louisiana law enforcement community. We're like family. Believe me, Bag of Hands is out there."

"Then I have to ask you again. You wouldn't happen to know what Bag of Hands looks like?"

"Somebody described him to me once...." Redge said, trailing off as he finally got his first good look at the salesman...

... who suddenly swept the hunting knife around-

- plunging it into Redge's chest, piercing the young man's heart in mid-beat. The hitchhiker would have gasped in horror. If it weren't for the fact that he could no longer breathe.

Redge grabbed the salesman's arm, gripping it as if onto life itself... which was leaving him rapidly.

As he leaned forward to gain leverage, pressing his shoulder against the wheel, the salesman focused on the road ahead. The car swerved a little but the salesman stayed on course, twisting the blade of the knife around inside Redge's chest.

The salesman could feel the hitcher's fingernails tearing through his white shirt, digging into his flesh... breaking the skin. As Redge breathed his last breath, the salesman let out an exasperated sigh. It was going to be a long night.

Two hours later Redge's remains dropped into a churning river just outside Barrington, Missouri. The salesman stared down from the bridge above. He was exhausted. He pulled off his shirt and casually tossed it down into the water as well. He looked at his right arm. The car's first aid kit took care of the scratches and lucky for him any long sleeve shirt would cover the bandages.

The salesman got back in his car and rubbed Redge's bootprint off the dash with a Baby Wipe. He never traveled without those things; they were good for cleaning anything off anything.

He caught a glance of the sour cream and onion potato chip bag on the passenger seat. It wasn't empty anymore. Seeing Redge's grimy fingernails poking out, he crumpled the top of the bag. What he wouldn't do for a chip clip right now.

God only knows why he had to take Redge's hands. He knew full well the river would wash away any blood or skin under Redge's filthy fingernails. Guess old habits die harder than people do.

The salesman fired up the engine and threw the car into drive. He'd had a busy day. Got a lot done. He was going to sleep well once he got to Barrington.

TO BE CONTINUED...

VICTIM TYPE

Lying on the floor of his own apartment, Paul Woodcove rewinds the events leading up to the second before this one and starts playing them back in his mind...

She had looked so helpless when Paul first saw her sitting on the other side of his cash register. Like a broken Barbie doll. It was the best fake ID in his twenty years behind the bar. He had even double-checked it under the infra-red lamp- standard at every Blacksmith Hometown Grillery- and shrugged when he saw the authentic strip on the driver's license illuminate. Kelly McGrath was twenty-five years old last August. If this is a fake, he had thought, the girl deserves a drink for the effort.

But Kelly had wanted more than just a drink hadn't she?

As the last hour of his shift wore on Paul would keep questioning his decision to serve her that rum-coke. She drank half of it right away and began to nurse the rest of it over that next hour, a queasy look on her schoolgirl face. For the novice drinker, this is tell number one.

Other tells appeared as that final hour rolled by. Tells that confused rather than confirmed Paul's instincts. A cockiness that masked her deep-seated fear of being discovered. For what, though? Being underage? That insecurity should have disappeared as soon as he put the drink in front of her and took her money.

The girl, this alleged twenty-five-year-old named Kelly McGrath was a little too chatty. Paul had seen that before too. Talking to keep herself awake, almost like. Or calm herself down. Drugs. That might have been it. Mix some pills with booze and you can get any manner of side effect, paranoia chief among them.

As the head bartender of St. Louis's only Blacksmith Hometown Bistro, Paul tried not to think about such things. The girl presented an ID that could fool any cop. He had no reason not to serve her. And if this girl collapsed on the bar from the synergy caused by the valiums or special k or oxycontin she was on and the alcohol she just ingested, the police would not hold him or Blacksmith Enterprises, LLC culpable.

Still... the bartender didn't like the police.

He had no reason to fear of the police. He was a fine upstanding citizen. Always obeyed the speed limit. All his bills were paid. He was a conscientious employee, not to mention friendly neighbor and avid churchgoer. He voted for the candidates who wanted to preserve this great nation's ideals. He was pro-everything-good and anti-everything-bad. He drove an American car. And if anything happened to Kelly McGrath he would be as cooperative as he could with the authorities. He had even helped them once, when those two college girls disappeared from his neighborhood. No, he was not the least bit afraid of the cops. He would rather not have to deal with them that's all.

"So..." Kelly McGrath asked as Paul as he rang up the second to last tab that was cashing out. Sitting close to the register was a tell of another kind. That of a petty thief. Was she hoping he'd leave the drawer open by accident? Not that the bartender of a suburban bar and grill ever uses the cash drawer anymore, where most customers pay with cellphone apps no matter what they're drinking.

Waiting for the credit receipt to print out Paul gave Kelly his best poker face.

"... do you get off soon?" she blurted out. Like it was killing her to ask, more not to.

That was the tell that sewed all these other incongruous tells together. Paul felt a rush of excitement at his discovery. So that's what you are... he thought as a smiled brimmed across his face.

He saw relief in her eyes. She'd taken his smile as a positive acknowledgment to her boldness.

He wanted to tell her the real reason why he was smiling. Instead, he pointed at a cozy couple engulfed in each others pheromones, saying: "Soon as the campers decide to leave..."

Kelly smiled, her eyes big, innocent. Like a little girl looking up at daddy. She put her lips on the cocktail straw and took a teeny sip of her rum-coke, unable to hold back a wince.

Paul grabbed the fountain gun and topped her glass off with straight coke. With the other hand, he peeled the credit card receipt away and strode down to the party who was just leaving, three businessmen here to watch the game that had just ended.

They'd never once noticed the girl sitting near the register. Neither had the cozy couple, who were so wrapped up in their own company, they hadn't seen Paul put the check down in front of them forty-five minutes ago. Paul gently tapped the bar grinning a grin that had won him so many friends here at the Blacksmith since its grand opening seven years ago.

"All set?" he said to the cozy couple.

They seemed to come out of a reverie, a little embarrassed. Time flies when you're on your way to getting laid. The young man nodded and threw down two twenties. On an $18.06 tab. Off Paul's raised eyebrows he said, "Keep it."

His generosity had the desired effect on his date, no doubt impressed with her prospective lovers' ability to throw money around. "RING THE BELL!" she giggled to Paul…

… who laughed back and, for the umpteen millionth time here at the Blacksmith Hometown Grillery, rang the stupid bell above the bar announcing to everyone in the otherwise empty cocktail lounge that he'd just gotten a killer tip.

The Cozy Couple never even gave a second glance to that lost little girl hiding in the shadows near the register. Kelly was staring at Paul, sucking gently at that little red straw in her rum-and-mostly-coke.

Paul stared back.

She smiled with a little hesitation.

It was on.

Paul stuffed the tip into the pitcher he kept on the bottle rack. He grabbed the pitcher by the handle. He'd count his tips later.

"Time to go," he said to Kelly, motioning at the door, then leaned in closer so only she could hear him, "Wait at the far corner of the lot. I'll pick you up in a few minutes."

Again, that look of relief. Like Paul had just saved her life. Her huge eyes radiated with gratitude, hope and most importantly… complete and utter trust.

Paul began feeling the blood pump to his groin. He suppressed the sexual response for now. Plenty of time for that after.

What was Kelly thinking as she shivered at the far corner of the parking lot, waiting for the bartender's car to drive up?

Paul didn't usually think of stuff like this. But lying on the floor of his apartment he wondered this now. What had been going through her mind?

Well, the narrator chimes in, at that time, the runaway-who's real name is so unimportant she might as well be Kelly McGrath- was thinking about how she could see her breath. How her legs and toes were practically numb. How the only thing keeping the rest of her warm was this big down jacket. The one she'd gotten off the last guy. Jed the plumber. He was the one who taught her about putting sugar in the drain opener too. She whispered thanks to Jed, "… wherever you are…"

Here came the headlights. The passenger door opened. What a gentleman, Kelly thought. She was sincere in her sentiment. She climbed in. The car was nice and warm. She put her hands up to the heating vents, smiling at her new friend.

"How about my place?" he asked gently.

She nodded. He already knew there was no "her place" but saved her the trouble of explaining why. A true gentleman in an age of douchebags? Nope. She knew this was just a part he was playing. That was okay though. He wasn't the only actor here.

Once Kelly drew her cold hands away from the heating vents, Paul adjusted the setting so that it blew on her legs. They were so skinny…

"Thank you!" Kelly gushed, doing a feline stretch before the vents. Like nobody'd ever done a thing for her in her life. "That feels nice…"

"No problem," Paul said.

They were silent for a moment. The girl absently bit at one of her black fingernails then...

"So..." the girl liked this word but always used it with the same amount of difficulty, "I, uh, don't really have a-a place to stay, uh, tonight..."

"That's fine," Paul said unable to watch her choke down any more of her pride, "I'll put you up."

"Not that it's about that," she said, afraid she was going to lose him or something, "I don't usually go around picking up guys to begin with, never mind using them for a place to stay..."

"Nobody's judging you," Paul said. He reached over and gently stroked her knee. Her skin was so soft. Like a baby's. His hand crept up, easing her legs apart. Her inner thigh was tense. But it relaxed under his touch becoming creamy and smooth as he made his way toward her panties.

"That feels so good," she whispered, putting her sweet head on his shoulder.

How old was she really? Sixteen? Fifteen? Hell, she may have been twelve. It was hard to tell these days. Young girls were dressing more and more provocatively these days. The fabric he was touching even now probably belonged to a thong.

He slid his hand under her panties now and had to suppress the biggest rush of blood to his groin yet. In those smooth folds and creases, he felt a touch of stubble. She shaved down there all right. Just not today. Good thing too. Paul liked stubble down there.

Her head was still on his shoulder even as they entered his apartment. He flicked on the lights and asked her to kick off her shoes so as not to make clomping noises and wake the downstairs neighbors.

He took her down jacket and admired her lithe dancer's frame. That dress could have been considered lingerie. There was nothing to it. Grabbing her elbow behind her back, she bypassed the expansive bookcase, opting instead to look over Paul's modest collection of video games.

"Can I get you something to drink?" Paul asked, putting to rest the idea that she's on anything. If she had taken pills earlier she would have passed out by now.

"Got any wine, barkeep?" she gave him a quick smile then turned back to the games.

"Coming right up, miss," Paul answered, taking a quick trip to the bedroom door.

The bedroom door.

He was careful not to make his movements too obvious. This was a fortuitous event, having this lovely young runaway stumble into his bar. But the balance was no less delicate. He had her trust. Something silly like the bedroom door could throw everything off. He opened it casually, tossed her jacket into the darkened room, heard it land on the bed just inside the doorway, then closed the bedroom door again. It clicked shut quietly.

She was none the wiser, looking at "Modern Warfare" under the living room light, where her face showed a little more age than he'd originally thought. Seventeen? Eighteen? Even in this light thought, that porcelain fragility sustained. This girl's spent her entire life a deer in the headlights.

What are you running from Kelly McGrath?

She turned the game over and Paul caught a glimpse of something on her wrist. A lateral scar. The tell of all tells. A suicide attempt that was supposed to get her attention. After all, if she'd meant it she would have sliced upward toward the crook in her arm. Poor Kelly.

She looked up and smiled again, "Hey can I use your bathroom?" she said, starting to bite another black fingernail in mid-sentence.

Paul gestured to the open door at the end of the hall...

... then switched his glance to a mirror reflecting the hall, watching Kelly pad barefoot toward the bathroom. As he turned to go into the kitchen, he made sure he saw her shutting the bathroom door in his periphery.

He would have deliberately watched, or said something to her, to make sure she didn't enter the bedroom by accident. But that would have called too much attention to it. Curiosity wasn't a major concern. She'd see the bedroom eventually. Just not yet. The bedroom was for after. No, Paul's major concern was fear. Not knowing was the fun of it. If she got afraid things would get messy and it would ruin everything. Paul knew stuff like this from experience. Things like reflections and peripheral vision have served him well over the past two decades.

In the kitchen, Paul got two wine glasses and a bottle of chardonnay. He was going to pour himself a glass even though he wouldn't be drinking more than one sip. This was turning out to be quite the conquest. He wanted to face it clear-eyed and fully conscious.

He set the glasses on the down on the coffee table and poured them each halfway. He corked the chardonnay and sat back, waiting.

He imagined her going to the bathroom right now. Sitting on the toilet, panties around her skinny little ankles. He started to fast-forward through what's about to happen. Her coming out of the bathroom. Sitting with him. Drinking the wine. And for the next three to four hours after that. However long it took after he got her into the bedroom. His shortest only lasted a half hour. His longest, eighteen hours. The sun came up and went down. He had to call in sick that day.

This time Paul didn't mentally withhold the blood rushing to his groin. In no time he is fully erect. He rubbed himself then immediately stops, afraid to spend himself too soon.

The ticking of the clock on the wall distracted him.

She's taking a long time in there.

Maybe now she was taking drugs? Shooting up? He hadn't noticed any track marks on her. Just that scar…

No. She couldn't be killing herself! Not Now!

Paul got up and started to pace, erection preceding him by a few inches. He agreed with every word the pastor says about suicide at church. It is the most selfish act in creation, making it the most damning sin of them all. How dare someone second-guess what the Lord has planned for them?

Erection gone as quickly as it came, Paul calmly strode toward the bathroom door.

"Everything coming out okay, Kelly?" he asked the door. No answer. He tried the handle. Locked. He had the key. In the bedroom.

He turned to get it… to see Kelly standing silently… in the bedroom doorway.

Behind her, the light was on. There were the pictures on the wall. The ones of the all the others. Decades of others. He was going to show her these pictures later on.

But now.

She had already seen them.

And now.

Her eyes were fixed on him. There was something different about her. She was the same person he'd been watching this whole time only… different. The fragility was gone. Replaced by something else. Purpose? Resolve?

Whatever it was, it was most unbecoming on such a helpless young girl.

Paul started out like he was going to explain what she had found in the bedroom, taking a few steps toward her. "Listen, Kelly, there's something …" he deliberately left the sentence unfinished, leaving her in reception mode. The easiest way to catch someone off guard before you take that one last step into striking distance and-

Paul did not even see Kelly's leg move when her heel connected with his jaw, sending him backward. Even as he sailed through the air he had to replay that one once or twice before believing she'd actually kicked him.

He felt the floor hit the back of his head hard.

As if that wasn't bad enough, the same heel that literally just broke his jaw was landing on his balls.

Paul tried to cry out, but his jaw was no longer working and his mouth was filling with blood. There was something missing too. Paul didn't have time to figure that one out. Job number one was the normal reflex of any man who's just been kicked in the nuts: hands over testicles.

Which is just what his attacker wanted him to do. With the speed and accuracy of a rodeo star she had his wrists and thumbs tied together with thin metal wire, then circled the wire around his ankles. Planting her butt on the floor and back against the wall, she pushed Paul onto his stomach with her legs and a loud grunt. And just as he was started to struggle… brought the wire up around his neck, pulling the wire snug. He tried to move but couldn't without choking himself.

"Careful," Kelly said for the first time since turning on him, "It's butcher's wire."

Paul began to whimper and realized why his mouth was bleeding so much. Darting his eyes to one side he could see a piece of flesh lying on the floor near his head. His tongue. His teeth must have sliced it out when she kicked him in the jaw.

Above him, Kelly went about her business. Every movement was concise and practiced. One second she was cleaning the bathroom doorknob with a Kleenex. A second later she was in the bedroom behind him. He could hear her putting on her down jacket. A second later, she was placing a small plastic cup in front of Paul's horrified face. It was a to-go kiddie cup, with its own plastic bendy straw. From the Blacksmith Neighborhood Grillery.

"It's Liquid Plumber," Kelly said, "I put some sugar in it so it would be easier to get down. Drink it all as fast you can, you'll be dead in less than five minutes."

He heard numbers being dialed on his cordless phone. Three numbers altogether.

The girl placed the phone on the floor in front of him and hit speakerphone.

Still hunched over, she looked him right in the eyes, a patient, mothering smile one her face. He noticed something about her hadn't before. A dimple on her chin. One of those two college girls who disappeared had that same dimple. Some said the authorities gave up their search for the young women. Paul was relieved when they gave up and pretty soon everyone else gave up on those two. A lost cause. But maybe not everyone gave up? Kelly with the dimple on her chin stroked the back of Paul's head and kissed him on the cheek.

"You're free Paul. And so am I," she whispered then scampered out of sight.

Utter dread cut Paul to the bone when he heard the voice come from the phone.

"9-1-1 what's your emergency?"

Behind him, Paul could hear bare feet padding toward the door to his apartment. Open. Close. Kelly McGrath was gone.

Paul began to whimper. Unable to speak. Unable to remain quiet.

"Sir are you okay?"

They'll come in, he thought. They'll come in before he's had a chance to get ready. Like he did before. They'll go in the bedroom. Oh. God, no...

"Okay, sir, stay on the line, we're tracing the call. Police and rescue should be at your location in less than ten minutes..."

OH JESUS GOD NO!!!!

Paul's done replaying the events that brought him to this moment, down to the finest detail. He still can't figure out what happened. Or why. It certainly was the last thing he was suspecting. The tables turned so suddenly and now here he is, faced with the choice of killing himself or... dealing with the police...

For the first time in his life, Paul Woodcove begins to cry genuine tears. Not the crocodile ones he had used on a few occasions when he needed something from somebody. He remembered using them on the last of the seventeen women he had brutally murdered in this very apartment. He told her he was acting so strange because his mother passed away the day before. The woman's suspicion seemed to vanish and she had cradled him in her arms. He remembered thinking how stupid she was for buying his act. Now there's nobody here to hold him. Not even Kelly McGrath, the clever spider who seemed to catch him in his own web. Paul Woodcove's alone. Settling for the memory of Kelly's little kiss on his cheek, Paul puckers his lips around the plastic bendy straw on the kiddie cup full of Liquid Plumber.

WIFE 17

Mack awoke from another dream about her. The two of them had been in an open field this time, playing like children- him chasing her, she looking back at him laughing. It was paradise.

But now Mack stared up at the ceiling, eyes misting. He wasn't afraid of crying anymore. Sometimes he wished he could turn on the waterworks at will.

But it wasn't in his DNA. Men aren't supposed to cry.

Now Mack laughed. Stupid Y chromosome.

His laughter trailed off and he stared at the ceiling a moment longer.

He wondered if there would be any news from the Clone Experiment in Stockholm today. His heart was pumping now. Anticipation was like a cup of coffee. Mack remembered coffee. It was still one of his favorite things, even though his last cup was twenty years ago.

Soon Mack was getting dressed inside his spacious uptown apartment. He threw back the curtains and looked down at the city of Manhattan, the way some Wall Street magnate from the Jazz Age would have. Rockefeller or J.P. Morgan or Dale Carnegie... But Mack was nobody like that. He had no fortune in oil or gold, no Swiss bank account, no tax shelters on the Caymans. He was just Mack. An ordinary man. Living in a desperate time.

The sun was rising. The sky was clear. It was going to be another gorgeous day.

Brushing his teeth, he peeked into the guest bedroom. It was empty, bed made, overnight bag gone. Wife number 6,820 had already let herself out. Mack shrugged. It was usually better that way. The morning after tended to be rushed and awkward.   The Husband Project's number one rule was "detached admiration."

Wife 17 had stayed the morning after. She didn't have time for breakfast but Mack gave her an apple for the road... She turned to him and just smiled as she walked out the door. No goodbyes. Not even a chance to tell her that in the months, years and decades to come, he would never ever forget her.

Now, running his toothbrush under the faucet, Mack started to cry.

"I envy you", Mack said to Drone Dan, the cook behind the counter. Dan's Diner was one of the last true restaurants left in the city. There were other places to eat here and there. They were called cafeterias and they resembled army mess halls. Worst of all the food was the same everywhere you went. The husbands were kept on a very strict diet. At least here, Mack could have the same thing but prepared with some character.

Three other husbands were eating breakfast at the diner. Gary, Chee, and Francois. They watched the female news anchor on the TV. They were all females on TV now. Every channel, every show. Completely populated with women, unless you wanted to watch reruns of very old TV shows or classic movies.

Drone Dan looked up from scrambled eggs in the frying pan. "You envy me." He was having trouble processing this. It occurred to Mack that people didn't talk this way anymore. Nobody felt envious of anyone right now. These were extreme circumstances. The seven deadly sins were a luxury of the complacent.

"You've got a wife," Mack continued, "One wife."

"I'm aware," Drone Dan deadpanned, taking a spatula and spreading the eggs onto a piece of Lavash bread. "You've had a harem, Mack. Who should be envying whom?"

"Not a harem," Mack said, "A procession of... partners. We call them wives because it makes things less... uh... clinical."

"What number wife are you up to now?" Drone Dan started folding the Lavash like an old pro. From what Mack understood, before the Anomaly began, Drone Dan had been a college professor. "Let's see, we arrived here almost twenty years ago so upwards of six thousand am I close?"

Mack just nodded and took a bite out of his breakfast wrap.

Drone Dan took a sip out of a Styrofoam cup. Mack's eyes widened.

"That coffee, Dan?"

Drone Dan decided to swig down the rest and crushed the cup, throwing it in the trash. "Grapefruit juice, just like you..." he said, breath reeking of coffee.

Mack just chuckled and took a sip of his unsweetened grapefruit juice.   He winced at its bitterness. Twenty years and he still hadn't gotten used to it.   What Mack wanted to say was: "Sometimes I wish I was sterile like you, Dan." Instead what came out was: "Good wrap today, Dan."

"You're welcome, buddy," Drone Dan the drone smiled.

Mack was content with his remark. He had made the right choice.

Just then, Gary, Chee, and Francois began shushing them from across the room.

Wild-eyed, Gary stood up and pointed at the TV, "They're going live to Stockholm!" He said in his thick Kiwi accent.

The TV screen switched to a young female reporter amidst a throng of female reporters. They were crowded outside a research lab.   All the reporters must have been about twenty-five but to Mack, they looked like preschoolers. Mack was closing in on fifty, just like every other man in this diner. Every other man in the city.   We're all over the hill, he thought with a shudder.

The main reporter spoke: "This is Ashley Jamison at the cloning project in Stockholm, Sweden," she briefly looked over her shoulders at the doors to the lab, "Where Dr. Wennborg is about to update us on what could be the first successful clone of a human male. Just a minute…"

The doors to the lab opened triggering a stampede from the herd of young reporters. An older woman slowly walked into the crowd. She was dressed in surgical garb, mask still clinging to her chin. Her expression was blank, weary, betraying nothing.

The men inside Dan's diner were on the edge of their seats.

"Dr. Wennborg!" our reporter Ashley was the first to put her microphone in the older woman's face.

The pause was pregnant as they get.

Then the older woman shrugged and spoke with a heavy accent, "I'm sorry the news is not good."

The energetic atmosphere outside the lab burst like a bubble.

There was another pause…

Francois barked "Changez!" in his native French. Gary reached for the remote to accommodate Francois' anguished request.

"Does this mean…" the reporter on the TV asked, "That the cloning project was not successful?"

"Not this time," the older woman with the accent answered, "But we will try again. We get closer every time-"

Gary switched the TV to CSN. The Classic Sports Network. Presently they reporter showing one of the old Superbowls. The New England Patriots versus the Chicago Bears. From some time in the late 1900's. Mack already knew the outcome of this one and, being a Pats fan, wasn't in the mood to see it again. He went back to eating.

"So," Mack said to Drone Dan, "Do you and your wife have, like, side-by-side plots at the cemetery?"

Drone Dan hesitated then shook his head, "Mack, Elaine and I just haven't thought that far ahead…" Drone Dan smiled and walked away from the counter leaving Mack to contemplate the fact that Drone Dan's only wife did not need a number.

Project orders dictated that jogging was the most efficient way to get your heart rate above a hundred forty bpm, twenty minutes a day. Jogging also got you from point A to point B.

Mack passed the Central Park Ranch. Turning Central Park into a farm was one of those great ideas that was obvious in hindsight.

Some blamed the Anomaly on processed food (technically, everyone blamed the Anomaly on all sorts of things. The ozone layer, car emissions, cell phones, sunspots, nuclear testing, Halley's comet, the shifting migratory patterns in honey bees, internet dating, witchcraft, microwaves, alien probing, certain kinds of men's underwear, the extinction of certain amphibious reptiles, ad infinitum). "A healthy man is made of healthy food," The Project declared. And healthy food should not have preservatives or any other foreign chemicals. Hence the farm. The eggs at Dan's Diner came from the chickens Mack saw just beyond the wrought iron gate. A gate now covered with, you guessed it, chicken wire. Mack waved to the man who was dusting the ground with chicken feed. Drone Rick- another one of the sterile men who performed menial functions here in the city- was one of the farmers who worked in the Ranch. A beautiful green-eyed woman their age came around the corner of the hen patch now. Dorothy, Drone Rick's wife. Also infertile. Sterile men were always paired with barren women. For some, the Anomaly had caused a return to the Arranged Marriage.

"Morning Mack!" she hollered as Mack jogged by. He waved to her too.

She started to tell Drone Rick something and he listened, throwing chicken feed on the ground at the same time.

Mack turned to face front again, feeling that pang of jealousy. Would he ever know that? To have that one person you're spending your life with just walk up and tell you something? It seemed so trivial, so mundane. And it probably was to Drone Rick and Dorothy. They were married shortly after they got to Manhattan twenty years ago. Was his wife's voice something that Drone Rick took for granted now?

Mack double-timed his pace fighting tears again. Of course, Drone Rick took Dorothy's voice for granted from time to time. He was only human.

Mack remembered Wife 17's voice as clear as if she were speaking to him right now. It was important that neither the "husband" nor the "wife" disclose anything too personal about themselves.

The Project's matchmaking program assigned wives based on a superficial compatibility. Common personality traits were used. Some interests, some aptitudes, just enough so there wouldn't be a lag in conversation... For example, Mack played guitar a little bit. Most of his wives also had musical interests.

Wife 17 was a pianist. He remembered how she waved her long fingers in front of him. Like a magician. "These are piano fingers," she said softly. Then, she put her hand in his, interlocking their fingers. He brought her hand to his lips and kissed it. He planted kisses up her wonderful arm, her beautiful shoulder, her glorious neck, her fantastic earlobe and... finally... when they kissed... everything else in the whole world disappeared.

His memory played back disjointed images of her. Like a Dadaist film. The lashes of her eye, which batted in slow motion, superimposed by her smile. That one tooth that was a little shorter than the rest. The echo of her laugh. Her caress.

His mind had kept her. Or maybe his mind was peering into his heart.

Their lovemaking had been desperately beautiful. Like the last wish of a dying man.

Every other encounter after Wife 17 paled by comparison.

She had ruined him for life.

In order to promote focus and efficiency, communication between Husbands and the Project was limited to emergencies. But one day, seven and half years ago, Mack tried to contact the matchmakers who'd set Wife 17 up with Mack. All he wanted was to pass a message along to her. The woman on the other end of the line chided Mack for veering from the protocol. "Emotional attachment causes undue stress. Stress affects reproduction!"

For a split second, Mack wondered if the woman on the other end of the line was actually Wife 17. But things like that only happened in old romantic comedies. And this was no time to be romantic. Or comedic.

Mack then asked if there were any way to get a picture of her. Wife 17. To see what she looked like today. He heard no reply. The call had already been terminated.

Then, two minutes later, Mack received another call from a Project Counselor, wondering if Mack needed to talk. Mack just laughed. What was there to talk about? The counselor gave Mack some contact information and encouraged him to call anytime. Mack never did.

At the end of his jog, Mack was taking the steps of St. Patrick's Cathedral two at a time.

Inside the cathedral, two hundred husbands sat facing the ornate chancel. It was completely silent. But each man was alert, his eyes trained slightly upward. Every few minutes you could hear the brief sound of someone shifting his position.

In the years since the Anomaly, men (literally) had found religion.

Roughly four decades ago there'd been a number of husband-cities. London, Paris, Hong Kong, those were a few Mack remembered when he was young... They were occupied mainly by fertile men for the sole use of reproduction. But as the male population kept dwindling and the female population kept growing, it became necessary to consolidate. Every five years the number of husband-cities was cut in half. About twenty years ago all the husbands were absorbed by Manhattan.

Manhattan. Get it? MAN-hattan?

When Mack first arrived in Manhattan, the silent meeting at the cathedral was standing-room only. The crowd would spill out onto the steps.

There was something so powerful in the silence of so many. Several thousand men, all waiting for an answer.

Today, the congregation was only a tenth of what it once was. Time was taking them all out.

A distinguished gentleman in the front row stood up. Pablo was one of Mack's oldest friends. Pablo was from Madrid, descended from royalty and the years had added a regal sheen to his appearance. He was the physician at the emergency clinic but mainly did check-ups these days. There had been very few actual emergencies since the Manhattan migration. Men were a lot more careful now, and not just because The Project told them to be. Humankind was teetering on a precipice. Mankind to be specific. Pablo spoke. He may have been born and raised in Spain, but he'd been educated at Oxford, so his English was fluent and with a slight British accent.

"My friends, I learned this morning of the death of a friend. Could we please all dedicate the last two minutes of this meeting to Brendan Phelps?" With that Pablo sat.

Cancer had taken Brendan out. Terminal diseases among the Husbands were growing exponentially. But then they were all getting older, these men. Life itself is a terminal disease and we all die from it someday... Still, the rise of viruses, cancers, and other degenerative illnesses added salt to the wound that the Anomaly had inflicted.

Forty plus years ago- because of poor record keeping in some regions, it was hard to say exactly when- male children stopped being born. It was sudden. One day (one day after Mack's birthday coincidentally) every hospital in the world reported every birth to be female.

Science was baffled. Pregnancies soon became closely monitored and it was clear that male children were no longer being conceived. Why? Well if anybody could figure that one out, they would win the Nobel Prize on the spot. The phenomenon was inexplicable. An anomaly.

From his early youth, Mack vaguely remembered "Henry". The artificially inseminated child of a Filipino couple, Henry became a global phenomenon in less than three months. Henry was the first male child in three years to have made it past the first and second trimesters. At eight months there was a huge celebration for Henry in the Philippines. At nine months there was a celebration across the world. The next week, Henry emerged on his due date, right on schedule… But there was no celebration. Instead, the world stood still for one devastating moment…

Henry was the last male baby ever to be delivered.

"What do you mean?" Pablo said after the silent meeting. He and Mack sat on the cathedral steps drinking purified water.

"One that you remember more than the rest," Mack said.

"They've all been interesting in their own way," Pablo responded, "Personality-wise, mentally, physically…"

"I know, I know," Mack jumped in, "But don't you ever think there's one woman you're meant for? I mean, we're men. not animals."

Being ten years Mack's senior, Pablo had been a mentor since the day they set foot on Manhattan. Mack had never had a concern that Pablo hadn't faced already. Never until now.

Pablo stared blankly into space at the moment. It looked like he wasn't paying attention. Then he nodded, "Mack," he turned to Mack and smiled, "I know exactly what you mean now. One wife for the ages."

Mack nodded back, excited, "One that wouldn't let you go. Once you thought you'd forgotten her, something would remind you of her."

"A sight, a sound, a smell," Pablo interjected.

"A dream," Mack continued, "And you'd feel that same connection as if you just had it a moment ago."

"It's called love," Pablo stated flatly.

Mack was silent a moment.

Pablo patted him on the shoulder, giving it a squeeze, "And I can tell you," Pablo's eyes welled up a little, "I've never felt what you're feeling for any of the wives I have had. You are a very lucky man."

Mack felt his heart in his throat now.

Pablo almost let out a paternal chuckle, "Cry if you want but I say again you are a very lucky man. Someday when all this ends and life goes back to normal, you might have a chance to reconnect with her. The Project keeps very detailed records. What was her number again?"

"Seventeen."

"So they'll check the calendar and give you all the information you need to know. Then you can go look for her. And if you managed to father a child with her then... you'll meet one of your daughters."

"What if that day never comes?" Mack asked.

"Then... you loved someone to depth and breadth of your being," Pablo said consolingly, "If I were a poet I would say 'tis better to have loved and lost than never to have loved at all. But you and the poets already know far more than I do."

Mack rubbed his eyes.

"Don't let these thoughts plague you, Mack," Pablo said as he stood up, "There is work to be done. Come on, it's time to meet the ferry..."

Twenty minutes later the two men were at the ferry landing.

Mack did a little research on this place. A few hundred years ago a small Irish Catholic family stepped off a cargo boat straight from the old country. Mom, Dad, and only six children. Small for an Irish Catholic family. One of the children, a little girl named Melora Talbott, was Mack's great-great-grandmother. Mack remembered seeing the daguerreotype picture in one of his mother's ancient scrapbook. Melora's father paid a photographer to commemorate the landing of the Talbott family in America. In the photo, everyone looked exhausted. Melora is asleep on her father's shoulder, a little dolly under her arm... the beginning of an epic adventure.

And that adventure will probably end in the very same place, Mack thought. Well... not end. Change drastically that's all. The sperm banks were all empty now, to no avail. Now, just a few hundred men were left, the Manhattan Husbands. The odds were getting steeper and steeper that a male child could ever be fathered...

Last year saw the first successful human clone. It was a female of course. So life would carry on that way. Maybe someday hopefully soon they would clone a male. in Stockholm or elsewhere... Who knew? "Only God knows anything," Pablo was fond of saying. But at this rate, the world was functioning fine without men.

Just as Manhattan was filled with men, so every other city on the entire globe was filled with women. The only difference was the parks were also full of female babies and children, the schools were full of girls. In every other place on earth, there was a future.

Not so on Manhattan. Just a dying past.

Mack watched the ferry coming. It was packed with wives.

Men of the past probably did have fantasies like this. A different wife every single day. And night. For the specific use of procreation. Someone to couple with, to love physically until you were both absolutely spent.

They kept getting younger to Mack, though he knew it was an illusion. The wives were always the same age. It was Mack who was getting older.

"You ever feel like a dirty old man, Pablo?" Mack said.

"Nobody's judging anybody anymore, Mack," Pablo was echoing the notion that had hit Mack back at Dan's diner, "We can't afford it."

Behind Mack and Pablo, husbands were approaching. Some power walking, others jogging. Some alone, others in pairs, still others in groups.

Mack stared at the boat coming. The wives were waving now, smiling. Mack took out his pic-viewer and looked at the picture of the redheaded girl the Project had sent him earlier. The number 6,821 appeared below the picture. In less than two hours the pic would disappear from his viewer forever. Mementos created that most dreadful of all demons: emotional attachment.

Mack looked up at the boat coming and thought he saw the freckled, redheaded girl. She was on the lower level, pale hand over her eyes. Probably Irish.

Mack smiled. She waved to him. Just as he'd gotten a pic of her, she'd gotten a pic of him. That's how it would stay too. No names, ever. He would call her "wife" she would call him "husband." If they clicked and got playful, maybe by the end of the night the names would evolve into "wifey" and "hubby".

She would be pleased. This was the first time in her life she would be with a man. Probably the only time.

She would giggle like a kid on the way back to his apartment. She would gaze upon him wide-eyed, jaw agape. Like a rock star's biggest groupie. Not because Mack was Mr. Alpha Male. No. In fact, Mack was unusually short, had a face only a mother could love and snorted loudly when he laughed. In Pre-Anomaly Days he was a trash collector no woman would give a second glance. But now, Post-Anomaly, he was nothing short of a god. And so far he had been with six thousand eight-hundred twenty adoring women. That would beat any rock star's record, he was certain of that.

Later, back at Mack's place, they would talk a little, just enough to break the ice. Then they would conjugate. Afterward, they would cuddle, maybe fall asleep, but before sunrise, he would leave her in her bed and go back to his room. That practice was a strict order from the Project.

Tomorrow maybe he would see her leave. Maybe he wouldn't. It didn't matter. It wasn't supposed to. They were to remain detached.

This was a physical task. A very, very important physical task.

Tomorrow morning, Mack's freckled redhead could be leaving Manhattan carrying the first male child conceived in two generations... or not.

Pablo interrupted Mack's musings: "What was so special about her? Wife 17?"

"What's so special about a snowflake?" Mack asked.

"It is one of many... but it is the only one like it..." answered Pablo.

Mack shrugged and nodded.

"Do you think of her when you're... you know?" Pablo asked.

"Yes," Mack said.

"You will think of her tonight then?"

"Probably," Mack nodded. At some point, Wife 17's face would appear over the redhead's. Then Mack would make believe he was making love to the woman he loved instead of performing a physical task with Wife 6,821.

"Lucky bastard," Pablo smiled a devilish grin. Sometimes Pablo had a way of saying things. Was he really jealous of Mack? Or did he just want Mack to feel better? It didn't matter. Nothing else was as important except the task at hand.

This was no time for envy. No time for judgment. No time for love.

Mack chuckled. "Pablo? You think when someone dies in their sleep they just... stay in whatever dream they were dreaming, you know, forevermore?"

"It's been postulated by some ancient religions and philosophers," Pablo returned. "Why?"

"Just asking," Mack smiled and waved again at the redhead on the approaching ferry. Behind her the brilliant orange sunset exploded in the sky, a cloud pattern so rich and layered, it was breathtaking. Mack realized this was the only time the sunset would look this exact way. Tomorrow would be different, the day after that different from the previous two days. Change is one of universe's few certainties.

Mack could think of one other certainty the universe has in store for all living things. Life itself is a terminal disease... And when that certainty happened, Mack hoped he'd be dreaming of Wife 17.

THE ENEMY INVISIBLE

I: RISING

It had been over a century since the planet Um 39 was discovered. Three days since it imploded. Now Human Civilization was on the brink of another fuel crisis. The wells went dry... for a second time.

It's November 22nd, 9:02am. Dr. Becker has twenty minutes to get to the Vaporizer. Lucky for him he got his NeuroPhysics degree at MIT Earth in Old Boston. He remembers a shortcut which will get him around the centuries-old "Big Dig", which ties up the JFK expressway to this day.

A new fuel source had been found on Um 39. It was a rebirth. You're probably too young to remember the end of the Fossil Fuel Era on Earth. But when the wells went dry- when the last drill coughed up its last drop of oil- there was panic. Accepting solar cells and electricity meant giving up speed and power everywhere. From the aircar to the gigantic andro manufacturing plants. Everything slowed. Nobody could travel as far nor as fast. People had to learn patience. They had to happy with less. It was awful. Human Civilization plummeted

into a new dark age. And when the Church rose to power...
complete blackout.

The funniest part was the oil supply hadn't dried up
completely. GASA (the now defunct Global Air & Space
Administration) had reserved earth's last hundred million
gallons of crude for its Beacon project. Right up until the
Beacon's launch, it was World Congress's best-kept secret.
Not even the Church knew about it. Church and State were on
pleasant terms to be sure. But by the time the Church caught
wind of the Beacon it had already passed the moon.

The Beacon launch was a crapshoot and World Congress bet
everything on it. This ship had the fastest, most powerful
engine ever built. To boot, its computer would utilize the
gravitational pull of every successive planet in Earth's system
to build momentum on its journey into deep space. Like the
atomic bomb, The Beacon had every scientist who worked on
it wondering exactly what would happen when countdown
ended and they finally hit "ignition". Some thought its engine
might propel the rocket backward in time. Others feared it
would shatter the atmosphere, stripping Earth naked and
killing every life form on the surface in a nanosecond. One or
two believed it would blow up, giving everyone a terrific
hundred million gallon light show. None of those things
happened.

*It is now 9:10. Twelve minutes before the bodies General
Hebert Corncrisp and four of his High Commanders are to be
vaporized. No funeral. No services. Not even one prayer for
their souls. Nearly every life form in the galaxy, Becker
included, wishes the five of them nothing short of eternal
damnation. "If there is a hell, may Corncrisp and his men go to
it..." is the sentiment.*

The Beacon shot into space early one September morning back in 2260. The exact date is subject to argument. After the launch, there was a big shutdown. The Big Shutdown new history books call it. Yes, the Church was involved damn them. Nobody went to work. Everyone piled their families into their landcars and made a beeline for World Congress when it was located in Old New York. When their cars ran dry of solar power or electricity, they hitched. And when they couldn't get a ride they walked.

All across the country power outages occurred- nobody was supervising the grids. Stratoplanes were grounded, nobody to fly them. Handfuls of frustrated shoppers stood at the doors of their favorite vendors, nobody to let them in. Exceedingly rich people (who had no idea what was going on) panicked and called their local Peace Station. But there wasn't a Peace Officer to be found. They too had joined the Big Shutdown and marched to Old Manhattan.

By the time the International Guard made it to Manhattan, a hundred million people had clogged the highways and skyways leading to the island. For hundreds of miles in every direction, all you could see was people. The Nondenominational Super Vizar (name unknown) stood at the front of the endless mob, demanding every member of the World Congress (names unknown). This was a revolution and as is customary in such uprisings, the mob was going to execute the old regime, very violently and very slowly. TV cameras picked up every frame of action because newscasters knew better than to not show up for work that day.

The International Guard could do nothing but stand before the mob. But the mob was quite serene despite the Super

Viz's threats- which were by the way delivered in a very calm fashion.

Okay, the Nondenominational Church was the end result of religions bashing one another. As if everyone began wondering who you really serving if you were a Jew-hating Catholic, or a Christian-hating Muslim, or a Moon-hating Hari Krishna? Certainly not God. Some hack had written this national bestseller called "Nondenominational Faith." People took to it like it was water in the desert like somebody had finally given words to what everyone was feeling. Nobody even questioned the fact that it was a so-so novel, Faith being the titular heroine.

The unification of beliefs is one of those things that looks good on paper. But all the Church did was create the biggest religion ever conceived, complete with its own hierarchy of "Gifteds". Holy Carrier, Holy Clerk, Supervisor, Officer in Charge and at the top of the food chain the Super Vizar- who was not at any costs to be confused with the more common Supervisor. Then there were the laymen of Church Doctrine, called a "Customer", although a few laymen did graduate to "Valued Customer", qualifying them to lead Church service. But they would have to be especially zealous to make that leap. The Gifteds numbered in the thousands. Customers numbered in the billions. Never have so many listened to so few.

9:12. Becker stands in the hypervator racing to the top floor of Vapor Central. "The Worst Go First" is the Vaporizer's motto. And, like society itself, the worst always wind up on top. General Corncrisp's body is located on floor five hundred just under the roof. Becker glances at his watch. This hypervator couldn't go fast enough.

84

Once the wells ran dry and the last gallon of oil was used (barring that extra hundred mill beneath GASA) serious fatalities began occurring. Those used to driving long distances suddenly found themselves stranded in barren areas to die either by a scorching desert sun, hunger or a pack of ravenous coyotes. Those who had no idea how to heat their homes would die in ineptly lit fires or else perish from the cold. Ignorance was not bliss after all. The machines that worked for people were permanently out of service. People had to take care of themselves now. Oh, how they hated that prospect and a global malaise began to brew.

This is when the Church quietly took over society. How did they do this? They told their followers the reason there was no more oil, the reason their houses would have to be heated with wood-burning stoves, why their electricity was rationed, why they would only be able to drive short distances very slowly, why progress was halting, why civilization was taking two gigantic leaps back and ignorant people were dying was this: because God was punishing them. Oil had become a drug that society abused and these were the consequences for that abuse. The punishment notion worked like a charm, bonding everyone to the Nondenominational faith no matter what race, color, sex or social status.

It took another five years after the wells went dry for GASA to launch Beacon I. So when it finally did in the wee hours of that September morning there was a shock-wave. The launch was captured live by a few lucky broadcast networks so most found out right away. It was supposed to be good news the Leader of the World Congress (name unknown) said later that day as he lay strapped to a table before the angry and incredibly huge mob that wanted to see his blood. This was a chance for us to reach out for help from the galaxy. "Someday in the not too distant future, a more sophisticated race will discover Beacon I and come to our aid". That was Beacon I's purpose all along. A call to someone out there who could give us some gas. With just one catch. A hundred million gallons of it were needed to make the call.

Like most religions before them, the Church became sensitive right from the very start. They knew they were right about everything because they had a rapport with humankind's Heavenly Maker. Why is it anyone who claims to have God on the other line gets very angry and very intolerant very quickly? The hundred million gallons of gas was merely the match. The fuse was the notion that there were one or more life forms out there comparable to ours. The Beacon launch wasn't just a waste of precious fluids. It was heresy.

So the Church began referring to the Beacon launch as "The Unforgivable Act".   Many had perished when the well went dry. Nonetheless, trusted leaders had hoarded fuel for their own sacrilegious rocket launch! It was cause for outrage. And as God had punished the rest of us for abuse, so the world leaders would be punished by the Church- acting on behalf of God.

Now, as oblivious as the Church was about the Beacon project, the World Congress was absolutely clueless about the discontent its own distant leadership had created. That and the Church... who laid waiting for the exact right moment to seize the wheel.

The World Congress Executions lasted well into the next day. The Church took over everything. Its first task was to put strict laws on power usage.

Freeways, skyways, and parking garages stood like dinosaur bones in some massive outdoor museum. Manufacturing plants were converted into living spaces and Nondenominational ("Nondy" for short) Churches. Things like cell phones, central heating, and power mowers became a thing of the past. Aircars, the biggest (and smallest) gas guzzlers ever built, were immediately stripped and used for parts to keep Land Vehicles running. Electricity and solar power had to be rationed so tightly that the use of an LV was reserved for only the direst of circumstances. People, who drove without just cause, used too much electricity or solar cells were branded Swine and had their reproductive organs removed without anesthesia. The Church did not wish to mutilate people for punishment or even for the fun of it. But they needed to send a message to the masses. The Customers caught on quick. Within days- hours even- nobody dared even think of the use of any kind of power whatsoever.

The Beacon launch was no longer referred to in any way. The Church erased all records - digital, paper, etc. - of it, the people involved and, while they were at it, all of history itself. The Unforgivable Act and everything preceding that was behind them now, the Church said, leave it there. But it sat in the belly of the mass consciousness, like a hunk of undigested cheese. There, malaise bubbled below the surface. "If only I had that hundred million gallons," all seemed to be thinking. "I could have visited my dying mother in Arkansas... I could be listening to favorite music and watching my favorite TV shows... the road would have been lit as I walked home from the bar and I wouldn't have fallen into that ditch..." It was as if the Beacon launch had cost a hundred million human lives. Looking back now it ultimately did. And a whole lot more.

It was about this time that the impossible happened. The word "miracle" was used at first but new history books are careful about any terms that have quasi-religious overtones. So... the "impossible" happened one spring morning. It literally dropped right out of the sky. Was it a year, two years, five years after the wells went dry? Timekeeping devices needed power to run so they were chucked out long before the impossible happened. And besides the world had already adopted the Church Calendar. The Church did not believe in years or months. On a roll with their burning of history, the Church decided that the passage of time filled humankind with useless anxieties so the Church calendar consisted of one five day week. No weekends. No months or years. Friday gave birth to Monday and week zero would begin again, into oblivion.

9:15 am. Becker is starting to sweat as he paces at the Reception desk. No one there. He presses the buzzer. "Just get to the Vaporization door by 9:20am. A second later and General Corncrisp will be really crisp," the Chief Vapor Tech had quipped. From his gurgled voice and inappropriate sense of humor, Becker figured him to be a Frazhic by way of the Orion Arm. Finally, the receptionist, a young Pleiadean in a suit and tie arrives at the desk. The Pleiadean's smile is unnerving though he's well aware their race's even disposition make them perfect for jobs like this. Becker produces a permission disk from Galactic Parliament to examine the late General Corncrisp. The Pleiadean scans it and nods. "Okay Dr. Becker, General Corncrisp's remains are in room A2..." the Pleiadean says, giving Becker a pocket map of Floor 500. Becker feels his eyes stinging from the sweat now as he breaks into run down the South Corridor.

Back in the late twentieth century, people said they saw things called flying saucers- crafts flown by extraterrestrial life forms more intelligent than man. Some claimed to be kidnapped by flying saucers and given body cavity examinations by the intelligent life forms who flew them. Pundits called these eyewitnesses "crackpots"- an antiquated term since the phonetic pronunciation is a Rorglian term of endearment, loosely translated it means sweetheart. In fact, it was the Rorglians, acting on behalf of the Galaxy Recognition Committee, who landed their flying saucer in the middle of a soccer field in Gary, Indiana. Looking back now the "crackpots" had it right. There was a reason why extraterrestrials stalked lone pedestrians or motorists- in isolated areas, in the middle of the night- and it wasn't because the people who reported them were crazy. These aliens really were observing the human race, waiting for Earth to intellectually "catch up" with the rest of advanced life in the cosmos careful not to interfere with humanity's development. So they kept their research to individuals. Of course, there were blunders where the extraterrestrial observers meddled a little too much, resulting in the creation of Atlantis, the pyramids in South America and Egypt, Stonehenge and of course some crop circles in what was once the state of Pennsylvania.

The first humans welcomed aboard the Rorglian vessel, coincidentally called "The Crackpot", were not important people. They were merely the first ten people brave enough to approach the ship. By the end of that day, it was learned that a Cygnian ship had landed in China. The Pleiadeans landed in Russia. And so forth around the globe flying saucers greeted earth with good news.

Humans were finally welcomed into the High Mind, a community of thousands of intelligent species throughout the Milky Way.

The world- almost all Churchgoers by now- was in shock. These aliens were, uh... people. Sure they looked a lot different. But they were intelligent, compassionate, and had goodwill and table manners. Not to mention they drove spaceships! Could it be God gave man cousins in the far reaches of the universe to play with someday? The Church remained circumspect. Polite but circumspect.

On that Gary Indiana soccer field, the Rorglian pilot spoke into has transvoker, expressing amazement at how such a scientifically advanced culture could have also embraced spirituality. "Never have I seen a race mesh thought and faith so completely..."

At first, the humans at the Crackpot's banquet table- all Customers- humbly responded with quotes from their literature and the rhetoric the Gifteds had drummed into them. They sounded pretty good because this is the way they were forced to talk Church talk all day. One of the humans took a hearty bite of his Starbat on a Stick and had to ask: "What do you mean by scientifically advanced? We use wood to heat our homes. We go to the bathroom in holes we dig into the earth. When we need to go long distances, we ride bicycles or sleds pulled by dogs."

The Rorglian pilot's blowhole spouted with laugh juice, "Humility is your race's calling card. I am talking about the Beacon!" All the Church Customers gasped at the vile word's utterance.

9:17. Becker winds his way through the maze of corridors on Floor 500. Each door looks the same as the last, and the room numbers seem to be out of sequence. He trusts the map and his desire to learn. Like many others, he bears nothing but hatred for General Corncrisp. But also like many others, he's perplexed as to why the highly decorated soldier took four of his men, hijacked that ooze freighter and drove it headlong into SkyChapel Beta two days ago. Dr. Becker could not care less what Vapor Central *did with Corncrisp's body. What he wants is inside the dead man's head.*

The spiritual confusion did not last as long as one would think. That day, which came to be called New Thanksgiving, was April 1st, 2300.

9:18. Breaking into a run now, Dr. Becker remembers that day. He was just a small boy but he never forgot when his dad came back from the store with something that looked like a book and hung it on the wall. "What's that?" Little Dougie Becker had asked his mom that day. "It's a calendar..." she replied choking back tears.

The Church lost none of their customers on New Thanksgiving. Just all of its power. They did not go down without a fight though, damn them. Valued Customers began breaking off into sects of zealots, renaming themselves VIPs. The VIPs believed the aliens landing was some kind of spiritual test. Man was still God's only. These were apparitions conjured up to trick us into thinking otherwise. Behind closed doors, the VIPs spoke of the church's return to power. It would have to wait for the perfect catalyst. But the Nondenominational Church would be back.

The rest of the earth was excited about this new circle of friends. Friends who came with medical advances that, once put to practice, tripled human lifetimes. They also came with a science far beyond anything even Albert Einstein could have conceived of. The slingshot theory behind the Beacon's trip was nothing compared to transportal navigation, light beam hitching, and recycled energy. What a smack on the forehead that was. Energy is the one thing in the universe that never dies, earth scientists had discovered that hundreds of years ago! Earthlings took this new technology and ran with it like heretofore stabled thoroughbreds in an open field.

Although the Nondenominational religion was a shadow of its former self, human spirituality played a role in its acceptance into any circle of alien cousins. Earth people and their serenity were welcomed everywhere. The human race began expanding, living longer, prospering, conjugating, populating every nebula and cranny- from the Sagittarian Arm to the asteroid rings of Planet Dark. Using the space travel technology the High Mind had shared, it only took a few decades for humans to knit themselves into the galactic community.

For a time Earth was the Milky Way's fair-haired boy. Every life form's favorite adopted son. From Perseus to Cygnus it was unanimous. The human race was rozzer, Rorglian for "the new cool kid who transferred from another school" (loose translation). For a while, copying Earth culture became the thing to do. There was nothing shocking about seeing Grook wearing a smiley face tee shirt or a Crab Nebular transport bearing a "Get off My Ass" magnet. Splotnik youths took to wearing gigantic afros. And if you didn't listen to "Earth Pop" you were definitely not rozzer.

So it was no surprise when election season in the year 2330 brought a new first for the human race: a seat on Galactic Parliament. To the sound of thundering applause.

How could things have gone so bad so fast?

II: FALLING

9:19 am. Dr. Becker remembers 2330 clearly. By then his mom and dad had settled into a Martian retirement community. It was a nice place furnished with its own telescope so they could always see Earth whenever they wanted. Having graduated from MIT Mars and now living in the Pleiades himself, Becker's just starting his BCR project- BCR being a monogram for "brain cell reanimation." The weathered briefcase clutched to his chest is the same one he started with back in 2430. "Please God," he thinks looking at his map, "Let me find this door in time..." He is hellbent on reanimating the dead general in spite of all that hatred. Over a hundred million humans died on SkyChapel Beta. A hundred million. One life for each gallon of gas used to launch the Beacon.

One day the human race was the darling of the cosmos. The next, it was a juggernaut threatening to destroy everyone and everything. Maybe it started when humans began representing themselves in Galactic Parliament. The first parliament representative, "Human I" (anonymous reps were referred to by species only), was a career politician who attempted to infect Parliament with "rhetoric"- ultimately called shnertz (origin Perseusian, meaning "that which puts pussworms in your third stomach"). Because most other species in the galaxy have sensory perceptors other than eyes and ears, style means nothing. They could not see Human I was photogenic or hear that sweet Baptist drawl in his voice. All they sensed was his shnertz. Luckily it only took seven more representatives to work this kink out. Human VIII was probably the first honest man ever elected. Things were supposed to go okay now. But they only got worse.

Because, besides being bad at government, humans have this inexplicable urge to take over stuff. If prompted they will use every tool available to achieve control over what they want. They will start with peaceful tactics, for example, shnertz. If that doesn't work they will eventually move to weapons of mass destruction. But in between the shnertz and the nuclear bombs, there is a step. Humans have to humalate. The Rorglians coined this word. It means to keep telling lies to yourself until you find one you can believe to the depths of your soul. In case this detail was missed, double-check humalate's prefix.

The year was 2437. A Human real estate expedition struck out for Tangent Far and found a planet. Absolutely desolate on the surface it was uninhabitable in every sense. Nonetheless, the real estate agents found natural pores on the surface leading thousands of feet below. Envirobots were dispatched into the pores. They came back with samples of what these wells contained. Preliminary tests revealed that the team of realtors were about to change professions forever. And that they would never have to suffer through another open house again. Did I mention each and every one of these realtors was human? I did? It bears repeating then.

9:20. Becker's finger jabs at the buzzer. Door A2 opens. Sure enough, a pink and purple Frazhic stands there sucking a cheeseburger into his vertical masticator. "Congratulations, Doc," he laughs through his voxer in a thick Old Boston accent, "We was just about to fry the bastid." Becker breathes a sigh of relief as he sees General Corncrisp's corpse lying under a gigantic metal nipple: the vaporizer.

The realtors were given resistance on their find. Perhaps they had been too quick to celebrate. Every race but the humans had known about this planet for a long time. It was called Umthrezvizydx!%k#. A mouthful for many species in cosmos- whether they had a mouth or not. It was eventually nicknamed Um 39. Humans were given the digested story of this strange and horrible planet. A visit to Um 39 brought misfortune to every race that had attempted to inhabit it since the dawn of time. No being could explain the phenomenon as it had been eons since an entire city of Warlords disappeared from its surface overnight. "And just who are the Warlords?" Human VIII asked in Chamber one session. "Exactly", came the response.

For the first time, humans began to laugh at their alien friends. All this wisdom. All this technology. And they were superstitious! Humans did their best to explain their own superstitions about a place on Earth called The Bermuda Triangle, where planes and boats disappeared and that science figured out it was all just crazy weather patterns! The aliens were confused by this response. Humans had trusted alien mentoring since the beginning. Yet now they thought they knew more about this place they had just "discovered" than those who had known about it for eons. How could this be?

The substance in the pores of Um 39 was christened bluck. It was bright green ooze, a lot like the stuff they'd sell to little kids at earth stores so they could gross their sisters out. But here's the thing. It was highly combustible. It was like something humans had seen long ago. Before the wells went dry. Word began to spread about this oozy compound. The realtors already had their ad campaign going before the first bluckpump was installed on Um 39. It was "Daylight Again!"

Earth's alien cousins, who were getting referred to as "non-humans" in some burgeoning circles, had to ask this: "When you were welcomed you only lived to be eighty of your years. You were riding bicycles and horses. Then you were freely given a wealth of new technology. This technology has enabled your race to live longer and travel to the far reaches of the galaxy with ease. What need do you have for more speed and power?"

The non-humans just didn't get it. Married with transportal navigation, light beam hitching and recycled energy this new fuel could give humans an edge over the competition. They could get to work faster. They could get home faster. They'd have more time. Not too mention a long-term goal that seemed to sit in every human's heart since they had struck out into the galaxy. Bluck would give the human race the ability to do something not even the most advanced race in the Milky Way had done. Travel outside it. To see what was beyond them... and the rest of the intelligent life forms out here, which had become yesterday's news pretty damn quick for some reason.

The intention was good. It was in the name of advancing past what was already had. "What's wrong with what's 'already had'?" was the non-human question. The answer was long, laborious and full of shnertz. Short version? What humans already had just wasn't enough. The discovery of bluck had stirred something within earth people. Something not seen in a great time. It was like an inbred addiction to some long-lost drug that suddenly turned up. The human race did not pick up this addiction where they had left off when the wells went dry. They started where they would have been had they never stopped. All the while there was much human laughter at the warnings of even the wisest beings.

So amidst the loud protests of non-humans (who some humans were now calling Inhumans), bluck was sprung onto cosmo-ciety. Customers began lining up to convert their space pods into superpods. Money started rolling in. Capitalism wasn't far behind. Turns out the realtors had not been thorough enough when claiming Um 39 and could only claim ownership to the bluckpump they had built. More professional people (some of them not even former real estate agents) began building bluckpumps on Um 39, dotting its surface like tiny, ravenous mosquitoes. Gluttonous is not a strong enough word to describe the bluck consumption that followed. Despite the seemingly unlimited supply found on Um 39, competing bluckeneers decided to gouge the hell out of consumers. Owning a vehicle with a bluck engine would surely make a rich man break a sweat. However, everyone decided they needed one, as though they'd been completely unhappy up until now. Curious.

This was an innocent time. Humans had finally carved out their niche in the galaxy. There was more productivity, more work, more time to do the things everyone wanted to do. More more more! And more more more was done really really fast... In the Bluck Age, the only way you could tell a superpod drove by was the sudden trail of green smoke (this green smoke would eventually introduce into the galaxy something previously unknown to alien species- lung cancer). But it wasn't just the pollution. It wasn't just the deafening hum the bluck engines made. It wasn't even the offensive smell. It was the accidents. Beings of all species were getting killed in senseless collisions. Collisions that could have been avoided if the faster vehicle had been traveling at a reasonable speed. Inhumans from every sector were beginning to fear the loud hum of an incoming craft powered by bluck. The name for this ominous hum came from the Sloorthian imitation of it. So it is by sheer coincidence the hum of a bluck engine is now called "the doom."

Um 39 was now the hot-button issue at Parliament. The Elder Reps demanded action against this new obsession with that green slimy ooze. It was becoming too costly. Parliament was not entirely sure what to do. Outlawing bluck would be a good start. Opposition to that idea started with Human VIII but quickly spread to the other Junior Reps. Its true, bluck power had introduced a dangerous element into the cosmunity. But humans and other beings, especially those who owned superpod manufacturing plants or any entities dependent on the fuel, began to worry about progress slowing down. Perhaps special lanes in the starway could be reserved for only high-speed vehicles. Surely that would eliminate accidents. When accidents quadrupled, a speed limit was enforced. Accidents did not stop happening but the fines paid by violators helped to ease the pain.

9:20. Dr. Becker is about to use his Injector again. On a brain, this time. Several decades ago he reanimated the hand of a man who had been dead for several days. He stood there, butterflies in his stomach, as the hand moved on its own. But hand cells are light years away from brain cells. He tried, again and again, to perfect his formula since with mixed results. He hopes today he found the right combination... Becker asks the Frazhic vapotech for a few minutes. But he's not sure how long it's going to take to reanimate General Corncrisp's brain. And even if the brain comes back to life, can Becker expect Corncrisp to be able to listen and communicate? All Becker has is his hand-held EEG. Hey, it's more than nothing. "How could a man knowingly extinguish a hundred million lives?" he wonders. Pretty soon he hopes he'll have his answer. If he gets that then the impending Nobel Prize and patented Brain Cell Reanimator will be the icing on the cake.

With nothing curing the galaxy of the horrific accidents- which seemed to double every day- Parliament now knew what it had to do. They had to somehow regulate bluck. In hindsight, it seemed like a great idea. But human bluckaneers took this as a slap in the face. Parliament calmly explained how the earth people had become a scourge in the solar system they encountered. Where once humans were considered pious and pure they were now seen as boastful, wasteful and devoid of any spirituality whatsoever.

Discontent between humans and Inhumans could only end one way. In God's name. In light of recent accusations that humans were "devoid of any spirituality whatsoever", Human VIII felt he needed to announce his religion to all in Chamber. That's right. Human VIII was a "valued customer" in the Nondenominational Church of Earth. The "of Earth" part was new but it was the same old religion that disappeared during the technology boom. Truth is they were always there behind the curtain. Getting stronger. "According to the book Nondenominational Faith, and I quote, 'it is the right of every human being to make whatever they find their own'. Um 39 was founded by humans, it is a place where humans toil and the only true accomplishment we humans have achieved since being welcomed to the High Mind. Um 39 is ours. God wants us to have it. Those who stand in our way stands in the way of God's will. And we will fight because He wants us to fight. Fight with every fiber of our being. Our human being." Human VIII sat. Though there was no applause, billions of earth people glued to the live broadcast burst into cheers.

So it was war? Parliament backed down. War had not been waged in eons. Not since... the Warlords...

It was cause for humans everywhere to unite and celebrate. God made the biggest governing body in the galaxy back down! For the umpteenth time in history, humans had found religion once again. Nondenominational SkyChapels began springing up all over the Milky Way. The patience of the VIPs had paid off. The Church was back.

9:21. Becker finishes shaving the hair off an area on Corncrisp's skull. Marks an "x" in the middle of that patch of skin with a red marker. Then Becker reaches into his briefcase and pulls out the oldest instrument in the history of Neurosurgery: the drill.

To the human race, things were fantastic. God was in their corner. They were enthralled with their superpods. They loved flying by the slower moving conventional pods the lesser races were driving. They were climbing the food chain once again. Once they were the dominant species earth. Now they were poised to dominate the galaxy. After that was done it would be time to launch the first extra-galactic rocket! Truly, God had created man in His image. Pre-ordained to rule the universe in His name.

Meanwhile, the rest of the galaxy began withdrawing from the people of Earth. In public, other species would shield their offspring from human children. They hid in sheltered communities. Places the humans would not find. It wasn't out of snobbery. It was out of terror. The human race and their "God" had become a cannon loosed upon all life, intelligent and non-intelligent. Ironically, there was much more prayer than ever before amongst the "Inhumans" who had rediscovered their gods as well.

Despite all that fear and hubris, it was a quiet time. But looking back, a human military man- perhaps General Corncrisp himself? - coined the phrase: "Peace is war without the fighting." In other words, there was tension. Something had to give. And one day something did.

It was an attack on a commuter transport headed back from Um 39. A nearby station in Cygnus 12 reported this message from whoever was at the ship's communicator: "Long live the Umlings, death to the swine, Mother Heart eternal in Um 39!" then drove the transport into an asteroid. Two hundred humans died.

There was an emergency Chamber. Human VIII informed all present that God was really unhappy about what happened to two hundred and one of His children today.

"Who are the Umlings?" he demanded of Parliament.

The answer was quick. "Nobody knows. Nobody has ever seen one."

Human VIII was dumbfounded. "I can only assume you are obfuscating."

"We have been honest with you and your species this whole time. We warned you about Um 39 a long, long time ago."

Despite heightened security and paranoia, the next Umling attack came the next day at an Earth bank on Planet

Manhattan's eleventh moon. There were no eyewitnesses but security cameras picked up a cloaked figure that walked into the lobby and shouted in perfect English "Long live the Umlings! Death to the Swine! Mother Heart eternal! In Um 39!" Static filled the screen a second later. Because that's when the figure detonated the Tri-Decimator under his cloak. The blast leveled the bank building. A thousand humans were killed, along with several Pleiadean tellers and a Mureenic custodian. A close-up on the cloaked figure revealed nothing but shadows.

The next emergency meeting of Parliament was called. Shifty-eyed and sweating, Human VIII stayed the course: "So that's what an Umling is, someone who doesn't like what we're doing on Um 39?"

All around the room, shrugging from species of all kinds. Finally the eldest member, Rorgl MMC stood up. "No..." he said, "According to the- what did you humans call it? - the superstition, an Umling is a native of Um 39..."

"There is no life on Um 39. Nothing could live on Um 39."

Rorgl MMC shook his head, "All I know is what I have been told by generations long gone now. The Umlings went under a different name though. Your ancestors have stories about things called gremlins. Invisible creatures that climb into machines and make them malfunction. My ancestors called simply called them 'the enemy invisible.' Retaliation is useless. I suggest complete abandonment of Um 39 if it's not already too late for your kind. I am sorry that is all I can tell you..."

Human VIII stormed out of Chamber. Gremlins?!

The next day a superpod plant on Rorgl itself erupted in flame, killing thousands. At that very moment, a message disk arrived at the office of Human VIII. He immediately called Chamber and made Parliament watch the contents of the disk. Representatives watched in horror as a shadowy face chanted at them all. "Long live the Umlings... Death to the swine... Mother Heart eternal... in Um 39." The Umling recorded himself standing at a pay-corder... right outside the Rorgl superpod plant, visible in the distance. As he moved closer to the recorder to end the transmission a gasp was heard throughout Parliament. The face looked human!

"Apparently these Umlings have fantastic mimicking abilities..."

"Or perhaps you have Umling sympathizers in your own kind!"

"Shut up!" Human VIII barked at whatever species said that "If any planet in the Milky Way is harboring an Umling we will blow it out of the sky. Uh... in God's name of course."

"You have our full cooperation in this matter."

"All right. Did anybody's ancestor ever give you a physical description of an Umling?"

"We've been telling you. Nobody knows. Nobody's seen an Umling since-"

"I know I know the f___ing Warlords. Well, I can tell you one thing about these Umlings that I bet you didn't know. Because none of you has said they're a bunch of sh__eating cowards who are too afraid to show their faces!"

Parliament had no comment but many members flipped through their translators, looking for words the galactic youth had picked up long ago. Human swear words were rozzer.

With no physical description available besides "fantastic mimicking abilities", Earth's armies, fueled by zeal for the Nondenominational God and poised for battle since Human VIII declared his religion, went into action. Every planet was under suspicion. No stone was unturned. Camps were built for displaced residents as tanks rolled homes into dust. The cries of mothers of all species and their offspring could be heard throughout the Milky Way. Some beings were taken into custody under suspicion of being an Umling "IMM" or "in mimic mode." Some of these were never seen again...

9:22. Becker gently removes the drill and readies a short hypodermic. It had taken 10cc's to reanimate that dead hand. Becker will start with that.

Every day brought another Umling attack somewhere in the cosmos. As deadly as they were baffling, each attack brought a higher death toll. Almost all the victims were humans. After one week the toll was at a hundred thousand. Humans everywhere were possessed by fear and anger. Despite the assistance from nearly every species in the galaxy, human paranoia and xenophobia were rampant. Yet through all of this, the aliens who had taken earth people under their wing prayed for their misguided brethren. Places of worship from the Pleiades to the Great Planet resonated with thoughts and prayers for those who were once the Golden Race of the Galaxy. How could creatures so erudite allow their brains to be harnessed by such frail emotions as greed, hate, and fear? Maybe their god really had made them that way.

Speaking of that human god, "Nondy" SkyChapels were getting packed to the gills nearly every day. People were wondering why this is happening. The answer was simple. God wanted them to fight for what was theirs.

Powered by the Church and obscene amounts of bluck, destroyers began patrolling the spaceways. Destroyers emblazoned with what had become the most recognized symbol in the universe. The Nondenominational Circle. It had started out as a peace sign. But that extra line at the bottom was removed for purity's sake and now it was basically a Mercedes Benz logo.

All efforts at turning up the elusive Umlings were fruitless. And with each attack, their recurring disappearing act became more and more baffling. Nonetheless, the bluckpumps pumped, the destroyers pushed forth. Deserted planets were reduced to ash. Not one Umling was found.

General Corncrisp himself was a visible character in all this, assuring humans everywhere "We will make this enemy invisible visible."

9:23. Using great care, Becker pulls the hypodermic from Corncrisp's brain. He'll wait one minute. If need be he'll inject the brain with 10 more ccs...

It all ended on a Sunday morning at approximately six o'clock. That's when the first bluckpump went dry. As in, nothing, empty. Within three hours every other bluckpump suffered the same result. It was doomsday for Um 39. The planet's stagnant atmosphere began shifting ominously. For the first time, work crews began to see clouds. Then lightning. Relentless hurricane winds began pounding the bluckpumps. Half of the workers got off the planet alive. The rest perished in their transports or on the pumps themselves.

One of the survivors was General Corncrisp who had been on hand to make sure the last of the bluck was allocated for his destroyer. He made it off Um 39 in that now infamous bluck transport.

Sunday at one after midnight the planet of Um 39 imploded.

At 3am, Rorgl eyewitnesses reported a gigantic contrail of green smoke appearing in their sunny sky. Whatever went past was big and powered by an enormous bluck-powered engine.

At six am Monday- half a million miles from Rorgl- SkyChapel Beta barely caught a glimpse of the bluck transport before it slammed headlong into a central generator. Having just had its bluck fill-up it ignited, causing a chain reaction. It only took twenty-two seconds for SkyChapel Beta to become history.

9:24. Seeing no movement on his pocket EEG, Becker readies 10 more ccs of Becker. Then... the EEG's readout flickers! Corncrisp's brain is alive!

Just before the bluck transport hit its target, it jettisoned a dinghy- a tiny pod capable of holding no more than five: General Hebert Corncrisp and his four conspirators. All lieutenants in Earth's army. In hindsight, the dinghy's launch was just a fraction of a second too late. A smoldering girder from SkyChapel Beta slammed into its undercarriage. Since none inside the craft had enough time to safely fasten themselves, they died from severe whiplash. At slightly after 6am (Rorglian solar time), four necks simultaneously snapped like twigs.

9:25. Corncrisp's brain readings are going off the map. So much so that Becker wonders if his pocket EEG's malfunctioning. Then... Corncrisp's head begins to move...

General Corncrisp was one of the most revered humans in the Milky Way. Though his high rank garnered him respect in the armed forces, General Corncrisp was known better as the human representative in Parliament, Human VIII. No being, human or otherwise, could even begin to explain how this man could have been seduced by the Umlings. Yet it had happened. A post-mortem DNA test proved him a man and not some alien mimicking a man.

107

9:25 and two seconds... Becker can't believe his eyes. Corncrisp is shaking his head from side to side! His eyes and mouth were still shut tight but... it's as if he's about to waken from a horrible dream shouting "no!" Becker's in his glory, success! And more importantly- Becker just knows this in his heart of hearts- the mystery of the Umlings is about to be solved. Then-

-General Corncrisp's head splits in half. Like a freshly hatching egg!

Becker is frozen in amazement. The brain is literally alive and... trying to crawl out its skull? No...

It's not a brain. Too green. Too slimy. What the-

Bluck! That's the noise the green slime made as it squoze out of Corncrisp's cracked cranium. Becker was still frozen in shock when the thing leaped onto his face. Becker's hypodermic and his pocket EEG hit the floor as the doctor tried to pull it off his face. It had already started siphoning itself into the doctor's nostrils.

Becker was momentarily blinded and deafened by the thing wrapped around his face. He opened his mouth to breathe and couldn't. But the panic only lasted a second. Becker's arms relaxed as it began to consume his brain. For a moment the Becker's thoughts intertwined with the thoughts of the Umlings. Memories of a dark, quiet place under the surface of

Um 39. Trillions of Umlings swirling together like jellyfish, swimming through one another, constantly dividing- reproduction by mitosis... like cells. From thousands of miles beneath the uppermost layer of Umlings the soothing heartbeat of Mother, the Queen Umling, could be heard. Her heart pumped out nourishment, life and most important of all: love. Mother Heart absorbed trillions of her sick and dying every day. And every day she pumped out trillions of baby Umlings. It was a glorious cycle of rebirth without end. Until three days ago.

The Umling inside Becker's head had many brothers and sisters, more than anyone could count. One by one they died when the pipes came down into the pores. The pipes began to rip the Umlings away from Mother's heart, killing them instantly. The Umling inside Becker's head had heard of an old trick. It was an alternate life forms version of "holding your breath." That way you could survive when you got to the top of those pipes. And, if you were lucky, you would encounter one of the murderous swine who operated the pipe. You could hijack their bodies by dissolving that useless mass of tissue inside their skulls, like the way the Umling in Becker's head was doing. Swine had hearts too. Little ones but just enough to keep one Umling alive. Their skulls were quite cozy too. The Umling and three of his siblings had been very lucky to find Corncrisp and his lieutenants the day his race was extinguished forever.

But inside that dead body, the Umling's luck had run out... he perished without Corncrisp's heartbeat. Then here came this new swine with something that could bring new life to dead things. And another kind of drill. Not like the kind of drill that destroyed his home. A good kind that could penetrate swine skulls. There was definitely hope for him. Probably hope for his siblings. And in the long run, maybe the Umling race wouldn't be extinguished forever after all. Daylight Again!

As Becker's brain dissolved Becker felt a little resentful. The Umling wasn't just eating tissue. He was eating Becker's thoughts, his memories, melding them with its own. In a flash, Becker's consciousness disappeared.

9:30pm. Briefcase in hand, the Umling in Becker's body walks up to the Frazhic tech who smiles- vertically of course. "Well, what's the verdict, doc? Can we zap 'em or what?" the tech says in that thick Old Boston accent.

The Umling in Becker's body makes Becker smiles back. "I got what I needed from Corncrisp. You may vaporize him. But I need to see the other four men he was with. Actually, just their heads would be fine."

"We like to zap them whole, so I'll wait till you're finished," the tech answers, "I mean it's not like this is brain surgery, right? Follow me," it laughs at its joke and pats the Umling's shoulder.

Following the tech down the corridor, the Umling considers itself very lucky indeed gazing down at its briefcase. "Uhh... could you call three of your associates as well?" Just for a few moments."

The tech shrugged, "Three of my guys are just getting off break, we'll hook you up."

"Yes," the Umling says under his breath, "Hook us up..."

110

THE FIRST AND LAST DAY IN THE LIFE OF A BULLFROG

"I need my wife." The words came together like a puzzle. His mind seemed to cry it now… "I need my wife!"

For the past thirteen years, it had been she who had needed him. But he needed her now. Desperately. The thought shocked Patterson as soon as it came to him. Pretty much like everything else that had happened in the past two hours.

Patterson splashed around in the basin of the water fountain a little more, trying to get as much water on his rubbery body as he could. Christ, the puddle was only an eighth of an inch deep!

"Mommy look a froggy!"

Ah, crap not again. This was like the fifth kid in the park who'd spotted him. Without even glancing over his shoulder Patterson leaped out of the water fountain and began hopping down a short tunnel, hoping he could lose his newest pint-sized pursuer in the dark. Hearing the little footsteps behind him Patterson gave it all his springy legs had. As he soared through the air he felt the roof of the tunnel graze his neck.

That was close. A little more oomph and Patterson would have splattered himself up there. Got to be more careful... Steven Patterson, million dollar soap salesman, could not die a goddam frog.

He hopped out of the other end of the tunnel. As soon as the sun hit him, Patterson started to feel it again. The sun's drying light, sinking in like teeth. Dammit. He knew the kid had given up but gave a really big jump this time, now that he didn't have a ceiling. He must have gone at least twenty-five feet.

Patterson's little eyes darted around. The kid was long gone. Good friggin' riddance! No sign of a human being anywhere. And- what was that he saw to his left? A birdbath. Yes! Patterson began hopping towards it.

A guttural noise hit his tympanums just before-

A goddam Rottweiler leaped in front of the birdbath teeth bared, snapping. "Shit!" Patterson croaked helplessly and leaped back about ten feet, his tiny heart beating like a hummingbird's wings. The gigantic dog lunged at Patterson then suddenly it reared back. Like a horse. It was being reined in by its owner, who had a good grip on the leash. "Come on, Levi!" Patterson heard the owner say, pulling the hideous beast away, "You just had lunch! Honestly..."

Funny how Patterson could no longer see faces. Just legs, shoes, ankles, toes. He needed to be at the right angle. High up. Or upside down on his back. And he definitely didn't want to be upside down again.

Patterson jumped straight into the birdbath and hit it with a splash. Ahhhhh... sweet, sweet water. This puddle was nice and deep too. It felt almost like home in a weird way. Ironic how a million dollar soap salesman- current employer: The Cherish Soap Company- would wind up taking baths every fifteen minutes in order not to pass out.

He hoped he would recognize Desiree's shoes. She had so many. But he knew where she'd be in an hour which was about how much time it would take to hop there. He didn't have time to worry about crossing streets or pedestrians or that bloody sun. He was very lucky it had rained the night before. There would be plenty of puddles he could stop at between the park and the Langue Fourche. Could he hit them all before he dehydrated? Of course, he could. He was a million dollar soap salesman. He was a survivor. Not just a survivor a goddam predator. Although right now he was nothing more than a goddam bullfrog.   He would definitely have to hit every puddle along the way. He couldn't die...

Getting to Desiree was the only way Patterson could become… Patterson again.

        …

Despite the obviousness of what had happened to him earlier, it took Patterson roughly five minutes to realize what that snake Glissant had done. And he'd done exactly what he said he'd do.

One second Patterson was standing at the edge of a pond in the park, with that French wannabe restaurateur. Glissant was the one that called the meeting. Patterson supposed Glissant wanted money to sink into the Langue Fourche again. Patterson hated giving desperate people money.

But it wasn't about money at all. There wasn't even any small talk. Glissant just peered into Patterson's eye and said something.

Patterson had heard it before, the equivalent of "presto" or "abracadabra". What was that stupid word? Didn't matter that info was of no help to Patterson right now. A waste of brain power he could be spending… oh yes, it was "voila!" Hang on. He said something else before that. No, he asked something.

"You know the story of the frog prince?" was the question Glissant had asked.

Patterson laughed, "Time's money, Glissant. I hope you're setting up a really good joke."

Glissant stood there staring at Patterson for a moment, studying him. Then he put his palm out to Patterson and yelled "voila!" A bright light that seemed to come from Glissant's palm blinded Patterson momentarily. And then, Patterson was on the ground. Almost in the ground. He looked up at blades of grass that seemed like trees to him now. And it had become insanely hot. Just like that. Confused, Patterson began to look around. The world had become a much bigger place, not just the grass. He looked up up up... at Glissant's dancing shoes. He could hear Glissant snickering uncontrollably.

Glissant's voice guffawed. "You are the joke, M'sieur Patterson!"

Still guffawing Glissant turned on his heel and walked away. All Patterson could see were the backs of Glissant's black restaurant shoes.

Of course, Patterson still had no idea what the hell had just happened to him. This is what he knew. He was still standing and everything was a hundred times bigger than normal. Then little signals hit his brain. His hands were on the ground too. He was sitting and standing at the same time. How was this possible? He looked down and, when he saw his green webbed hands, distinctly remembered going to the bathroom on himself. Only it didn't matter because he was stark naked too.

Patterson attempted to walk but instead took off, springing upward. Adrenaline kicked in and when Patterson realized he was airborne. For a quick second, he thought he was able to fly. The back of Glissant's neck was looming just ahead. Looking like a moving tree. WHAM! He hit Glissant's neck and plummeted to the ground. Apparently, he was bouncy now so the double impact of Glissant and the ground did not hurt too much. Just knocked the wind out of him and disoriented him further.

Patterson was on his back, upside down, so now he could see Glissant's head and shoulders.

Reacting to Patterson's "strike" Glissant turned around a flash of anger and a wince of pain. Glissant rubbed the back of his freshly hit head and started to laugh again.

"Oh you want to fight Patterson, you feeling 'froggy' now?" Glissant raised his fists and laughed some more, "Come on!"

Glissant went back to guffawing and turned away again, this time breaking into a run.

The sun had begun to sear Patterson's soft white underbelly causing him to roll over- which was not as easy as it sounds mind you. By the time Patterson was upright and had gotten his bearings Glissant was nowhere to be seen. It was just "Froggy" Patterson. Alone in this clearing.

That was a little after 5:30 this afternoon. He was supposed to meet Desiree at Glissant's incredibly mediocre bistro, the aforementioned Langue Fourche, at 7:30. Patterson had not seen a clock but judging by the twilight it was probably almost that right now. How long would Desiree wait for him before she left? Anytime he'd been late for a date with her she always waited, the poor thing.   That didn't happen too often. But the last time he had kept her waiting was on their anniversary. After that night she told him he had fifteen minutes. She refused to wait a minute longer. But then, Desiree was a woman of ultimatums. She would close the place waiting for him he was sure of it. Hell, there was that one time he'd forgotten they'd had a date. They'd gotten home at the same time, practically. He just looked at her...whoops! She gave him an ultimatum then. If he forgot her one more time it was over. Des and her ultimatums. Heck, it wasn't like he was cheating on her. He was a million dollar salesman! The Cherish Soap Company had to be his home away from home every now and then.

Patterson was staring down the barrel of another ultimatum right now. He was not sure what the lifespan of a bullfrog was. All he knew was that he was a fully grown one, so that lifespan was already considerably shortened. Time was not on his side.

Luckily he had gotten this hopping thing down pat. It had taken him about ten minutes to figure out how to aim himself and how to land without throwing up. He was covering quite a bit of ground now.

But he was at the street entrance to the park now. He was about to leave safety and hit the streets. Never mind cars. People's shoes terrified him. Especially the women in the spike heel numbers. Ironically, stiletto heels were a personal favorite of Patterson's. You might even say he had a fetish. Nothing like a little hottie in high stilettos.

Wait a minute. But Patterson said earlier that he didn't cheat on his wife. Hey, it's not cheating if you're just looking at another woman. Oh, Patterson had gotten Des to wear stilettos once. She just didn't have the ankles for a spike heel that's all.

So you get it, Patterson thought stilettos were hot. But right now they were weapons that could easily puncture his delicate frame.

He hung back, momentarily out of energy. But then a powerful odor hit his nostrils. Food. And then another odor, even more powerful than the first. Shit.

Steven Patterson, the number one salesman for the Cherish Soap Company five years in a row, craned his bullfrog head until he was staring at: a fresh pile of dog feces, literally covered with flies.

It's a buffet, he thought, all I got to do is get past the smell. Wouldn't be the first time.

Moments later Patterson's bullfrog belly was full. He probably had too many. Again, wouldn't be the first time.

Springing toward the nearest intersection, Patterson started praying it would rain again. Or at least get a little more humid. It was twilight time but those scant few rays of summer sunlight were like a blowtorch.

He thought he'd seen the glimmer of a puddle at one point but it was just some shattered glass in the street.

The city was still a mess, Patterson noticed from his low level. Covered with trash. The former mayor what's-his-name, well he'd done the best he could. Too many people making too much garbage and not enough places to put it all.

There it was! Patterson's little eyes lit up. He could see the red marquee of the Lange Fourche on the left side of the street. Probably about five blocks away he estimated. All he had to do was not get run over or stepped on.

He smelled water close by. It was just on the other side of the street. He waited on the far end of the sidewalk for the OK to cross signal. Luckily no pedestrians were around to block his journey across the street. The signal flashed and Patterson leaped. One. Two. Three times.

Splash! He hit the small puddle. It was full of soda, cigarette resin, and oil. He didn't care. He was cool again. At least for the moment.

Suddenly an incredibly loud noise hit his tiny bullfrog ears. It was the wheel of an oncoming car rolling on tar!

Patterson leaped up and bounced off the car's hood. As he passed the windshield he couldn't believe his tiny eyes. Desiree was behind the wheel... and that douche Glissant was in the passenger seat! Neither of them saw him. They seemed preoccupied.

As Patterson sailed back down to the sidewalk he was a different frog. Well, the same frog physically. But with a different purpose namely this: what on God's green earth was going on?

Desiree's car- or more precisely Patterson's car- rolled down the street toward the Langue Fourche. Wasn't she supposed to be waiting there for him already? They'd had a seven thirty reservation.

Patterson huddled against a building. He recognized this corner. There was a large face clock halfway down the street on the left. Because of his recently adjusted height, he could not spot it right now. He boinged straight upward, focusing on that specific part of the street. He could see the clock. But came back down to quickly to register the position of the clock's hands. So he boinged up again...

It was almost eight!

With newfound resolve, Patterson began leaping down the street toward the Langue Fourche sign. So close, so far away.

Desiree who could never show up late was already a half hour behind. And Glissant, the toad who just turned Patterson into a frog was with her.

It took him fifteen more minutes, three more street puddles, five houseflies, three moths and a ladybug to get to Jardins. He looked up at the marquis panting. He wasn't sure how much or little he had left in him. This little bullfrog body seemed in constant need of insects and water. Desiree didn't always prefer to eat on the patio around back but it was a nice night. And besides, how would he get into the restaurant's dining room without causing a riot? To the amusement of some passers-by, he hopped a few times in place, getting good looks into the front window, making sure that Desiree, in fact, was not in there. She was not. Good.

He bounded into an alley toward the Lange Fourche's back patio.

A hanging pot provided the perfect vantage point. Patterson leaped up and landed in it perfectly, causing very little sway. Boy, he had really gotten this trajectory thing down. But then there was very little Steven Patterson couldn't master.

He sat in his perch looking down at the only couple on the patio. Desiree and Glissant.

Frogs have an amazing sense of hearing and since Patterson was a frog (well, for now) his sense of hearing was vastly improved. He noted if only on a subconscious level that he could hear Desiree's high-pitched voice through his ears and Glissant's low pitched guttural utterances through his skin.

Glissant had literally gotten under Patterson's skin…

"The man will not arrive I assure you…" Glissant said confidently.

"My husband is always late, I haven't shown up on time in years and I always beat him," Desiree said.

Patterson was struck by this. Desiree had always told him she'd gotten to their dates on time. But then, Patterson thought, he had always assured her he would get there on time and never did.

"I don't think you understood," Glissant nodded, "I said the man will not arrive.   Your husband will be here sooner than you think." Glissant began searching the surrounding area, never thinking to look up at the planter. "He may already be here…"

"What do you…?"Desiree trailed off, then gasped, "You… Henri, you promised me you would not cast my spell…"

Glissant busted out cackling.

Patterson didn't know what made him angrier. That Desiree was privy to this ridiculous spell. Or that she was calling Glissant by his first name now.

"I trusted you with that!" Desiree cried and stood.

Glissant grabbed her arm, forcing her back down. Were Patterson warm-blooded, his blood would be boiling right now.

"Whoa chillax, ma petite…" Glissant said in a tone that sounded way too romantic. It seemed to work on Desiree. She smiled back and reluctantly rubbed her neck. Did they just get done screwing? Is that what they were doing? If so where? In Patterson's house? In his bed?

He looked down. And saw on her chubby-ankled feet… stilettos! Patterson thought she'd gotten rid of those things. Images began to roll through Patterson's bullfrog brain now. Images of those spike heels jutting skyward. Only they weren't turning him on at all.

"Henri how could you do this? You knew this was a very important dinner for me and my husband," her lip was trembling. "I was going to give him his last ultimatum."

"Ultimatum! You were just going to talk again," Glissant said, "All you do is talk. Blah blah blah. It's time to," snapping his fingers, "What's is it…? Put your foot down!" He pounded his fist on the table scaring her. "I need money and you need to free of that poor excuse for a husband!"

Patterson was a little green spotted ball of mixed emotions now. Jealousy, rage, fear… and deep down underneath all that, something else. Something he couldn't put his small webbed finger on. A feeling for his wife he never knew he had.

Glissant put his hand on Desiree's and she pulled it away, shocked. "I think somebody's gotten a little too high on himself. You and me aren't going to happen, Henri."

"Oh no?" Henri grabbed her and pulled her toward him, kissing her full on the mouth. She pushed him away, aghast. Henri started looking around, "See that you worthless little reptile! I just kissed your wife!"

That's it! Patterson had his target and already plotted his trajectory. He leaped right at Glissant's face, bracing himself for impact. This was going to hurt. But it was going to be so worth it.

. . .

120

Desiree Patterson shrieked when the frog slammed into Henri Glissant's face. He yelped equal parts pain and shock.

The bullfrog ricocheted and plonked onto the table right in front of her.

As Glissant tried to stop the bleeding from his freshly broken nose, Desiree peered down at the frog in front of her. Its belly puffed quickly like that one act had completely exhausted it. Then... she looked into the frog's eyes.

"Steven?" she uttered in disbelief.

The bullfrog croaked back at her.

"I don't know," Desiree said, "This could be a major coincidence..."

"Of course it's him!" Glissant each nostril plugged with napkins. "He's here to prove his undying love for you!"

Desiree smiled weakly at the bullfrog in front of her. "Steven if it's really you... do morse code."

Amazingly the bullfrog made three short croaks, three long ones, three short ones. SOS.

"Awww it is you!" Desiree said.

"Finish the fairy tale if you've got the stomach for it!" Glissant spat out.

The bullfrog's eyes flashed with recognition. As if it had heard Glissant's words before.

Desiree picked up the bullfrog and kissed it.

There was another look in the frog's eyes now. Anticipation, excitement.

Only... nothing happened.

"That was a kiss goodbye, Steven", Desiree said matter-of-factly "This is not the tale of the frog prince."

Then Desiree Patterson suddenly winged her husband at the nearest wall where his frog body splattered. The bullfrog's body wheezed with alarm as it began its last moments.

"This is the fairy tale about a sleeping beauty", she continued to her dying amphibious mate, "Who finally woke up."

Desiree stood over the dying bullfrog and put the spike heel of her stiletto over his heart.

"Henri was right about one thing," Desiree said, "This is not the time for talk. It's time for me to put my foot down."

And that she did.

...

Moments later Desiree and Glissant ate quietly in the patio. Glissant attempted to play footsie with her but she pulled her feet away.

"Don't you dare," she said coldly, "I was going to tell you the time and the place to use the transformation spell if I needed it."

"You were going to need it and you know it," Glissant said rolling his eyes, "Everything worked out fine, n'est-ce pas?"

Desiree took a sip of wine. "Walk out on your feet while you still have them, Henri. I turned you into a man and I can easily turn you back into a snake…"

Glissant pushed his chair away from the table and hissed (pun intended), "Bien ssssur, madame." He walked back into his restaurant.

Now here was Desiree. Contemplating the rest of her life in peaceful solitude. She smiled and said to herself: "Everything did work out fine, n'est-ce pas?"

A waiter walked up to the table.

"So. How are you enjoying your frog's legs?" the handsome waiter smiled.

"Delicious", Desiree said smiling back at the young man.

"Cuisses de Grenouille is always better when prepared fresh," the waiter remarked. "By the way, I wanted to express my condolences. When Mr. Glissant brought the frog into the kitchen he said you were in mourning."

"Yeah," Desiree said, acting like she was holding back tears, "My poor husband croaked."

THE SOCIOPATH

Webster's definition of "sociopathic" is brief:

sociopathic "of, relating to, or characterized by asocial or antisocial behavior"

So brief is it, in fact, the curious word-hunter is forced to look up asocial ("a: not social, b: rejecting or lacking the capacity for social interaction) and antisocial (1: hostile or harmful to organized society; esp: being marked by behavior deviating sharply from the norm. 2: averse to the society of others.)

A school doctor once used this term to describe The Sociopath when he was seven. It was after the squirrel incident. The Sociopath's parents refused to believe the doctor. After all the boy seemed normal up until that day. His parents transferred him out of that school and they sent him to another. This appeared to solve the problem. The Sociopath no longer exhibited any behavioral abnormalities. Life went back to normal. And normal it stayed. Normal.

What his parents did not know (and never would know) was that life only went back to normal for them. Their young son on the other hand, well, he learned something important that day in the playground. It was kind of like in that book "Through The Looking Glass" when that girl did what the title said. The Sociopath went through the looking glass that day. Up was down, black was white. At the tender age of seven, The Sociopath had learned he was most definitely not normal.

He had spent his first seven years observing the behavior of his family, his peers and the rest of the world. He concluded in that short time that everyone was like him. Actors. People who "pretend" to laugh and cry and care because it was something to pass the time away.

When he was six his parents cried a lot when his grandma died. Especially his mom. His dad cried too but stayed strong, held his mom and let her weep on his shoulder.

The Sociopath had to look in the mirror for a few minutes, tapping into the stuff that made him cry. Getting stung by a bee. Being hungry. Not getting his way. The tears came. He went out and sat on the couch crying next to his mom. She took him in her arms, kissing away his tears. She looked thankful to be distracted from her own crying.

The incident confused him a little. What if she wasn't pretending? That his mother had been touched deeply by someone else dying.

It was weird...

Loss, the sociopath realizes, watching his wife and children eat dinner. Kylie is eighteen, Kirsten, fifteen. His daughters are beautiful. He knows this because people tell him what beautiful daughters he has. To him, they look no different than anybody else's daughters.

That is what his mother felt. Profound and unequivocal loss! But of what exactly?

People live and they die. The sociopath read a poem in college about days being born and dying. But would we weep because the sun is setting on what has been just another day?

"Pass the tartar sauce, hon?" his wife Maggie called out, bringing him out of his brainstorm long enough to smile politely and pass the shaker of salt to her.

"Thanks, hon," Maggie said.

The Sociopath nodded back, pushing a forkful of battered cod into his mouth. Mmm, he loved Fridays. You can't beat fish and chips.

Now, where was he? Oh yes... People live and they die. Just like bugs, plants, animals... squirrels.

When he was six and a half The Sociopath discovered he could catch them. He was always athletic. He was the youngest karate student Sensei Ryan had ever awarded a yellow belt. The boy had incredible discipline. Patient. Focused. Capable of a stillness that eluded most adults. The sociopath was not easily distracted. Not like squirrels, who would freak out at the slightest noise.

The Sociopath would lean against the tree in the backyard of his parent's Vermont home. He would wait. It would take a long time but one would scurry up to the tree. It wouldn't notice the boy standing against it. Squirrels have brains the size of peas. Unable to discern the details that separate a motionless boy from the tree trunk, the squirrel determined that both are one and the same.

Sensing no danger, the squirrel began darting up the tree, about two feet at a clip.

The Sociopath would always knew exactly when to strike. It was while the squirrel was in motion. By the time the squirrel came to rest for that split second, the Sociopath's hand would be around its neck.

The boy had been bitten a couple of times. He would welcome the pain. It was a sensory experience, manna from heaven to our little sociopath. Nonetheless, he had learned to grab the squirrels a certain way though. His index and middle fingers cradling the head, ring finger under the chin, locking its mouth shut. The other hand would go for the tail so he could pull the little creature taut as he brought it to the ground. He would then kneel gently on the squirrel's back (he had learned not to put all his weight on it thus ending the experience prematurely). Letting it writhe underneath him he would twist its little head. The animal's movements would become more and more panicked until he heard the noise. Like a twig breaking. Snap!

The squirrel would be no more. Maybe a couple of cartoonish twitches then... nothing.

He'd drop the remains into a stream behind their Vermont house. Putting his baseball cap over his heart he would watch the current carry the squirrel-du-jour's remains out to sea...

How many times he had done that before the day in the schoolyard? Thirty? Forty? Whatever the number this particular squirrel would be his last.

"I can too!" he shouted back at Ronnie Brewer.

Ronnie put her hands on her hips and scrunched up her face, "You can not! Now stop saying you can!"

The Sociopath took another look at the squirrel sitting on the stump just outside the yard's perimeter.

"I'll show you..." he said.

The Sociopath walked the long ways around the playground, approaching the squirrel from behind.

"Hey over there, doofus!" he heard Ronnie yell. He did not even respond. He'd never responded to distractions, "You're going the wrong way!"

The Sociopath was very quiet, reading the squirrel at about twenty paces he got down on his belly and inched up on his prey like a snake.

The other kids had stopped playing. They all gathered around Ronnie as she waited for the Sociopath to look like the complete idiot she insisted he was.

"He says he can catch squirrels," the Sociopath heard her say. He was about four feet away. He watched the little thing feed its tiny face. He moved a little closer and the squirrel froze. The Sociopath froze too. Maybe Ronnie was going to have the last laugh after all. The squirrel started eating again. Whew. The Sociopath smiled and got within striking distance.

The other kids were spellbound. Even Armie Armstrong, who always had to go to the bathroom in the middle of recess was standing with his legs crossed. He was holding it instead of missing this show!

The Sociopath lay for a moment at the stump watching the squirrel's bushy tail twitch above him. He took three deep breaths and-

"BOO!" Ronnie shrieked at the top of her lungs, scaring the squirrel off the stump.

The Sociopath glared at Ronnie, who stuck her tongue out at him. Even at his young age, The Sociopath felt more victorious than frustrated. Yelling boo was Ronnie's way of admitting defeat. In a sense, the Sociopath had already won.

Show over now, the other kids in the playground had all laughed and gone back to playing. The Sociopath could have gone back to play with everyone else and take Ronnie's continued taunting. Instead, he chose to stalk that squirrel, which now sat at the base of a nearby tree.

The Sociopath formulated his attack.

It took almost the rest of recess. About half an hour. Mrs. Crabtree was telling everyone to line up, that it was time to go back inside.

Just as Mrs. Crabtree was about to ask where he was, The Sociopath came out of the woods behind all of them shouting triumphantly:

"HEY RONNIE!"

Everyone turned.

He was holding the squirrel taut, by the head and tail. The animal was squirming violently, threatening to scratch him. At first, everyone looked nothing short of amazed. Even Mrs. Crabtree was absolutely speechless.

The Sociopath could have stopped there. Ronnie would never doubt The Sociopath from here on out. But where was the fun in redeeming himself before his peers? He needed to go all the way. To hear that sound. Like a twig breaking···

Snap!

Everyone's face went from awe to horror in the time it took for the squirrel to stop squirming.

Armie Armstrong wet himself. But he wasn't the only one. Ronnie let go too, her terror liquifying through her eyes as well as she began crying.

Mrs. Crabtree instinctively told the rest of the class to file into the room and do the study exercise on the board. Then she walked up to The Sociopath and gently took his hand.

Here there is a moment of confusion.

It lasts as long as it takes to get him to the school doctor. Like most of the other schools, they had a nurse on hand for cuts, stomach aches, and temperatures. But The Sociopath's parents had seen fit to give their boy the best of everything. so he got to go to the best elementary school in Vermont. They had a doctor there too. A doctor who specialized in kid's thoughts and feelings. She probably earned her year's salary in that one afternoon after recess.

Dr. Phillipa Young smiled a lot. She asked questions. She had a very friendly voice too. The Sociopath has learned since that only 33% of communication comes through words. The other 67% comes from posture and tone. The Sociopath opened up. The only time in his life, to her. There were lots of questions.

"About three times a week", was the only response that seemed to ice Dr. Young. The glare of disbelief went away as she cleared her throat and resumed her friendly interrogation.

"Why do you uh... catch these squirrels?" was her next question.

"They're hard to catch."

"So it makes you feel good to catch one?"

"I don't know... It's just a thing I do."

The doctor peered into his eyes a while. She continued smiling. Then she looked away.

"You're very good at that," she said. Finally, something that wasn't a question.

"I know I like catching squirrels", he said.

"I was talking about the way you can look people in the eye until they look away," Dr. Young said. She took her glasses off and cleaned them. "Does that make you feel good when you do that?"

"No", The Sociopath, "I didn't even know I did it. I figured people look away when they're done talking to me."

The Doctor put her glasses back on.

"Can you tell me about something that happened to you..." Dr. Young shifted in her seat a bit, "That made you feel very bad?"

"Sure," The Sociopath said, "Well I got stung by two bees at one time in my backyard."

"Good", Dr. Young smiled, "Anything else?"

The Sociopath thought. "I wanted some chocolate last week and my mom said it was too close to dinner. That made me feel bad."

Dr. Young nodded.

"Or like this one time when I wanted to go to a hotel with a pool and my mom and dad laughed and said I had school tomorrow."

"Anything ever," Dr. Young tried to put some words together, "Make you feel really really bad. Like horrible. Your grandmother died last year, how did that make you feel?"

The Sociopath shrugged and shook his head. He didn't understand.

The Doctor went on, asking questions about the way he felt. The Sociopath began closing up on her then. He started feeling like the more he said the less she thought of him. That was important. To look good in everyone else's eyes. To be perceived as being good. He began making things up.

When Nathan the class bully picked on him on the first day of school it made him feel really really sad. When his mom made him cookies on his birthday it made him really really happy. And so on...

Dr. Young seemed to relax a little. But not completely. That would never happen because he told her how killing squirrels made him feel neither happy nor sad. That it didn't matter to him if something was alive or dead. He would never see Dr. Young again. But it would bother him that he never entirely won her over. But perhaps Dr. Young remembered him and tracked the progress of this little boy she had helped forty-two years ago. Maybe somewhere along the way he had won her over. If she was still alive.

God what a great old-fashioned meal, thought The Sociopath. How was it that good tasting food made him feel more than somebody living or dying? Ah, he was thinking too much now, time to give it a rest... At the moment his family's servants were cleaning the dishes from the table. His wife and daughters dabbed their mouths with cloth napkins.

The head servant finally approached The Sociopath, "Are we ready for coffee and dessert, Mr. President?"

The Sociopath nodded. When he took office, he told his staff to ship his favorite coffee ice cream from Vermont. It was a Friday ritual. And for the past one hundred and eight Fridays, it had been in the White House freezer, fresh and without fail.

If Dr. Young could see me now···

INTERLUDE

YOUR LAUGHTER IS MADE FROM THE FINEST AMBROSIA

Your laughter is made from the finest ambrosia

It flew about me beating joyous wings

Ran through me barefoot throwing open each shade and curtain

Until the light was blinding

Your voice is made from the coolest turquoise

It caressed a windswept shore

Where I laid to forget the day's trifles

Remembering what was important, nodding with every crash

Your silences are made from the brightest shimmers

Pinned to a jet black cloth, wrapped around mason's jars

Where I caught all those fireflies

Who rejoiced in their newfound freedom

You are made from your laughter, your voice, your silences and infinite else

A colossal collage of earth and magic. Untamed and uncharted

Expanding such that the universe begins to bend around you

And without you is but a frame. Sharp. Motionless. Empty.

You are the discovered enigma, the answer's riddle, the catalyst for the thunderstorms and rainbows, the myths and the eons. Every lost gaze toward the horizon, every sonnet from every quill, every sigh, every song, every moment where it all made sense, every term of endearment ever uttered across time, they were all meant for you my love.

All for you.

YOU ARE QUITE THE BARGAIN

A taste of you is worth a thousand king's banquets

A touch of you is more soothing than the countless embraces of countless rare beauties

A scent of you would be the greatest gift to the most fragrant garden

A murmur of you could teach a choir of angels

A glimpse of you is why God created eyes

And a memory of you makes my broken heart seem like a mere pittance

ALLEGIANCE

Were I

Uncertain would I believe for thee

Wealthy would I slave for thee

Impoverished would I give to thee

Weary would I stand vigil for thee

Famished would I feed thee

Suffering would I comfort thee

Terrified would I fight for thee

Freezing would I blanket thee

Hobbled would I carry thee

Drowning would I swim to thee

Dying would I my very last breath give to thee

Thou art my queen, my castle and my country

And for my allegiance do I collect the richest of all rewards…

… the honor to serve thee.

I WAS ICARUS YOU WERE THE SUN

"I will always love you!" I cried falling eyes afire.

CONVERSATIONS WE'LL NEVER HAVE

How your hair cascades down your shoulders creating a haven
around your neck

That careless giggle that always ends in a high note

How happy you make me

How happy you would make me for the rest of my life

The feeling of your hand in mine

The sunset

The way your eyes flutter in the first morning light

What kind of toothpaste we should buy

How one of us would feel should the other die first

The fact that now whenever it rains I smile

The fact that now whenever I see a used bookstore I have to
run in and browse

How I bought a body pillow after that one phone
conversation... the one where I gave up waiting for you ...

How you destroyed me so sweetly, neatly and so completely
for anyone else ever

That you are now my muse until my dying day

DO YOU WANT TO KNOW HOW YOU DIE

"Hey Mister, wanna know how you die?" she asked. The little girl had the most adorably lisp due to the missing two front teeth. She was no more than six. Her sky blue eyes were big with excitement and her lips were curled up mischievously. She held a dolly with blonde hair just like hers.

The traveler looked over at the girl's mother seated next to her. The mother was napping right now, her hand on her chin.

"Oh please don't wake mama!" the girl suddenly pleaded in a lispy whisper, "She hates it when I tell people how they die. She wishes I wouldn't but it's so cool! I have never been wrong once!"

This was just the traveler's luck. First, his flight gets delayed. Then the only vacant seat at the gate turns out to be next to this chipper child of the damned.

"Actually," the traveler said, "I'm going to get some rest."

"I can write it down so you can read it later," the girl said, "My penmanship's real good but mommy says I need to spell gooder."

"Look I am not-" the traveler started then paused. The conversation could end right now, "Sure okay, yes write it down for me then. I will forgive your- not good spelling."

"Hooray!" the girl chirped and went into her little backpack.

"Here's the thing though," the man said, "I need to sleep so when you're finished just fold up the paper and leave it under my chair. And please don't wake me."

"Of course not, silly!" the girl giggled pulling out a cute little crayon and notepad set.

The traveler set his backpack down, went into one of the side pockets and pulled out a small spongy pillow that immediately expanded. It fit perfectly in the crook of his neck. It was the prototype for his patented invention. The Sleep-Thru he called it. Once upon a time, he was going to sell it and be filthy, stinking rich. Now it was just another reminder of his many failures. Here he was once again. On the next flight back to...Cranston.., ..Rhode Island.

The traveler dreamt of his wife. It was the only time he saw her anymore.

He opened his eyes to the announcement that Flight 1402 to ..Providence.. was now leaving.

"Shit!" he said. He'd been asleep for an hour and a half! The traveler ran to the jetway entrance in disarray. The boarding pass was clamped between his teeth as he stuffed the Sleep-Thru back into its pocket. Just another day in his life.

He was almost at the jetway when he stopped, turned and saw the little piece of paper folded up underneath the chair.

"Sir you'd better hurry!" the gate attendant said waving him through.

The traveler tried to fight the urge but had to see. He ran back to the chair and scooped up the piece of paper.

He bolted toward the jetway again.

The attendant held out her hand for his boarding pass. He handed it to her and she fed it into the electronic reader, checking him in.

While she was doing this the traveler could no longer fight the urge to look at the paper. He unfolded it, read it and chuckled to himself. Creepy kid, the traveler thought. *God bless her little imagination though.*

The machine gave the attendant an annoying beep, "Uh-oh!" the attendant said.

"What?" the man said.

"The flight's leaving sir," the attendant said, "You're too late."

Out the window behind her, the traveler could see the 727 taxiing away.

The displeasure in the man's eyes gave the attendant some incentive. She walked him over to her computer and found another flight to Providence leaving in twenty minutes.

"It's on the other side of the airport but if you hurry-" the attendant didn't need to finish. The man was already gone.

.. ..

The next flight to Providence was practically empty. The traveler didn't need his Sleep-Thru this time. He splayed out across three sets, head comfortably on the soft pillow, blanket over him. He was having another dream about his wife when the shaking woke him up. It took him a second to realize what woke him up wasn't the airplane shaking. It was the fact that he had just hit the ceiling of the plane. And it was starting to hurt.

As he processed the fact he should put his seatbelt on, the oxygen masks   deployed. He heard screaming. Then-

-the plane went dark.

Out the window, he saw in flashes of lightning that one of the plane's engines was on fire.

He pictured his wife and held onto the mental picture. It calmed him.

There was this escalating mechanical whine now. And the unmistakable sensation of falling. It went on forever. As the feeling became more intense the plane seemed to detach itself from any physical laws. The man did not see much in the flickering light but could feel the plane moving all around him. He reached out in front of him and touched the ceiling again. A chair's headrest bumped his knee. He collided with someone else. It was like a dream. Everything whirled so fast and so slow. Just before the thunderous slam that knocked him out he thought, *Looks like Little Miss Morbid was wrong for once-*

The traveler came to in the aftermath. Just for a moment. He could not see nor hear but felt rain pelting his broken body until he couldn't even feel that anymore. He could only feel one thing now. Relief.

The traveler's journey was over. He was home.

Good thing it was raining that night or the park would have been jammed with people. But if it wasn't raining that lightning bolt wouldn't have hit the plane's engine. Whenever a tragedy is autopsied, the variables always wind up turning back on themselves in infinity. Like a hall of mirrors.

The strangest thing was that passenger who had been catapulted from the midsection of the plane. He had landed a considerable distance from the crash site. They found no ID on the dead man's person. Only a folded up piece of paper with a poorly spelled message on it written in crayon, decorated with cheerful flowers: "U wil die in a hanted howse!"

The two first responders felt an inexplicable chill. The moment passed and they pulled the dead man from the very spot where he had landed. It was the entrance to the House of Horrors ride.

CANT W8 2CU

"There is something about me you need to know," his voice said in her ear. "Something I want to share with you..."

"What?" she spoke.

"It's a secret," his voice, so calm and soothing, whispered, "I can't tell you until I know I can trust you."

"You know you can trust me," she said, barely aware of her heart hammering in her chest.

"I won't know that I can trust you with this," his voice said, "Until I see you."

Silence. Then breathing. It wasn't an uncomfortable pause. It excited her to the point where she needed to break it. "Why can't you just tell me what it is?"

"It's a secret," his voice resonated in her ear, echoing into her very soul. He repeated the words, "Something I need to tell you face to face."

More breathing. Her hand trembled, along with the rest of her.

"I can't wait to see you," she whispered now. It was contagious.

"Five past midnight on the steps of the old church."

She could hear him smile as he spoke. She tried to

imagine his face but found a silhouette. He was tall, she imagined. She pictured dark wavy hair, broad shoulders, small waist. Was he wearing a long coat? She convinced herself she had been reading too many cheap novels. He would look nothing like she imagined. But he would be perfect. She knew this because to her he already was...

"Five past midnight on the steps of the old church," she confirmed.

Nothing. Not even breathing anymore. Then a loud beeping noise. He'd already hung up.

Lydia Miles had never engaged in phone sex before. But her conversations with this man named Michael had her ready to climax. Already thanking God she had not gone with her gut in that singles chatroom, she pocketed her cell phone. Then opened her eyes to the harsh glare of the fluorescent lights above her. She looked at the clock on the microwave. Damn it was only ten thirty! Still, an hour and a half left on her shift. Then a five-minute drive to the old church and she would meet him. She broke it down in her mind. Ninety-five minutes. Only ninety-five minutes until she would lay eyes on this mysterious man who had come into her life only three short days ago. She couldn't wait to see Michael. Absolutely couldn't wait. She sent him a text it hoping he'd want to call her back when he got it. After a minute or two she finally dragged herself out of her chair and trotted for the door...

Lydia emerged from the solitude of the break room and into the chaos affectionately known as the Snake Pit. The registration department in any emergency room is grueling enough. But this was Crescent County Memorial. No further explanation needed. And if you're not from Crescent County you wouldn't understand anyway. Suffice it to say "the double C" was the strangest place Lydia had ever visited in her thirty-four years. One thing about Lydia was she had never actually "lived" anywhere. That implied the notion of settling down.

No. Lydia had visited places sometimes up to two years. New York, Santa Barbara, Chicago, Philly, Omaha, Taos, El Paso. Nice places to arrive at, all of them. And when it was time to move on, nice places to leave.

So what had brought Lydia to the double C? It wasn't the sprawling scenery. There wasn't any of that. It wasn't opportunity. At no time in history had Crescent County been considered a "boom town". It was famous for its truck stops, roadside diners, and a "world famous" dinosaur museum, which resembled a children's playground- only with dinosaur shaped everything. The only distinction Crescent County could claim is that it once made The Horror Channel's Top Ten Most Haunted Places in North America. Which, if you believe in that sort of thing, could explain why Crescent County was... Crescent County. If you believed in that sort of thing.

"Lydia Miles to patient registration please, Lydia to patient registration," the PA barked. Sandy, Crescent County's most diligent triage nurse, loved watching the clock. If Lydia said she'd be back in ten minutes, she'd hear Sandy calling her name at ten minutes and one second. "I love my job," Lydia reminded herself.

As Lydia walked by the triage cubicle, she exchanged sarcastic smiles with Nurse Sandy. "That cell phone bill's gonna be a doozy," Sandy said. Presently Sandy was screening a sobbing Russian woman. Thick black mascara ran down her cheeks as she wept.

Lydia pretended not to hear Sandy as she sat at her own cubicle. In front of her was the window to her world. The Snake Pit. She didn't have to gaze out at the sea of faces to know everyone was looking at her, the lone registration coordinator with no one at her window to register. Instead, Lydia grabbed the computer mouse and scrolled to the next incoming patient's name. "John Smith" read the computer screen. Smiling out at the sea of hungry faces, all of them looking hopeful they'd be next, she used her nicest voice to call "John Smith?"

"I love your voice", Michael had said when they first started talking- which was about sixty seconds after they had logged out of that blind dating app heart2heart. This was just three days ago. Michael told her he could listen to her voice all night.

Lydia looked at the clock. It was 10:32. Damn. She and Michael had made a deal. No identities. First names only. No talk about where they worked or lived, or anything else that wasn't on their profiles at www.heart2heart.com. The ordinary person would think, what else is there to talk about? Lydia and Michael had clocked in nine hours of talking in three days. Trifle things... they were both voracious readers, took their coffee black, preferred to sleep late, and had a particular weakness for the sound summer rain. Whatever they talked about, no matter how mundane, made everything outside their little cell phone conversations seem mundane. "I can tell just from your voice you have a beautiful soul," Michael told her at one point. Despite the fact that he probably stole the line from a romantic comedy, Lydia remembered catching her breath. After saying that this man could have admitted he was an ax murderer and she would have still fallen in love with him.

"Hey!" Lydia looked up at a disoriented-looking gentleman whose head was caked with blood. He'd stumbled up to the window and plopped himself across from her desk. "I cut my head," the disoriented man said. He reeked of... something strange. What was that smell?

"Mmhmm," Lydia said, looking over at Sandy. She was still busy with the weeping Russian woman, whose running mascara was beginning to make her look like one of the

146

Insane Clown Posse. Lydia turned back to the disoriented gent. "Can I have your address please?"

"I can't remember anymore, I cut my head... see," the man said, lowering his head so she could see.

Underneath his tousled hair, something shimmered gold. Hmm. Lydia had to squint and adjust her eyeglasses to make sure. Yup. It was a small crucifix, jammed into his skull. Like someone had shot it in. She could see the crucifix's chain dangling next to his right ear. If this were any other hospital her stomach would have probably been backflipping. But this was her second year at Crescent County Memorial.

"Oh-kay," Lydia said and quickly scrolled down to the description, seeing the description Sandy had typed in: small cross lodged in cranium. "Do you have any identification at all sir?" She waited a moment looking at the screen then turned back to the man. He still had his head lowered. Uh-oh. "Sandy?!" she yelled out, "A little help!"

Seeing what was going on, Sandy had the PA phone in her hand like a shot and barked, "Gurney stat to registration!"

Lydia took another look at the man. He let out a belch and she was hit with another wave of that smell... what the hell was that?

Sandy left the weeping Russian woman to assess the man with the cross in his head. Just then, the elevator doors opened and two stocky orderlies- Dave and Boogie- wheeled in a stretcher. Lydia got their attention and pointed to the man with the crucifix stuck in his skull. As Dave and Boogie loaded him onto the stretcher Lydia called out to them. "See if he has any ID, wallet, anything?" Dave, Boogie, and Sandy did a cursory search before Dave came up with a blood-soaked feather.

That explained the smell. It was raw chicken. None of them batted an eyelash, having seen much stranger. Outside of New Orleans, Crescent City had the largest subculture of voodoo worship in the United States.

Lydia shrugged at the orderlies. "John... 'Cross', address unknown..."

"MCU," Sandy told the orderlies and they wheeled him off.

Lydia raced through the registration form, guessing his age, weight, height, and so forth. Then she got to the magic question. Insurance? She wrote what she had gotten so used to writing in this box. UND. Undetermined.

At Sandy's cubicle, the Russian woman burst into tears again. Lydia did a double take, realizing for the first time that wasn't mascara running. It was the woman's tears... they were black. Sandy pushed a Kleenex box toward the woman and turned to Lydia. "Least you got his name," Sandy said, "Hey you know we only have nine Unknown's and it's almost midnight!"

"I wish it was almost midnight," Lydia said, immediately regretting it.

Sandy's smile broadened as the Russian woman sobbed loudly. "Why what happens at midnight honey?"

"Shift change. I get to go home and go to bed," Lydia said. God, she hated having this annoying woman know her business.

"With who?" Sandy chuckled.

"When using a preposition it's whom," Lydia replied. "Not who."

"Fine be that way," Sandy laughed. The Russian woman had regained her composure and was ready to give Sandy more info anyway. Black tears. Yeesh.

Lydia sighed in relief and turned back to the snake pit. "Okay..." she said aloud scanning the faces. They all looked sad. They all looked like they wanted to tell Lydia their sad story. Before Lydia could look at her computer to see who was next-

-"Respiratory stat to the CPR room!", the intercom blared. A moment later came the siren and the red and white lights reflecting off the ER's gurney entrance. Everyone else, whose problems had been so important just three seconds ago, craned their necks to see. Even a guy wearing a neck-brace.

The sliding glass doors flew open and two EMTs wheeled a gurney past. A blond haired EMT looked Lydia's way, wide-eyed. Lydia grabbed her laptop, running after the gurney and its entourage.

Lydia stood at her laptop as she watched the doctors go to work over the unconscious man. They already had him on oxygen and a plasma drip. He had no I.D. on him. In fact, the pockets on his tattered clothing came up empty. "Unknown #10" she typed into the registration form. She looked the man over. He was in a johnny now. From what the EMTs said, he was completely naked when they got to him at Goddard Park. Cops guessed he was some bum who was trying to get a free bath in the pond. The man had a single gunshot wound in his chest. The x-ray showed the bullet had missed his heart by a fraction of an inch.

"They were chasing the alley cannibal," the brown-haired EMT said peering over Lydia's shoulder.

Lydia grimaced at the EMT.

"He's been all over the news haven't you heard?" blondie piped in.

TV challenged individual she was, Lydia just shrugged.

"He's this freakishly huge dude, built like a gorilla... He's been, like... eating homeless people, throwing the leftovers in dumpsters!" brownie went on, "Tonight he moved up to people with homes. Some lady came out of a bar and decided to take a shortcut through the alley behind the Dew Drop Inn... They found her head first then about twenty feet away they found her arm. Her purse was still hanging from it!"

Lydia felt chills go up and down her spine. This was even

gruesome for Crescent County Memorial. The last time she had this sensation was her first night at the Snake Pit...

...when the lady with the bumblebee in her ear came in... That was a fine introduction to Memorial. The mother of all shockaroos. After that, a man with a crucifix in his head and woman crying black tears seemed normal. She could picture the lady with the bee in her ear now. *Screaming as if she were in labor...* Lydia pushed that memory away right quick. She needed to concentrate on this man laying on the gurney in front of her.

All right- name, Unknown #10. Address, homeless. Age? She pegged him at early to mid-thirties. Height, weight, not tall not short not overweight not underweight. This was just a normal guy. She regarded him a moment. His eyes were closed. His breathing faint. Unknown #10 was going to need emergency surgery this much was certain. Though the doctors, nurses, and Lydia maintained an optimistic air, they knew deep inside he was pretty much a goner.

Apparently, the cops had been chasing this Alley Cannibal and were just about at the pond when they started firing on him. Of course, it was dark and their target was dressed in black and moving very very quickly. One of them fired into the dark. They'd heard a shriek and thought they'd hit the cannibal. But when they arrived at the spot they found this homeless Unknown number ten there instead. A double tragedy. First of all, an innocent man had been shot. Second, the Alley Cannibal was still out there.

"But he's clean shaven," Lydia said out of nowhere. The EMTs stared at her a second. "Homeless men don't shave do they?"

"Well he was taking a bath in the pond," the brown-haired EMT said. "He probably had a razor too. Like an old one he found in a dumpster?" His partner nodded too. Made sense to them...

Lydia felt those chills again and had to drive them away. Finished with the brief physical description she saved the registration form to the computer, which automatically assigned Unknown #10 a registration number.

It was time to go back into the Snake Pit. Lydia looked at the clock. It was 10:55. Just seventy more minutes till she met Michael at the old church. She gazed down at Unknown #10. For a reason she could not fathom at the time she put her hand on his and whispered, "Good luck, Unknown 10." Nobody else saw his eyes flutter open. He looked straight at Lydia for a split second, then before Lydia could call attention to it, his eyes closed again. By the time she got back to the Snake Pit, she convinced herself she'd imagined it.

The clock on the wall said 11:01. Sixty-four minutes to go. Lydia passed Sandy who gave her a sideward glance. "Hey, I had to register that guy in ICU..." Sandy just shrugged. The Russian woman who cried black tears was gone, rushed into MCU apparently. She was replaced by an extremely old Jamaican woman now, flanked by her granddaughters. Sandy smiled a venomous smile at Lydia, "Your future husband's sitting at your desk." Lydia rolled her eyes.

She sat down across from "her future husband", an EtOH - the chemical abbreviation for Ethyl Alcohol. In layman's terms, he was a stinking drunk. Like, all she could smell was alcohol and vomit. Save a few swear words the man was incoherent. But what he lacked in annunciation he made up for in loudness. It's funny how she was the only person in that room who was paying any attention to him. And that was only because it was her job.

Unknown 10's eyes haunted her memory. They were sparkling green. Eyes the color of some hidden tropical place far away from the Snake Pit. Lydia felt a knot in her stomach. Her Internet friend, Michael... Remember him? How could she forget? No sparkling green eyes could eclipse the heart of a man like Michael's. She still wanted to meet him. Or... did she?

"Do you hear me?" the drunk stammered. "I said..." he repeated the same unintelligible thing he'd said before when he thought Lydia had been listening.

Lydia nodded patiently and smiled, "I hear you, sir, and I understand," she said. Well at least the first part's true, she thought.

The drunk stood up and lurched across the table, going for Lydia.

"Security!" she yelled as the drunk reached to the side of her, grabbing one of her pens. Out the corner of her eye, she could see the husky security officers, whom she called Starsky and Hutch because she was so bad at names.

The drunk held out his arm and shoved his sleeve back, revealing a large brown splotch on his forearm. This only took a second but for the first time in many moons, Lydia gasped... as the drunk pushed Lydia's pen into the splotch, penetrating his skin and coming through what appeared to be a matching dark splotch opposite the one he pushed the pen through.

As Starsky and Hutch restrained him he said the same thing he'd been saying before. Only now Lydia heard him plain as day. "I got the Fallen's mark!" he yelled, "The Fallen marked me! WHY?!!" Tears welled up in the man's eyes as he began to sob.

The security officers pulled the EtOH into a detaining room off the ER. And Lydia could see something on his face she'd been missing. Abject terror. The "mark". That was a new one. But at least he didn't have a bee in his ear.

It was about then Lydia saw the flashing lights outside the ER entrance. There was a blue light in it. Not an ambulance this time. A police car.

Lydia called the next name, "Dorothea Palm?" It was the elderly Jamaican woman Sandy was screening earlier. She was helped out of her seat by her granddaughters. Lydia smiled as they helped her up to the desk.

The granddaughter on the right spoke first pointing an accusatory finger at Lydia and spoke with a slight Jamaican accent, "We need to see the white-haired doctor now." Her tone was firm and final.

"Umm..." Lydia was used to bad first impressions but this kind of rudeness always demanded an extra dose of tolerance, "Can I get some insurance information first?"

This time it was left granddaughter's turn."My sister's very, very sick, you understand?"

Lydia nodded, "I under..." then her brain caught up with her mouth. "Sister?" she blurted. "But-"

The old woman's voice was raspy. "The white-haired doctor knows what to do..." she said, "We been here before. Please hurry."

Lydia looked at the screen again. "According to my records, this is your first visit."

"Look in the manifest," right granddaughter demanded, "Last time we were here was before the computers."

"I'm sorry," Lydia said, "I'm not familiar with this manifest you're talking about. All I have is my computer data which is telling me-"

Left granddaughter rummaged around in the old woman's purse and pulled out a driver's license. She slid it in front of Lydia. The license pictured a young woman who could be either of the granddaughters. "Look at the name!" Left granddaughter left pressed.

Lydia read it, "Dorothea Palm?" she looked up at the old woman.

"It's her, man!" right granddaughter hollered at the top of her voice. "That's what she looked like at three o'clock this afternoon!"

"All right what the hell-"

Left granddaughter was beginning to cry, "Just get the white-haired doctor, lady! My sister going to die if we don't see him NOW!"

Lydia was going to get into trouble for this. She knew who they were talking about. Tall, ancient, head ringed with wispy white hair. Like an angel. She grabbed her phone and hit the public address button. "Dr. Stoker to admitting please..."

"NOW!" Right granddaughter yelled.

"... stat! Dr. Stoker stat to admitting, thank you," Lydia hung up and looked at the old lady. Could it be Dorothea looked even older than she did when she came in?

Lydia pointed the three women to a restricted entry door on the other side of the emergency room, "Wait there, he should be down in less than a minute."

The younger women helped the old woman out of her seat. Out the corner of her eye, Lydia saw something shiny leaning against the wall to her side. "Wait!" she called out to them. They turned to see Lydia hoisting a wheelchair onto her desk. One of the younger ones rushed over and grabbed it. "Thank you, lady," she said without emotion and, unfolding it, rolled it over to the old woman.

Lydia sat back down and tried to comprehend what she just saw. Every day seemed to bring more moments like this. The brain catching up to the event, trying to rationalize and process simultaneously. She'd stayed long enough at Memorial. It was time to move on.

A man's voice brought her back to reality. "Excuse me... Lydia?" the voice said. Lydia looked up and the most beautiful man she had ever seen was smiling back at her. He removed his police cap. "Officer Mike Hitchcock, Crescent County Police..."

Mike... Michael? Lydia looked at the clock. It was eleven thirty. Her knight in shining armor had come to rescue her twenty-five minutes ahead of schedule.

...

At age 26, Officer Mike Hitchcock hadn't been a cop long.

Only two years. But he came from a family of blue knights. Ever since 1911, when his great granddad moved the family to Crescent County, there had always been a Hitchcock on the force. Cop was in Officer Mike's DNA. There was no question about what he wanted to be when he grew up. Or what he was expected to be. Mike's dad and grandfather began schooling him since he could remember. Not just about law enforcement. But about they called "protecting the peace in Crescent County." And it involved a lot more than a blue uniform.

"Michael? What a surprise..." the woman behind the desk smiled at him as if she'd known him all her life. "It's me, Lydia!"

Hitchcock had gotten used to really weird things happening in Crescent County. In just two years he'd already seen some stuff he knew he'd be taking to the grave. No pun intended. But it was always the mundane stuff that threw him. Awkward moments like this. He smiled back embarrassed, trying to remember how or if he knew this woman. Of course, her name was Lydia that's what the ID badge on her neck said...

She suddenly stood and grabbed his hands. "How nice to finally meet you..." There was something very forward in her demeanor. The way she smiled and looked up at him coquettishly. Like she wanted to throw him on the desk and have her way with him. She was an attractive woman too. Mike had to remember one of those mantras his dad and grandpa taught him should the situation arise... "attraction means distraction" ... Officer Mike had a job to do.

"You look so young", she cooed through full pouting lips. He laughed a little. This was getting weirder. Did this woman work here or was she some psych evaluation case who stole that nametag. Was there a registration coordinator named Lydia locked in a closet somewhere in the hospital? "I'm sorry, this is really embarrassing, uh, Lydia but-" Hitchcock started.

"And you sound so much different on the phone..." her voice trailed off pretty much at the same moment that ecstatic expression fell from her face. She pulled her hands away and covered her mouth. "You're not Michael. I mean not the Michael I thought you were..."

"I would guess not," Hitchcock shrugged.

Lydia slowly sat back down, assuming her professional air. The coquette was gone. "Uhh sorry..." big forced smile, "What can I do for you?"

Hitchcock smiled back in a boyish way. She looked to be about in her mid-thirties so he knew exactly how to begin: "Well, first of all, miss..."

Lydia couldn't resist blushing a little. It had been a while since she'd been called that.

The handsome policeman continued. "I have your John Doe's personal effects, least we think they're his. Must have fallen out of his pocket when he was getting ready for his midnight swim..." He lifted a small plastic Ziploc. It contained a pen, a thin wallet, a money clip, loose change...

Lydia's smile went from polite to broad. "We have ten Unknowns tonight but I know exactly which one you're talking about. Unknown number ten..."

Hitchcock always thought it ironic how men like this "Unknown #10" could make a woman smile like that. The devil must be a man, he thought to himself.

"Those are his? I can take them," Lydia said. She took the bag, studying its contents for a moment.

"I already looked in the wallet for a driver's license or some ID, couldn't find anything but a calculator..."

"Calculator? And a money clip huh? I thought he was supposed to be homeless," Lydia said.

Officer Hitchcock chuckled, "We I did too... probably just had one too many and tried to sober up with a little skinny dip."

Lydia giggled like a schoolgirl.

Hitchcock went on: "I need to know which room this Unknown #10 is in..."

Lydia put Unknown #10's Ziploc in the appropriate drawer and gave Hitchcock a puzzled look. "He's in trauma right now. The doctors are trying to resuscitate him..."

"For the hospital's safety," he continued, "When he comes to, there might be a little trouble."

"Oh security sees trouble here all the time," Lydia laughed.

"Not this kind of trouble," Hitchcock said. He was dead serious too. "Could you tell me where he's located?"

Lydia felt an unease. He looked kind and gentle- in a very manly way of course- but something told her he could turn on a dime. Do what he had to do in a moment's notice. Of course, he's capable of that, stupid, she said to herself, He's a policeman, he has to know how to do that!

"He had to have emergency surgery," Lydia said.

"No doubt," Hitchcock said. That concerned look on his face seemed like a mask though, "I remember them loading him onto the ambulance. There was a lot of blood."

"Well," Lydia said, "Surgeons don't like interruptions."

"Miss," Hitchcock's jaws were clenching now so the compliment was overshadowed by its hissing noise, "I've been here before. I have good hospital manners. I just need to know where you're hiding Unknown #10 that's all." That last part was delivered like a joke but Hitchcock's expression was dead serious.

Lydia shrugged, smiled and turned to her keyboard. Nonetheless, Lydia took her time at the computer screen. "Hang on this'll be just a sec," she said in that voice that could buy her about thirty seconds. What to do? What to do? She scrolled through the computer screen. Above her, Hitchcock seemed to try to crane his neck so he could see the screen. She hated when people did that. She was glad Officer Michael Hitchcock wasn't her Michael. Lydia put on a good show- pointing, clicking, punching in a password here and there. She actually accessed the hospital cafeteria at one point. Mmm, beef kabobs. Too bad she never at the hospital. She never would either. With all the germs floating around here she'd sooner eat off the floor of a gas station restroom. She sighed and looked up at Hitchcock. "I'm sorry, there's a conflict," she said standing, "They've got several patients assigned to the same room and he's one of them. And I know he's not sharing a room with anyone. Could you wait right here? I'll go get that information for you..."

Officer Michael Hitchcock could not hide a look of suspicion now. The police generally had access to the hospital, no questions asked. Why was he getting stalled? Hitchcock wondered if somehow that beast with the bullet in his artery had gotten to her. He absently rubbed the handle of his sidearm. He had put one special round in it in the car. Now he was wondering if would need more.

Lydia walked up to Sandy, who happened to be eating the policeman up with her eyes. "Could you watch that policeman for me, San?" Lydia asked.

"All day long," Sandy smiled back, sizing the policeman up- then did a double take at Lydia, "Where the hell do you think you're going?"

"I never got all the information off the...", in her mind

Lydia went through the list of people she'd seen, "... drunk guy who stuck the pen in his arm", and made an abrupt exit.

Any other time Sandy would have told her to worry about that when the Snake Pit slowed down. But Lydia knew Sandy couldn't resist a man in uniform.

"Hurry up!" Sandy said, then glanced back at the handsome police officer.

In order to make things look good, Lydia had to through the cubicle area behind registration, where the drunk was being treated.

On her way, yet another pungent smell hit her nostrils. It was kind of like, what... seaweed? She nearly tripped over a bucket sitting outside one of the cubicles. It was filled with black muck. A nurse wearing surgical gloves came to the bucket and wrung more muck out of what used to be a white towel. Craning her neck, Lydia could see the Russian woman laying on a table. Her eyes were wide open, black tears rolling from them at an alarming rate. The Russian woman was crying anymore. Hell, she wasn't even blinking. Lydia nodded apologetically to the nurse and moved on...

... past another cubicle where a familiar gentleman sat, his head in a turban-like bandage. In his right hand, John Smith clutched the crucifix which had been lodged in his head. Boy, that neurosurgeon worked fast on him, Lydia thought, and right there in the cubicle apparently! Then she remembered Dr. Moore was a devout Catholic. Pays to have Friends in high places, Lydia mused...

A baby's cry startled her. She paused and, looking over her shoulder, she saw a cubicle where the white-haired Dr. Stoker apologetically handed a tiny black baby to Dorothea Palm's sisters- who were seemed shocked beyond rational thought. "Dorothea...?" one of the sisters said, holding back tears, "That you, girl?" Dr. Stoker noticed Lydia watching the scene and suddenly pulled the privacy curtain.

Lydia shook off the creepy feeling and marched toward the last cubicle. "Just another night at Memorial..." she mumbled to nobody.

She finally arrived at the cubicle where the EtOH lay and froze in her tracks. The drunk had been completely undressed, the hospital johnny bunched up around his private area. He still had his socks on that, was it. Lydia felt that same feeling she had on her first night at Memorial... when the woman with the bee in her ear came in. The EtOH's stomach bore the same kind of brown splotch he'd stuck his pen through earlier at her desk. Only the one on his stomach was the size of a dinner plate. The EtOH was unconscious. At least that's what she told herself. Lydia did herself and everyone else in the vicinity a favor by pulling the privacy sheet across the cubicle.

She'd seen enough for one night and there was still about a half hour to go. She broke into a run as she headed for trauma... Despite her efforts, the memory flooded back in. Her first night at Memorial...

The lady had come in screeching as if she were giving birth. No, worse than that. Lydia almost vomited when she saw the bee wriggling around inside the woman's ear. "It's stinging me!" she screamed over and over again.

Those screams haunted Lydia even now as she broke into a jog toward Emergency Surgery.

The hospital had immediately admitted the lady with the bee in her ear.   Lydia never saw her again. The rest of the night she overheard snippets of what was happening from orderlies, nurses, and doctors. It all happened so fast too. First came the x-ray. Turns out the bee had not flown into the woman's ear. It was trying to fly out. The x-ray showed something that had even the most experienced doctors, yes, even Stoker, completely baffled. The woman was filled with

160

the pupae of thousands of bees. They were just underneath the skin. Under her arms, her legs, her face. The x-ray also revealed a hive... inside her torso. It had started between the lungs and just behind the stomach. Then got connected to all of her vital organs. Strangely, this woman had experienced no health issues in spite of the honeycomb, and all of its inhabitants, inside of her. The medical staff had no idea how to deal with this unprecedented condition. That bee in her ear was removed and examined. It was an ordinary yellow jacket... that had somehow gestated inside this woman and was burrowing its way into the world. The woman really was giving birth! And had about a thousand more labors to endure. The next night Lydia worked the lady with the bee in her ear had died. The rest of the bee pupae had chewed their way out of her. And the woman had been conscious right up until the very end... Her remains were mercifully cremated.

Lydia had to wear a mask in order to enter the emergency OR. She stood behind two nurses and two surgeons, who were still trying to remove the bullet lodged in Unknown #10's chest. From what Lydia could hear #10 had been hanging by a thread just two minutes ago. But his vitals were getting stronger by the second. He was a fighter. Lydia's heart swelled. She knew a man with eyes like that wouldn't give up.

Again came that knot. She wanted to see Michael. She really did. She started wishing Officer Mike had been the same Michael she'd been talking to on the phone. She would have no trouble breaking up with Officer Mike for Unknown #10. Wait a minute, she thought, "breaking up..."? Lydia, you just met Michael three days ago. Now you're protecting this dying man who may very well be a wanted criminal because he has sparkling green eyes? What the hell was Lydia's problem all of a sudden? For what seemed an eternity no men in her life at all. Now two in the span of seventy-two hours! Maybe it was a hormonal thing. She didn't have her period. She was way too young for menopause. And she wasn't pregnant. Yep, she admitted to herself with a bitter grin, not even a remote chance of that.

Peeking through the nurses' shoulders she could see his face under the oxygen mask. So peaceful. Like a child sleeping. Then, as if he sensed he was being watched he turned his head and opened his eyes... looking right at her! More than at her... through her. Unknown #10's eyelids fluttered before sinking closed again.

Lydia heard a clank and realized the doctors had just removed the bullet from his chest.

One of the nurses turned to look at Lydia. "Everything okay?" the nurse asked.

Lydia nodded quickly, "A police officer is waiting to talk to the patient..."

The nurse shook her head and turned back to the operation.

"Is he going to be alright?" Lydia couldn't resist asking.

"Too early to tell," one of the surgeons barked, "Wait outside please."

Lydia took another look at Unknown #10 and left.

Outside the OR, Lydia stopped and put her hand in her pocket, feeling the cell phone in there. She looked at her watch. It was already eleven forty. Just minutes ago she couldn't wait to leave the hospital. To meet with her dream man, the mysterious Michael. Now her mind- as well as her heart- had no room for him. She had become obsessed with Unknown #10. "Shit..." she said out loud. She looked around. The hall was empty. Nobody had heard her. She needed to call Michael.

She ran into the nearest one-seat ladies' room, guaranteeing privacy. It was the least she could do for the guy who had shown her it was possible to love again. She dialed his number. One ring. Michael usually picked up after two rings. Two rings. Okay, any second now. Three rings. Lydia started playing with her hair. Four rings. Lydia couldn't believe it. He had caller ID! Five rings. And for the first time, she got Michael's voice mail. "Hey, it's Michael. Leave a message..." Lydia was so caught off guard it took her a moment to realize she had to leave a message. She hung up. She couldn't do it. Just hearing Michael's voice made her weak again. She had to see him. Just had to. "Lydia Miles you officially a wreck! " she said aloud.

"Lydia Miles stat to patient registration!" came Sandy's voice over the PA. Lydia groaned. It was time to go back to work.

When she returned to the Snake Pit, Sandy was glaring at her. It seemed like the size of the waiting area had doubled. And the noise had tripled. Babies were crying, mothers yelling, EtOH's ranting drunkenly.

"I hope you got that drunk's life story, Lyd," Sandy snapped.

Pushing the image of that splotched stomach out of her head, Lydia's eyes darted around the room. Something was missing. "Uh, Sandy?" Lydia asked quietly. "Where did the policeman go?"

"Back out to his car..." Sandy said, growing impatient.

"Did you tell him where Unknown #10 is?" Lydia asked, trying to maintain.

"Why wouldn't I?" Sandy barked, "It was the first thing he asked! Now finish out your shift! You're on til midnight remember?"

Lydia looked at the clock. It was eleven fifty-three pm.

Presently a glassy-eyed gentleman with no shirt waited at the registration desk. He was covered with tattoos. As Lydia approached she noticed two things. The first was, once again, a foul stench. The other was the man's inability remain still.

He wobbled back and forth, side to side. It was the exact moment he looked up at her that she figured what was causing this haphazard swaying. Something very long was slithering around inside his torso. As if the man's intestines had come to life and decided to swirl on their own. The man spit up a little black bile as he grinned a toothless grin at Lydia. She stared at his roiling guts... his guts...

A long time ago Lydia's grandmother decided to tell her about true love. "Always trust your gut, Lydia. Your head will create fear and your heart will create foolishness. But your gut will never let you down."

A loud beeping from the drawer momentarily distracted her. She threw the drawer open. The beeping was coming from the Ziploc containing Unknown #10's personal effects. Adrenaline began to race as she opened the bag. The wallet was beeping. No, something inside it. The calculator? Rifling through the wallet she found the source off the beeping. She knew what she was going to see before she saw it.

But when she saw what she knew she was going to see, she gasped anyway.

Lydia Miles suddenly pictured Officer Mike passing the ladies' room where Lydia had made her call. Right now he was probably standing outside the OR waiting to "talk" to Unknown #10. Standing... or pacing.

Meanwhile, the toothless man with the belly-urchin rummaging through his innards looked as if he was about to pass out. What was the snake doctor's name? Oh yes. Lydia got on the PA and made the announcement: "Dr. Cranston stat to patient registration!" She smiled at the shirtless gentleman with the reptile in his bowels. "The doctor will be right with you sir."

The gentleman nodded as if he understood, bobbling and wobbling the whole time. As gross as she thought that was it still wasn't the lady who came in with the bee in her ear. Nothing could top that that one...

Lydia then hurried back past Sandy, "Where do you think you're-" Lydia shoved Sandy aside and made her way back into the hospital, toward the OR. She broke into a run. The PA blared: "Lydia Miles stat to registration!!" Lydia mentally blocked any further announcements out. She just didn't have time to mess around anymore and damn the consequences. You only come around this way once. She knew one thing now about Unknown #10. That she was meant for him, for all eternity.

Standing outside the OR, Hitchcock kept hearing that announcement "Lydia Miles stat to registration!" What had gotten into that woman? He had seen that waiting room fill up with every other dreg in Crescent County Memorial while Lydia had been away from her desk. Some looked to be in really rough shape, especially the guy with the snake in his belly. It was times like this Hitchcock thought of that expression "a chain is only as strong as its weakest link." It was as true in the business of saving lives as it was in law enforcement. Hitchcock was glad he had run out to his car for that extra bullet. He also remembered to screw on his silencer. Keeping things like this on the down-low came part and parcel with police work here.

"You have to forget who they are," Harold Hitchcock had told his grandson Mike some twenty years ago, "And remember what they become. That makes pulling the trigger an easy decision." Hitchcock's grandad had taught him a lot about keeping the peace in Crescent County. It involved much more than chasing your garden variety criminals around and making sure they wound up behind bars. That's for damn sure. He'd been chasing this Alley Cannibal for three months now. But it was only tonight that he figured out just what the Alley Cannibal was. When he'd fired upon the big hulking creature near the pond then found the body of a man lying on the ground.

If he'd only figured it out when the reports started coming in... about human limbs being found in alley dumpsters. Unknown #10 would have been on his way to the morgue where right now instead of having his life saved so he could kill again. Because Hitchcock would've made sure to use the right kind of bullet the first time. Crescent County hadn't seen anything like this in two generations. Hitchcock determined Unknown #10 was definitely an out-of-towner. Every baby born in Crescent County was secretly vaccinated against lycanthropy and every adult who had a blood test was secretly screened for it. Here in this very hospital.

The doors to the OR swayed open. The doctors and nurses were about to walk right past Hitchcock. "Excuse me," he said and they turned, pulling their masks off. "I need to talk to your patient. Is he awake?"

One of the doctors shook his head, "He died during the surgery. I'm sorry." With that, he caught up with the other doctor and the nurses, who headed toward the elevators.

Not yet, Hitchcock thought. Adrenaline would restart Unknown #10's lupine heart within minutes if it hadn't already. This time Officer Michael Hitchcock would be ready for it, silver bullet and all...

Lydia knew she should have taken the stairs. Only four floors up but the elevator stopped at every floor. A very old man on a walker got on at the second floor. Of course, he took so long Lydia had to hold the "door open" button for him. And, of course, he had to get out on the third. She had to resist the urge to push the old geezer out the doors. "Thank you, young lady," he said smiling at her. He patted her shoulder and just before the doors closed Lydia felt a moist spot where he had touched her. She gagged in disgust. His palm had been bleeding and there was a nickel-sized blood stain on her uniform. Great. Now she was going to have to stay a little longer tonight to get an HIV test. But when the blood stain disappeared on its own accord so did her disgust. As if the man's blood had never been there. Just another night at Memorial.

The elevator doors open and Lydia flew out racing down

to the end of the corridor, taking a left... just at the end of that corridor was where she saw Officer Mike Hitchcock entering the OR. "Wait!" she cried. Either Hitchcock didn't hear her or he didn't care.

Lydia had been right on the first count. As Hitchcock entered the now empty OR he was completely focused on his mission. To take Unknown #10 out. He found the lock on the OR door and latched it.

He took out the peculiar sidearm he had brought specifically for this occasion. It looked a little like something from a wild west show. It was a revolver- heavy, shimmering, extra-long thanks to the silencer. He double-checked the cylinder. Two rounds of pure silver. He raised it at the thing on the bed. It may have looked like a man (well the corpse of a man right now). But Hitchcock had seen the beast this man became. Technically, Hitchcock believed it was the beast that turned into the man in order to maintain anonymity. Sure this poor bastard was once human before another beast bit him. But now his human form was a cheap disguise for what lurked within.

Hitchcock quietly took aim. The man's body was motionless right now so he could afford a little time. Didn't want to make too much of a mess... He squeezed the trigger and-

The scream from outside the door came so loudly it almost defeated the purpose of the silencer on the end of his gun. Hitchcock looked behind him and saw the crazed woman from the registration desk. Lydia.

Hitchcock turned back to Unknown #10 and realized he had missed the shot. A bullethole now sat in the headboard of the hospital bed.

She started pounding at the door. "No! Let me in!" she screamed. This was going to get messy. He no longer had his second bullet. He would have to improvise. Lydia was obstructing police business, a cuff-able offense. He would take her out to his car and do her there. Still, he cursed himself for not taking any extra silver bullets from the glove compartment.

Hitchcock raised his weapon at Unknown #10 again. Who would have guessed he'd have to have more than one try at a point blank shot?

A rattling noise now added to the chaos. Hitchcock didn't have time to wonder what this new noise was, he just focused on firing that silver bullet into Unknown #10's head...

... which was now vibrating. His whole body was vibrating! The sheets once covering him fell to the ground and Hitchcock could see he had run out of time. This was Officer Michael Hitchcock's last-second alive and he already knew it.

Hitchcock squeezed the trigger a second time just as Unknown #10 changed his shape and lunged from the hospital bed, pouncing like a tiger onto Hitchcock.

Outside the room, the orderlies Dave and Boogie were now at the door with Lydia. Boogie had just put his skeleton key in the lock when they all heard the loud thud come from inside. The three of them froze for a second... and then came a blood-curdling howl that could come from no animal on this earth. Then came the screams of a man. A man who was being ripped limb from limb. Once the blood splattered on the door's narrow window, Dave and Boogie both began to back away. With a loud snap, the screams abruptly stopped. It was quiet again.

Lydia knew in her heart she had to go into that room no matter what. Her heart was telling her so. She turned the key.

Upon entering the stench of blood filled her nostrils. She nearly slipped on something. Looking down she saw it was a kidney. Entrails were strewn everywhere. She moved up to the thing that crouched on the floor, just above what was left of Officer Michael Hitchcock. The crouching thing had its back to her but she could clearly see it was not human. It was not an animal either. Something in between. Skin could be seen under waves of long brown hair along every inch of its body. Its feet looked like enormous paws.

The thing swung its head around with lightning speed. But Lydia didn't even flinch. She knew what she would see. Those two sparkling green eyes. Now they were surrounded by fur, jutting bone and a long, wide mouth filled with razor-sharp teeth and dripping with blood. In fact, the whole front of the thing was matted with fresh gore and insides.

Then Lydia could see not all the blood belonged to Officer Hitchcock. There was an oozing bullet hole in the werewolf's forehead. A hint of silver flashed from the bullet embedded in its skull.

Suddenly the werewolf raised one of its hideous claws and swiped at Lydia, slashing her chest. She heard her clothes and skin rip and fell backward a few steps. Then she felt the warmth of her own blood seeping onto her blouse.

The whole time she never took her gaze from those green eyes, which almost looked sad as they began to roll up until Lydia could see only the whites. Then... his eyelids closed for the last time.

The werewolf dropped to the floor, landing on the remains of its prey.

Lightheaded, Lydia looked at the clock on the wall. It was 12:01. They had never made it to their rendezvous. But had been brought together anyway... by destiny.

The huge wound on her chest pumped blood like a waterfall. The droplets spattering onto her shoes, she fell onto the body of a naked man who was once a werewolf. So that was the secret he had wanted to share with her. She realized she knew nothing else of this man. Where he lived, worked, spent his idle time. As she lay there dying she realized none of that was important. For once in her life, she had loved someone with all the depth and breadth of her being, if only for a short while. With her last breath, Lydia whispered into the dead man's ear, "Goodbye Michael..."

Something that looked very much like a calculator fell from Lydia's hand. It was actually the old school blackberry she'd gotten from Unknown #10's personal effects. It displayed the last text message it had received. It read "cant w8 2cu".

MISSED CONNECTION

It has been ten years since Journal-Bulletin reporter Elizabeth Kale boarded the subway one summer night and was never seen again. Recently, a striking piece of her puzzle surfaced. Laying in the archives of a now-defunct personals website called "Missed Connections" was a mysterious thread that asked as many questions as it answered. Those who knew Liz Kale do not recall any correspondence with its main "author" David Suffolk and are chilled by the connection between the thread's urban legend and Liz's very first newspaper article. To fill in some blanks The Journal-Bulletin has not only inserted subway records but blurbs from its own archives- some authored by Liz herself eerily enough. Nonetheless, the biggest blanks remain blank. So why add to the mystery, the reader wonders? Perhaps publishing this will help it reach someone who can fill in those blanks and help to locate her. Liz's family and her friends here at the Journal-Bulletin miss her and at this point seek nothing more than closure and peace.

Editor In Chief

The Journal-Bulletin

June 1st

User: david_suffolk

To the dead lady in the wedding dress who rides the subway:

You know who you are. I was riding eastbound last night. The car was crowded but when the lights went out it was like everybody else disappeared. And all I saw was you, glowing there on the other end of the train. You wore a wedding dress, veil and all. I couldn't make out your face but I thought we had a moment. I felt something. A connection. It's like you and I were the only ones on that subway car. I instantly felt like I wanted to see you again. I realize things would have to be a little different, you being ectoplasm at best. But I'm cool with that. I would love to see you again. I remember the number of that car. Thirteen. Which happens to be my lucky number.

I have no idea if ghosts can read internet message boards. I am assuming that they can sense when someone is trying to contact them. Perhaps you'll "read" this from that world beyond ours.

And perhaps I'll see you again when I ride car number thirteen again tomorrow. Until then.

June 2nd

User: david_suffolk

Dear ghost bride... I was there. Where were you? I actually stayed on car thirteen to the end of the line and rode it back again. The ride was intriguing. I could have stayed longer but the conductor kicked me off when I got back to central station. The whole ride I thought to myself "so this is where she lives" or in your case "this is where she's dead". I took in every nook and cranny of the subway car. The chairs, the handles dangling from the ceiling, the plastic seats with the torn micro-thin pillows. All these things people who ride that car every day take for granted. Not you though. It's your home isn't it? Or your tomb? How did you get there anyway? Did you die on the subway?

I'm sorry. If you're reading this I suppose it could be making you uncomfortable. Is there discomfort after death? Listen. I am convinced what happened was not a chance encounter. It was meant to be.

I just got home and it's really late now. Yesterday when I saw you I was having a bad day and you turned my mood around, a hundred and eighty degrees. Maybe you supernatural types can't read these posts. I hope you can. I will give you one more chance. Tomorrow night I will get on the train after midnight. That way too it will be just the two of us.

June 3rd

User: david_suffolk

Dear ghost bride... thank you, thank you, thank you, what a rush!

At first I thought you had stood me up. But you were just playing hard to get. Lucky me.

I was alone one minute cursing my bad luck with women for the umpteen millionth time. Then the lights went out, everything went dark and there you were sitting across from me. I could see your veil silhouetted in the window. I saw the distinct shape of a bouquet in your lap. I heard your gentle weeping and felt your need. There is discomfort after death isn't there? My heart was beating faster than a hummingbird's. It still is as a matter of fact...

But then the lights came back up and you were gone. I should have introduced myself. Or told you how beautiful you looked. My name is David by the way. And you did look beautiful.

I will be on car thirteen again tonight. And when I see you again I will say something.

PS: I will also have my phone handy. I hope you don't mind having your picture taken. I don't even know if ghosts can be photographed! I just want to be able to see you anytime I want. If I can.

June 4th

User: david_suffolk

Dear bride of car thirteen... What happened?

I must have been on your subway car for about four hours. I had a cup of my strongest coffee with me too in case I started to nod out. You were a no show! Every time the lights went out my heart would start beating. I'd pace up and down the darkened train car and I would take a picture with every flicker of light. I must have taken about forty pictures! But no sign of you, your wedding dress or your bouquet.

Was it something I said?

Was it all that talk about me wanting to take your picture? I guess I am actually coming on strong for once in my life. Usually I'm too afraid to approach women. I can't even muster the courage to look a woman in the eye. Especially the ones I am attracted to. But for some reason, I have no problem being bold with you. Ironic yes? Most people find comfort in the living and are afraid of ghosts. I'm the exact opposite here.

I guess it's because I have always believed in ghosts, big time. That's the main reason why I can see them I think. And even when I can't see them I can feel them. It's been happening my whole life. My best childhood friend was the ghost of a long-dead distant cousin- Tommy Suffolk, whose family disappeared in the woods behind my house before I was born. He was the coolest kid I ever met and the only real friend I ever had. Since then the thought of ghosts has brought me comfort. I have to believe in an afterlife. I come from a family that has suffered much tragedy over the years. And it continues. A death in the family is what brought me to the city (my last living relative, a great uncle who I'd never met made me sole beneficiary of his meager estate).

That night I saw you I'd had a horrible case of insomnia and throbbing headache (I spend all day entering data into a computer and I work under fluorescents so yeah). But when those lights went back on my insomnia and my headache were gone. Unfortunately so were you.

When I heard you crying I felt your need. I mean that.

Do you feel mine?

Being a bride you are familiar with vows. Here's my vow to you. I vow to continue riding car thirteen every night until I see you again.

June 5th

User: david_suffolk

Today I was deleting the pictures I took on car thirteen last night. As I remember none of them showed anything but an empty subway car. Then I got to the picture where I accidentally got my own reflection in the window. Now I see something behind me. Something I originally thought was a trail of a streetlight outside the car. Now I see what could be bouquet at the end of the trail? I don't want it to be a trick of the light. I want to believe you are there behind me. A tease would be better than what I have right now. Which is nothing at all.

June 6th

User: david_suffolk

Dearest Bride,

I'm revisiting an old and not-so-dear friend right at the moment. Her name is Rejection. Two nights in a row. Perhaps I was seeing things two nights ago on car thirteen. Maybe I was just overtired and thought I saw you. Or maybe it was a dream.

Stop me if you've heard this before but I don't want to believe those things. Here's what I want to believe. That you may be shy. That you may not be used to someone showing you this kind of attention. That perhaps you are used to quote-unquote scaring men away. And that you are shocked someone would actually respond to the sight of you by wanting to see you again.

I need to know we are communicating somehow. If you are reading this from the other side please give me a sign. I will ride car thirteen tonight. Could you please lower one of the windows in the car for me so when I get on the car I'll at least know you are real?

Please be real. This is more that a crush. It is an obsession. Maybe it's no good for me but it sure doesn't feel that way. I have some very powerful things happening inside me because of you. And I will not rest until I see you again.

June 7th

User: david_suffolk

I just came across this chain post elsewhere. Superstition and the supernatural are connected by more than just the prefix. I have never been a big fan of this sort of thing but I guess I am getting desperate. If I don't do this I may always wonder what if... anyway maybe it will work. Here goes:

"If you repost this message on another city's board then tonight at midnight your true love will realize they love you. They will let you know tomorrow. You will get a big surprise- a good one. If you break this chain, you will be cursed with relationship problems for the rest of your life. If there is someone you once loved, or still do, and you can't get them out of your head, repost this in another city within the next 5 minutes. It's guaranteed to work. Repost this titled as " I Truly Do Miss You". Whoever you are missing will surprise you. Don't break this, for tonight at midnight, your true love will realize they love you and something great will happen to you tomorrow."

I am posting this in the city where I was born and raised... Worthington, Ohio. If there was only a way to convey to you how not like me this is. That's how strong the feelings are that I have for you. Sure I feel like an idiot. I will feel like a bigger one if this doesn't work. But I may be in the company of every man who believes he has found his soulmate. And will stop at nothing to make her realize it too... no matter how stupid he looks.

See you on the train?

June 8th

User: david_suffolk

Yes. I was feeling like a complete ass. You have to know that my heart sank in my chest when I stepped on that train and all of the windows were up. I have been stood up, rejected and dejected over the years.

In case you could not tell I am something of recluse who can only express himself on his computer's keyboard. My laptop has been my confidante since my family moved away from my first home and my ghost friend Tommy. I could never make friends in school. The only interaction I had with my schoolmates was when the bullies cornered me in the bathroom. Also I am not much to look at. Girls used to tell me I had a face only a mother could love. But even my mother would tell me that looks aren't everything. Does wonders for a child's self-esteem. Sometime during college I decided I could either continue being dissatisfied until I found my better half. Or I could start enjoying being single. It was not easy at first but over the years I have found that there are many pleasures one can share with himself.

I spend a lot of time at museums, the library, the theater. Ticket for one please.

Every now and again someone would want to set me up with a co-worker, a neighbor or an aunt who for some reason could not land a boyfriend. I never turned these opportunities down. I was not an isolator. Anyway I met some women who had a lot of potential this way. Unfortunately none of them thought I had any potential, and moved on.

They would usually not tell me they had moved on. They assumed I would figure it out from their unreturned phone calls and stand-ups.

It has been roughly four years since I've been out on a date.

The night I first saw you I was coming back from a midnight showing of some cult movie from the nineteen thirties I had already seen about eight hundred times. Up until that point, just another night. Then the lights went out...

In case you couldn't tell I am endlessly disappointed by the living. Women with a pulse really let me down in every way. So being ghosted by an actual ghost was the ultimate in rejection.

Now you can imagine how discouraged I felt as I got ready to get off at my stop. I was literally staring at the floor when the sudden noise jolted me. Then I felt the breeze.

Every window in the train had been opened at once!

As if this wasn't enough just before the train stopped they all went up again with a slam! Needless to say I was overjoyed. And I will never break a chain e-mail again. I can't believe that worked.

I will be riding on your car again tomorrow night. Hope to see you. I wish I know more about you bride of car thirteen. I want to know your story...

June 9th

User: david_suffolk

Ask and ye shall receive so sayeth the Lord. My bride I feel closer to you than ever before. I had to buy a new rail pass last night and I took the opportunity to ask the old man in the ticket booth about car number thirteen. He looked like he was going to have a heart attack! Luckily there was nobody behind me in line. So he was able to tell me the story some old custodian told him when he first started working there.

Still reeling from the story I ran back home and looked it up online...

"FROM THE JOURNAL-BULLETIN

May 23rd, 1980

ELDERLY COUPLE FOUND DEAD ON SUBWAY CAR

By Elizabeth Kale

Authorities are trying to find the family of an elderly man and woman, both in their seventies, who both suffered massive heart attacks while riding the subway. Because they were not found until the subway had reached the end of its line, it is difficult for authorities to guess exactly where the couple was headed. Medical examiners estimate the man and woman died at the exact same moment, prompting police to suspect some outside influence. However, upon investigation, police found no trace of any other passengers or disturbance to the train car which would cause two people to have sudden heart attacks at the exact same moment."

It didn't say in the article but these two unfortunate seniors happened to be riding in your train car that night. As I will be tonight. See you then?

June 10th

User: david_suffolk

I could feel you tonight although I did not see you. Feeling is enough. For now. To be riding alone in the dark and to feel your presence. Such power. You left a lot of business undone when you shed this mortal coil. I wish we were in the park under the bridge, sitting on one of those quaint benches, the river and the skyline behind us. You would tell me all about yourself. And I would hang on every word.

Sadly we cannot communicate the usual way. Ours seems to be a long distance affair. With me in this world you in the next.

I have found the Department of Transportation's website and intend to hack into it. I understand they've scanned just about every page from every log on every subway train in the city. Maintenance, schedule consistency, complaints... sightings of unexplained phenomena? I intend to find out. I will not sleep until I find more about you.

Until next time...

June 11th

User: david_suffolk

Eureka! This is the most important piece of your puzzle to date. I studied the logs of all the conductors working on your train (the "6 train" of which number thirteen is the last car), dating back since the subways first opened, roughly sixty years ago. The first five years the 6 train rolled without incident. Breakdowns, minor repairs... no fires, no derailings, no holdups like you see in the movies.

Then on the night of June seventh about fifty-five years ago, a lone passenger riding the train spoke of seeing (this is straight from the log) "a lady in white crying in the back of the train. He got up to check on her but by the time he reached her seat she was gone. Fearing she had thrown herself off the train he reported the incident to me (conductor's name). An investigation turned up no evidence of another passenger at that time and it was supposed passenger one was hallucinating due to working a long shift and being overtired."

Hoo-ha! There's more....

On the night of January seventeenth, roughly nine years later, a group of "juvenile delinquents" was "having a marijuana party". Then according to them the lights in the train went out. And that's when somebody or something crashed their little party. The conductor on duty reported that the emergency button in car thirteen was "flashing repeatedly" until he stopped the train. When he went into car thirteen he found four boys huddled in a far corner of the train, clutching one another for dear life. They were all staring at one of the windows: the one window that had been smashed and whose jagged corners had been smeared with blood.

When the conductor opened the doors for them to get out they scrambled off the train like they were "waking up from a nightmare". The surviving teenagers then told the conductor (before the police arrived) that after the lights went out they sensed "a presence". Then one of the boys started screaming at the top of his lungs and, to the shock of his friends, jumped through one of the windows. This was a feat the conductor had trouble believing. The windows on every subway car are made of Plexiglas and would be impossible to break without the aid of a bullet, heavy object or machine like a jackhammer. Of course the conductor suspected foul play when the police finally arrived.

I had to cross reference this case with the police file from that night. Four teenaged boys were taken in for questioning concerning the death of the fifth boy, James Smith. The four boys seemed "rattled and contrite" and, when questioned separately, each told the same story. They got on the train, smoked a joint, then the lights went out... and they saw their buddy James jump off the train... through the window... backwards... yelling "no" repeatedly...

The more I know the more there is of you to love. The brief glimpses are enough for now. But I will not stop until I find out who you were in this world.

PS: See you tonight?

June 12th

User: david_suffolk

Ever since our first encounters I have rode your train hoping to see you again. How you tease... Nonetheless if it weren't for your elusiveness I would be digging so feverishly to find out as much as I can about you.

I am at a dead end with the conductor's logs. Aside from the elderly couple having simultaneous heart attacks and the young boy being hurled from car thirteen, there really is nothing more to "write home about". No more ghostly encounters. None recorded anyway. I don't know what exactly I was hoping for. But with each tidbit I read I feel as if I have a shared experience with you. Some common frame of reference. My next goal is to read the records that the subway builders kept. Perhaps something interesting will present itself...

In the meantime here is a strange coincidence. I have been going through my recently departed uncle's effects and have found a genealogical history, a sort of narrative family tree. One of his own uncles is named James Smith just like the boy who was ejected so abruptly from car thirteen all those years ago.

My eyes are itching. I must turn in now so that I may ride on car thirteen again tonight. Until then...

June 13th

User: david_suffolk

My bride I thought I saw you on the train last night. Sadly I was asleep and dreaming about you. I could not even feel your presence car thirteen. It is disheartening. Plus it makes me question my own sanity. Am I that lonely? That cut off from the rest of humanity? Am I that much of a... what do you call it... "loser"? Perhaps this is how hermits dealt with their isolation. Having dreams about the ghosts of women they'll never meet anyway? I am having no luck with the DOT's website. I am going down to city hall today to see if I can find something else on car thirteen. I'll pore through everything they've got on the construction of the subway. Wish me luck. If you are real. And Happy Friday 13th...

June 14th

User: david_suffolk

Just got back from city hall, what I found out today has my head reeling. I don't know if I can write anything yet. I am in shock. And for the first time completely without words. Please show yourself to me again tonight!

June 15th

User: david_suffolk

Okay I've had twenty-four hours but still at wit's end. Got a solid night's sleep. Unfortunately it was all done on that train car. No sign of you. Why? Does the gender thing apply in the afterlife? Are mortal men from Mars and ghost women from Venus? Is stuff like this what Freud was talking about? Or are you just playing a game? I have heard about people who play games. Manipulators. Both sexes are guilty of that I suppose. I have no experience in this department. So there is a first time for everything. By the way you heard me right. No experience. None whatever. At the ripe old age of thirty-two I am still a virgin. I don't know what compels me to tell you that. Maybe you'll show me a little pity?

My God you taunt me. It's like you own me, heart, mind and soul. You must know we have more in common than a chance meeting on the subway. You must know what I find out yesterday. You have to know about how car thirteen- your home for God only knows how long- was built in a small Midwestern town, once famous for building train cars. That town's name is Worthington, Ohio. That's right. My great grandfather was a welder at that manufacturing plant. He may have even worked on car thirteen!

How odd is that? Do you think that falls into the small world category? Of course you don't. You showed yourself to me for a reason. And now you play games. Just like a real woman. How disappointing.

I think I need to take a break from all this. Tonight I will be getting some much needed rest. In my bed.

June 16th

User: david_suffolk

Decided to pick up a copy of today's paper out of the blue. I never buy the newspaper can you believe that? To quote one of my favorite literary characters things are getting "curiouser and curiouser". Here's a copy of one of today's articles, which I found online:

"LIGHTNING STORM ON SUBWAY CAR

Three passengers riding the 6 train were treated to a little more than a ride across town last night. Several minutes into their trip downtown (names withheld) claim that the lights inside their car went out. "What happened next is hard to describe," (name withheld) said, "It was like a sidewise lightning bolt that went from one end of the car to the other." All three claim the source of the freak lightning bolt was actually a person. "It looked like a woman," (name withheld) added, "she was wearing a dress…" The three passengers were rushed to the hospital when they had trouble exiting the train due to temporary loss of vision. All three were released from the hospital with no permanent injuries. Subway conductor, (name withheld), claims there was no evidence of a fourth passenger but reported burns on the rear interior of the subway car."

If you really do read my letters I have one word for you. Communication. It should not matter that I live in this dimension and you live in the next. Our two dimensions obviously intersect at a point known as car thirteen.

I've been open and honest and shown you my feelings. This is literally the first time I have done such things for a woman. I am just learning how to express myself as I'm going along. I don't know if I'll get compassion from someone as otherworldly as you. But based on what I know and what I have read and I have been told by the very few women in my life, this is what a man needs to do to prove his love. To show his feelings. Am I mistaken? Are you looking for someone who does not show his feelings? Who chooses to hide them from you?

I ride your subway car for several nights in a row. Nothing. Then, three jerks from nowhere get on the train and you treat them to lightning! Funny too you should choose to display yourself with lightning. Worthington Ohio holds the record for the most lightning storms every year. Is this another strange coincidence?

Maybe I am not the one that is mistaken. Perhaps you just enjoy playing with men who are attracted to you. I have known a woman or two who liked to do that. What a sad and lonely life (eternity in your case) that must be. Stop me if you've heard this one before but I'm getting too old for that crap.

I will give you one more try. You intrigue me in a way no one else ever has, living or dead. I can forgive you for ignoring me. I can forgive you for throwing your affections to others. But please, please, please communicate with me tonight. I'm begging you on bended knee. Please.

(Excerpt courtesy the Municipal Transit Authority)

Conductor's Log, Train 6,17June, Hour 0350.

En route to central station saw bright flashes from the back of train reflected in windshield. Made unscheduled stop to inspect and immediately heard someone running from last car, number thirteen. Ran to car thirteen but it was too late. The passenger was already gone. Train did not appear damaged. Followed protocol and reported incident to shift supervisor.

MISSED CONNECTIONS

June 18th

User: david_suffolk

I want to create a word. It has to describe the way I felt last night right after the lights went out. And you appeared wiping away any doubt I ever had about you. I am sorry I ever harbored any anger or mistrust toward you. You are real. And you are so worth the wait. How can I put words to the rush, the electricity, the white light! Is psychorgasmic a word? Because that's how I felt.

Maybe it's a little too soon but I do feel, let's just say, a certain way about you. I've never said the words I want to say to you. Not to anybody. And I don't think I will yet either. I do not want to scare you away- said the mortal to the ghost. I want the timing to be just right.

I don't play games. Maybe if I was younger I'd be eager to engage in some cat and mouse thing. But I am not looking for that anymore. Games are for the immature, the shallow... the living. I want a sense of permanence. I don't want to guess. Again, I have to wonder if that's what every man- correction, what everyone wants.

This evening I will be freshly showered, shaved and have on my finest suit. I want this to be an official date whether you want it to or not. Okay I can't hold out any longer. I have to say it.

I love you my bride. You may be dead but you are the only thing that I am living for.

My thirst for you is unquenchable. I long for you so much I've started having fantasies about killing myself. I think I would have already if I were absolutely certain I would join you on car thirteen. I can't conceive of spending eternity in some place where you were not. No matter what that place was I would call it hell.

Until tonight.

(Excerpt from "The Journal-Bulletin" archives June 18th)

STRANGE LIGHTS AND BLOOD ON SUBWAY CAR BAFFLE FIREFIGHTERS

Responding to several 911 calls that a subway train caught fire, local firefighters came to the subway station downtown, only to find it was a false alarm. What they did find baffled them even more. Smudges of blood, presumed to be human, scrawled in geometric patterns on one of the windows. Witnesses from the street claim the train car had one passenger. But the car was empty when firefighters arrived. This is the second time the fire department was called because of this particular train. Two nights ago three passengers reportedly saw a lightning bolt inside the subway car.

June 19th

User: elizabeth_kale

RE: the bride of car thirteen

Dear Mr. Suffolk- My name is Liz Kale. I am a reporter for a national publication and am doing a piece on urban legends. Presently I'm in town and have read all of your posts so far. Imagine my surprise at seeing the first article I ever wrote, when I was doing an internship for the Journal-Bulletin! The coincidences do not stop there. You will be intrigued to know my piece begins in your hometown, where a strange and tragic wedding occurred in 1939, almost fifty years before you were born.

Please contact me on this message board. I am curious about your recently deceased uncle, Nolan James. He may provide a missing piece to the legend I've been researching. Sincerely, LK.

June 20th

User: david_suffolk

Still bleeding. Still writhing in joyful pain.

My blood forms in pools.

The blood of a virgin no more. And more than just make love.

More than any earthly experience, you inside me. You take me over.

My hands cut me but you were the pilot. You did the cutting, the painting, the spell.

We are one.

June 20th

User: elizabeth_kale

Mr. Suffolk, I don't know if my last post is showing up on your end. I need to meet with you in person the sooner the better. I've got a deadline coming up and there are some facts I have uncovered about your family you will want to know. Those two elderly people who died on the subway of heart attacks were actually brother and sister. Their last name was James, same as your uncle. I realize it is morbid but this stuff sort of thing sells newspapers, even creates best sellers. Interested?

June 20th

User: unknown

I know how I can be forever with you now.

June 20th

User: elizabeth_kale

Is that you Mr. Suffolk? If it isn't do you know where I can contact him?

June 20th

User: elizabeth_kale

Mr. Suffolk, I guess another party has decided to leave messages on this board. I will ignore them and wait until you contact me personally.

Before we meet I was wondering if you had a genealogical chart done, or was in possession of one that someone else in your family had done. I ask this because I worked for a genealogist when I was in college and took the liberty of creating a family tree for yours.

I was in for quite a shock when I discovered the extent to which tragedy and bad luck runs in your family, the Suffolks and your cousins, the James'.

According to my notes, every one of your ancestors has met with an untimely death or protracted illness. Even the branch of your family that moved out to the city- your uncle, the elderly people who died on the subway- no longer exists. More puzzling is the fact that this run of misfortune began in the same year as the tragedy which occurred in your family's home town of Worthington, Ohio.

Unless you have any siblings or cousins I am not aware of you are the last of your family. I do not believe in curses but this information is provocative and would make for a wonderful article.

June 21st

User: elizabeth_kale

    Mr. Suffolk- I am still waiting for your reply. Perhaps you have not read my previous e-mail or have me written off as some kook who wishes to horn in on your inheritance. I assure you this is not the case. I am a reporter and your family figures into a little known urban legend that sprang from the Midwest. Most of the citizens of your home town are either too young to remember this event or have chosen to forget it entirely. It is the legend known as The Lightning Bride.

    In the mid to late 1930s, a fellow named Maxwell Suffolk (coincidence?) was to wed a woman named Constance Eldred. She grew up in an orphanage where the young Mr. Suffolk took work as a custodian. According to the legend, Mr. Suffolk and Miss Eldred struck up a friendship when she was still very young. During that time Mr. Suffolk whimsically promised the very young Miss Eldred that when she turned eighteen he would marry her. Unfortunately for both of them, the little girl took this promise very seriously.

    On the morning of her eighteenth birthday, June 23rd 1937, Miss Eldred bought a wedding dress and went to the chapel where the pastor informed her that Mr. James was already engaged to another woman, a Miss Hattie James (coincidence?). Refusing to believe this she went to a local bar where Mr. Suffolk had been drinking a while. His reaction was hardly polite or understanding. In fact, he burst out in laughter, along with the rest of the bar.

    Constance Eldred was heard to have said she would rather "marry the devil" then ran out of the bar in tears.

    Apparently, her next stop was the playground at the orphanage located just behind the church, where she sat on one of the swings. Being too big for the swing she broke the seat and fell to the ground. When she stood up again she was said to have cursed God. She then took one of the stray swing chains and hanged herself with it. Of course, there was a terrific lightning storm on the way and Constance Eldred was hit by a bolt of lightning. And since everything was made of metal she was literally cooked in less than a second.

In light of this event, the James-Suffolk wedding was postponed until a few years later, 1939 to be precise. The wedding was held at the same church where Mr. Suffolk vowed to wed Miss Eldred. Did I mention that the church ground abutted the playground where Miss Eldred died?

There were no lightning storms forecast for the second wedding day. Nonetheless, Mr. Suffolk, his new bride Miss James and everyone inside the church perished in a lightning storm that took place... inside the church. Just after the vows took place. Police noticed the backdoor of the church had been blown in, as if a lightning bolt had shot in-horizontally.

Supposedly just before the interior lightning storm occurred, the wedding photographer had walked outside to have a smoke. He had his camera with him and figured he'd take an exterior shot of the church.

According to my source, a one-hundred-year old woman who taught at the orphanage, claims a picture exists which shows a bolt of lightning coming from the swingset in the orphanage's playground. It belonged to the wedding photographer, who happened to be the new bride's cousin... your great grandfather.

As you are the last of the Suffolk branch of your family tree, your uncle was the end of the James branch. Being that he was a widower whose only child succumbed to crib death, all James heirlooms would be in your inheritance.

As a side-note, I read how your uncle died. He was shaving with an old-fashioned straight razor and sliced his jugular by accident. I am not sure you are aware but the last company to make straight razors just went of business. It was located in Worthington, Ohio. Do you see now why you need to contact me?

I am almost done with my research and the wedding day photo- if it exists- would make a great finishing touch to the article.

Please get back to me at your earliest convenience. If I do not hear from you today I will try to find other means. I hope you don't mind it is in the interest of journalism and nothing else.

June 21st

User: david_suffolk

Ms. Kale this is David. Meet me on the 6 train tonight. Car thirteen.

June 22nd

User: elizabeth_kale

Mr. S, David- So good to finally hear from you! Tonight when? Just after dusk? Or later on?

June 22nd

I will be on the train at nine. If you don't show within an hour I will assume this was a joke.

(excerpt courtesy the Municipal Transit Authority)

From the Supervisor's Request for Psychiatric Evaluation on PM Conductor, Train 6, June 23rd.

...I spoke with (name withheld), pm conductor on the night in question, about the incident in which he was found unconscious in the last car. The following is his version of events in his own words as dictated to me.

"I saw bright lights from the back of the train again (See June 17 entry). Stopped train to investigate. Took flashlight. Train was completely dark. I turned the flashlight on to see two people, a man and a woman- man, early thirties, woman early fifties, talking to each other. From what I could make out, the man's hands and neck were bandaged, like he just got hurt. The two people were not speaking English or Spanish or any other language I'm aware of.

They did not look at me, like they were hypnotized. I could not get their attention. The woman finally looked at me and I found myself in what you could call a twilight sleep. Like I was on ether. I was speaking this other language now. It became like a dream. I was conducting a ceremony. No. Someone- something else was conducting the ceremony through me. When it was done the man and the woman were facing each other again. I blacked out. Like I was hit in the head. When I woke up, police were there and the train was empty..."

(excerpt from the Journal Bulletin archives, June 24th)

SUBWAY RETIRES "HAUNTED" TRAIN CAR

The transit authority has announced it will retire the 6 train's now infamous "car thirteen". According to sources, the car was in constant need of repair and lately people did not feel safe riding in it. Anyone who rode the 6 train could tell you car thirteen was the bumpiest ride. Some even admit to believing it was haunted by a woman in a wedding dress. The car will take its last ride aboard an Amtrak. It's final destination will be a plant specifically used for recycling unique metal items large and small, from ship hulls to old playground equipment. It is located in Worthington, Ohio.

(from the Missing Persons Alert, June 29th)

A 51-year-old woman from West Greenwich has been reported missing. Journalist, wife and mother Elizabeth Kale is 5-foot-7, 135 pounds, has long blond hair and green eyes. Anyone with information is urged to call the West Greenwich Police Department. She was last seen boarding the subway at central station on June 23rd.

THINGAMABOB

A Novella

Chapter One

His was a world of corners. Cool. Smooth. Snug. Endless angles. No days, no nights. Except for the occasional window the crawler's life was one long dark tunnel. The crawler did not know if he liked the windows. They showed views of dangerous places. Harsh light. No corners. Nothing to cling to. Scary. He crawled up to a window now. Stared down through the slits in the wall. In the blinding light, he saw two giants. Their mouths moved but the crawler heard nothing. The crawler had no ears.

"Hayes," Mysti answered.

Mrs. Daniels smiled and nodded when she heard Mysti's last name. Mrs. Daniels was one of the polite few. Usually, when people heard Mysti's full name their eyes would bug out they'd say something like, 'What was your mother thinking?' or 'Bet you can't wait to get married...'

Mrs. Daniels simply smiled and nodded and let Mysti into apartment 210. "Pardon me if I seem a little nervous," Mrs. Daniels said leading Mysti into the small but pretty dinette, "I haven't had a babysitter since..." Mrs. Daniels couldn't finish.

Mysti's dad had told her about the late Mr. Daniels. He was a policeman who got between two gangbangers last year. Got shot to death in the crossfire. Funny how the two shooters lived and the one who tried to stop them died. That's a cop's life though, Mysti thought. When Mysti got married it wouldn't be to a cop. Or any guy whose last name that had anything to do with fog.

"I understand," Mysti said.

"I keep wondering if this is too soon," Mrs. Daniels said.

She looked at Mysti. Mrs. Daniels was a pretty lady, especially all dressed up and made up.

"My dad says a date is just a date," Mysti told her, "Not 'till death'."

Mrs. Daniels nodded and smiled again, the exact same way that she did before. "Let's meet the little men." Mrs. Daniels led Mysti into the living room, "Robbie! The sitter's here, say hi to Mysti."

Mysti saw the nine-year-old boy laying on his stomach in front of the TV, watching an old Dracula movie starring some British actor as the immortal bloodsucker. Robbie wore Captain Spaceman pajamas and his haircut was so short he was almost bald. He had the kind of face you wanted to pinch. He barely gave Mysti a look, waved at her then went back to Dracula.

"He's a cutie-pie," Mysti said.

"He's got about nine valentines in his classroom," Mrs. Daniels said. "The girls just love Robbie don't they baby boy?"

Robbie barely looked at his mom then went back to the TV again.

"It's a weekend night so I just let him doze off in front of the TV," Mrs. Daniels said leading her down the hall toward the baby's room, "He'll probably be out by eight o'clock anyway," Mrs. Daniels dropped her voice to a whisper, "Only thing is he's a light sleeper. And he can wake up with a start too. It'll scare you at first but that's just the way he wakes up in the middle of the night."

Night terrors, Mysti thought, a condition usually reserved for older people. But as she passed by pictures of a handsome man in a police uniform in the hall, she figured little Robbie had reason to feel unsafe when the lights were out. Still, it always struck Mysti sad when she heard about a child suffering from a grown-up condition. Like migraines or ulcers. It seemed so unfair. She was going to become a pediatrician someday. Already had the grades at Filmore High to prove it. Four-oh GPA, eight hundreds on her PSATs and college credits even though she'd only just finished her sophomore year. The summer between junior high and Filmore, Mysti's dad had told her she was going to need a plan. "I don't care what that plan is," he'd said, "As long as you follow it." Mysti always loved kids and they loved her. Someday she was going to have a child or two herself but that was way far off.

Mrs. Daniels got to the end of a short hallway, arriving at the baby's room. She looked at Mysti and put a finger to her lips. "This is little Huey," she whispered and stood aside letting the light from the hall illuminate the crib just inside the doorway. Mysti tiptoed in and saw the infant, no more than eight months old, all bundled up and completely still except for his chest which was almost imperceptibly rising and falling.

"Hey Huey," Mysti said smiling down at the baby boy's beautiful face.

The crawler moved down to another window and looked down. Down at another little one like him. Trying to sleep in his little prison. The two giants standing were next to the prison now. According to the crawler's sense of smell, the older giant was the little one's mother. She and the other giant suddenly abandoned the little one, leaving him alone. The crawler would cry if one of his numerous eyes could produce a tear. This little one in the crib and him, they were brothers. Brothers from mothers who didn't want their babies.

Mysti was at the dining room table now, unloading her bookbag. Mrs. Daniels was checking herself one last time in the mirror.

"You look great," Mysti said. "He'll feel lucky to be sitting next to you tonight."

Mrs. Daniels smiled, "I don't even know this guy. Never even seen him."

Uh oh, Mysti thought and said, "How did you get fixed up with him? Internet?"

"A friend from work," Mrs. Daniels said, "My friend says he's a widower himself. No kids. He's a little older but he doesn't look it… supposedly."

Mysti raised her eyebrows and nodded, "Supposedly."

Both of them laughed. Mrs. Daniels checked herself in the mirror again, "I just have two rules. Rule one: in case of an emergency call 911 first then call my cell. Two: no friends in the apartment. Especially the boy kind. You got a boyfriend, Mysti?"

In her mind's eye, Mysti saw Derek Woods. Tall, long legs, broad shoulders and eyes the color of bronze. After seeing him smile everything was a do-over. Staying focused, Mysti looked Mrs. Daniels in the eye: "It's all about school right now. Boys can wait."

"Smart girl," Mrs. Daniels said.

There was a knock at the door. Both women looked at each other wide-eyed. Then Mrs. Daniels stood up and regained her composure. "One second!" she shouted.

A muffled male voice came from the other side of the door, "Take your time!"

Then Mysti and Mrs. Daniels looked at each other mouthing the words "take your time". They stifled giggles as Mrs. Daniels went to the door and opened it.

On the other side was one a man who looked old enough to be Mysti's grandfather.

"Is everything okay?" the old man on the side of the doorway said.

Mrs. Daniels turned her look of shock into surprise, "Oh I just- heard you were handsome but you look even better than I had imagined! Come on in..."

Wow, Mysti thought, Nice save!

Mrs. Daniels' date "Phillip" (not Phil) was as polite as he was old. And like most old folks he considered talking about himself a civic duty to young people. In the short time, it took Mrs. Daniels to finish getting ready Mysti found out Phillip had served in Vietnam, in the 11th Cav (just like Mysti's grandfather) that he liked rhubarb pie and that his favorite TV show of all time was The Mod Squad.

Mrs. Daniels allowed Phillip to put on her coat as she said a few last things to Mysti, "Huey sleeps through the night but if he wakes up hungry there's a bottle in the fridge it just needs to be nuked for twenty seconds. Robbie already brushed his teeth so no more snacks. He should fall asleep in front of the TV but if he's still up at ten put him to bed lights out," then as she was turning to go out the door with Phillip she said, "My cell phone number's on the fridge. Anything goes wrong you call 9-1-1 first then me."

As she turned to go out the door with Phillip he turned to Mysti, smiling like an old gargoyle: "I'll have her back by sunrise..."

Mysti waved as the door closed behind them. She stood there a moment enjoying that special moment only babysitters know. The time between when the adult leaves and when the kids start whining.

A minute later Mysti had her homework splayed out on the kitchen table. She would start on it right after she did quick checks on the baby and on Robbie.

Huey was sleeping like the innocent little angel he was. Mysti touched his little baby cheek and he stirred only a little then became still again.

Mysti then went down the hall to peek in at Robbie. She expected to find him lying on his stomach in front of the TV. He wasn't there now though. She looked on the couch. He wasn't there either. "Robbie?" She called out. On the TV Dracula had a nubile maiden by her pale neck and was about to sink his fangs into her jugular.

She thought she heard something. Grabbing the remote she muted the TV.

Scritch-scratch.

Mysti froze.

Scritch-Scratch.

It was coming from above her. She looked up at the vent and swore she saw something behind the slotted metal grate just before it disappeared. Then Mysti heard the scampering of tiny feet on metal, becoming more and more distant until... nothing.

"Stupid rats," Mysti said aloud, startling herself. She turned to go when-

-a tiny hand from under the couch clasped around her ankle! It was Robbie's. Laughing, she crouched down and looked under the couch.

"You scared me half to death..." she trailed off when she saw the look on Robbie's face. "What's the matter, honey?"

"You saw him too didn't you?" Robbie sputtered out.

"Who?"

Tears began streaming down the little boy's cheeks, "Thingamabob..."

Chapter Two

The top of the riding box was one of the crawler's three favorite places. It was dark. A little more open but still in a tunnel. And it took him to his two other favorite places. At the moment it was on its way down to the hot place. The crawler looked down through the window and saw the baby's mother standing inside with another giant. A man giant. Like his father. The mere thought of his father made the crawler very, very angry...

"He's white you know," Robbie said looking up at her from his pillow.

It had taken a few minutes to pull Robbie out from under the couch. He was so afraid of that slotted vent cover. Mysti kept saying there was nothing up there but a cute little mouse. Like the cartoon mouse, big ears and all. Even after she got him out from under there Robbie insisted on clutching to her, burying his face into her Filmore High sweatshirt. Mysti noted with concern that he was shaking.

"Who's white?" Mysti asked gently

She felt his tiny hand squeeze hers (he made her promise she wouldn't let go of his hand until his mommy got home), "Thingamabob!" He started crying again. Man, this kid was tired.

"Shhh," Mysti said stroking his forehead, "Okay! It's going to be okay. Can we talk about something other than...?"

"His momma was so poor she took money to get experimented on when she was pregnant..." he whispered now. "She took all these needles in her belly the whole time. They were for helping a baby live through a nukuler war. But when they finally looked at it with a ultrasound they saw it was a total mutant. Too many arms, no legs. Wasn't a girl or a boy. Had no head neither. Just a neck with a big mouth. And eyes all over his body..."

"Eww..."

"Thingamabob's daddy told her to get a abortion. So she paid a doctor or somebody to give her a abortion but it was too late. Thingamabob was too big. The doctor got him out but Thingamabob was still alive and he was mad. He killed the doctor."

"How...?"

"Thingamabob bit the doctor's neck so deep there was nothing left of it and his head just fell off."

"Robbie you have to stop watching those movies late at night..."

"But Thingamabob loved his momma. She was screaming and covered with blood but he cuddled up to her. She knew her husband would never accept his son. So she brought Thingamabob here to this building that night all wrapped up in a towel. She went into the basement and threw

Thingamabob into the thing that heats the building," Robbie paused for dramatic effect. "She thought he was dead. She thought wrong. Takes more than fire to kill Thingamabob. It doesn't need food or light or air either. It just walks through the vents looking for babies. Thingamabob feels bad for babies that get left alone. A baby without its momma. Thingamabob hates that more than anything. It takes those babies and brings them down to the heater inskinerator."

"Incinerator, honey," Mysti said and shook her head.

"Remember that Rosevelt baby?" Robbie whispered.

How could Mysti forget? Only three months old. Mrs. Rosevelt had put Baby Monica in the crib and took a nap in the living room for a half hour. She awoke to find her baby gone from a room with no windows and no other entrances. An exhaustive month-long search turned up no evidence and no suspects. Other folks in the apartment complex started thinking Mrs. Rosevelt got rid of the baby herself. It wasn't too long after that the devastated Mrs. Rosevelt and her husband quietly moved out.

"That night she went missing," Robbie continued, "I heard a baby crying up in the vents. Thingamabob doesn't know regular babies can't live in the- the incinerator like he can."

This kid watched too many scary movies. If Mysti had the mind to she'd tell Mrs. Daniels' when she got back. Mysti smiled and said, "Hey Robbie? What's your favorite bedtime story?"

"I like the three bears. NO! The three pigs."

"The three pigs it is..." Mysti said in her softest voice. She told the story of the three pigs nice and slowly, decreasing the volume of her voice as she went. By the time the wolf blew down the first pig's house Robbie's eyes were fluttering. By the time the wolf banged on the third pig's house, Robbie was snoring.

That's when Mysti's cell phone suddenly went off, blaring the top ten hit "Good Love" by J.P. She literally jumped up, took out and silenced the phone with one hand, never letting go of Robbie's with the other.

The little boy's eyes fluttered slightly then he settled again. After another moment he was snoring again. Whew. Mysti pulled her hand away from his and the boy rolled over. Double whew.

Exiting his room she looked at the phone's caller ID. She smiled despite herself. It was Derek. He just went to voicemail. Good. He can just wonder for a little while.

Mysti padded down the hall to the baby's room and peeked in. Precious Huey was right where she had left him. Like he'd be anywhere else? Mysti walked up and looked at him for a moment. Was he breathing? She felt fear rise in her throat then- Huey's chest fell and rose ever so slightly. He was still breathing. And that's when "Good Love" by J.P. started playing again at top volume!

Now Huey stirred and made a whimper. Mysti cursed to herself and silenced the phone again praying Huey wouldn't awaken. He didn't. Mysti hurried out of the room as quietly as she could.

Walking toward the kitchen she looked at the caller ID. It was Derek again!

She pressed talk and put the phone to her ear.

"Hello?" she said not bothering to veil her frustration.

"Oh hey Mysti," came Derek's smooth voice, "Everything okay?"

"I'm just trying to put a couple of kids to bed here," Mysti said.

"Oh sorry," Derek said, "So you don't have time to talk right now?"

"Well, I do now."

"Cool," said Derek, "Cause I'm waiting outside apartment 210."

What? Mysti thought. "What?" Mysti said.

"I was in the neighborhood."

"You live all the way up the hill in Hunter's Crossing," Mysti said, "And you were just in the neighborhood."

"My grandma lives in B building," Derek said, "I have dinner with her every once in a while…"

Awww, Mysti thought, Boy has dinner with his grams. She quickly shook off the warm fuzzies. Mysti's dad told her all about the things boys say to a girl. "That's nice," Mysti said, "But I'm not supposed to have boys over here."

"I'll stay outside the door," Derek said, "Promise. I just want to talk a second."

"Derek…"

"Look, whatever you're going to say can't you just say it to my face?"

And what a face it was. Mysti and Derek stood at the threshold to apartment 210. Right this moment Mysti was gazing into those light brown eyes. She had trouble keeping that same stern tone with him face to face.

"If Mrs. Daniels steps off that elevator," Mysti said pointing down to the elevator end of the hall, "And sees me standing here talking to you she will never call me to babysit again."

"First of all, the elevator isn't working right now I had to take the stairs. Number two, I'm outside the apartment," Derek stressed, grinning. "I could just be some guy- you know- a door to door salesman."

"Yeah? What are you selling?"

Derek suddenly broke into a spot-on imitation of J.P., dance moves and all, "Good Love," he sang, dancing up to her.

Mysti pushed him back and he burst out laughing, then stifled his laughter when he saw the look on her face.

"Are you drunk or something Derek?" Mysti chided.

"I'm sorry!" he whispered loudly, "Sorry, sorry sorry. And no I'm not drunk, girl. You think my grandma's going to give me a bottle of wine with dinner or something?"

Mysti could do nothing but smile and gaze at Derek. It's a good thing she was babysitting. She would have pulled him into the apartment and thrown him on the couch right then and there.

"You should go, Derek," she said finally. "And I should get back to these kids."

"I just want one more thing," he said and opened his arms.

Mysti opened her arms too and they hugged. Only he wasn't letting go. Not that she wanted him too. With Mysti deep in his arms, Derek started slow dancing with her now. "Good Love..." he sang in her ear, moving closer. Mysti remembered five words:

"It's where babies come from." Her father's voice rang as loud in her ear as the day Mysti had asked him the question. She was about six and the news was on. There was some scandal about a famous politician having "sex" with a woman besides his wife. Mysti had looked over her shoulder. Her father was in his favorite recliner doing the crosswords. Daddy, what is "sex"? Mysti asked. Her father looked up at her then at the TV then back at her. Nothing you need to worry about right now, sweetheart. He went back to his crossword then looked up again. Actually, there is something you should know right now. It's where babies come from. Anybody tells you babies come from doing something else they're lying. Babies come from a man and a woman having sex. That's all you need to know about sex right now. Her father then got the remote out, switched the TV to Nickelodeon and went back to the crossword.

Mysti pushed Derek away. "Goodnight, Romeo," Mysti said, giving him a theatrical wave. Derek tried to take a step toward her again but she backed off, readying the apartment door.

"A kiss goodnight, Mysti, please?" He put on this pathetic little boy face that Mysti saw right through. Boys.

"One more step and your kissing this door goodnight, dude," she stated.

Derek smiled then backed off. He blew her a kiss then did the "call me" gesture.

Mysti nodded and started to shut the door. Derek held her gaze and the two of them peered at each other in the ever-narrowing crack between the door and the frame. A sort of silent movie routine that ended as the door clicked shut. Mysti waited a second. Then she opened the door ever so slightly. Derek was no longer there. Then-

-Derek's face poked out from the opposite side of the door frame, grinning and cackling insanely! Mysti screeched and shut the door again.

And that's when she heard Huey crying.

"Dammit, Derek, you made me wake the baby!" she whispered and almost kicked the door. Maybe that would awaken Robbie too.

Instead, she turned and tramped back toward the baby's room.

By the time she got to the crib, the crying had stopped. Actually, it was a little stranger than that. The crying faded away. It got softer and softer until it was not heard anymore. Mysti barely noticed the phenomenon at the time. But she recalled it plain as day when she looked in the crib and moved the blankets around suddenly realized...

Huey was no longer there.

The baby was gone.

Chapter Three

Mysti then did what almost every mortal does when it realizes it has completely lost control over a situation. It summons its Creator: "Oh God!" she gasped.

Easy does it, a calming voice assured, *you just heard him a second ago and he's just not in the crib that's all, you haven't looked everywhere yet.*

Mysti's eyes darted around the room. If he fell out of the crib he couldn't have gotten that far. She looked under the crib. He was not in the room at all. But-

"Mysti?" a little voice called from behind. Mysti whirled around. Robbie stood at the doorway rubbing his eyes, "Is Huey all right?"

She immediately smiled and nodded, "Huey's fine honey I was just looking for another pillow to put in his crib isn't that right Huey..." She gently patted the empty blankets on the crib. Robbie was too short to see that the baby was no longer there. "Now get to bed sleepy-head," Mysti poked his little nose.

"Okay," Robbie muttered then turned and went back to bed.

Forty-five seconds later Mysti was pacing the kitchen floor tapping the cordless phone to her chin.

She should have never started the inner debate now it was eating her alive. She should look harder for the baby shouldn't she? He had to be somewhere in the tiny apartment. Somewhere she hadn't looked. Screw it. She held the phone out in front of her and dialed 9 then 1 then-

-she stopped and hung up again.

What was she going to say? That she lost Huey? The baby she was hired to take care of for one night? As soon as word about this got around she could forget about babysitting again. Never mind that what university was going to take a baby loser as a prospective candidate for a pediatrics degree? Mysti's future was-

"This isn't about you," Mysti said aloud, "This is about Huey."

And every second she waited counted for the worse! If there was ever a time not too self-centered this was it.

She dialed 9 then 1 then... 1...

There wasn't even a ring: "What's your emergency?" the operator's voice said.

"Uh. I- uh..."

"Take your time..." said the operator in a calm tone.

This just made Mysti more nervous. The words were hard to find and even harder to put together... "I am a babysitter and I have- uh... lost one of the kids- a baby. I am the babysitter and I lost the baby."

"A child has gone missing then?" the operator asked.

Mysti suddenly started to cry as she answered, "Yes!"

"What's your address, hon?"

Mysti told her between sobs.

"We'll get a car out there right away miss..."

"Thanks..." Mysti said and hung up. She noticed she was shaking.

Now for the really tough call.

Looking at the number on the fridge she hit the first six digits on the keypad then... to a deep breath... and hit the last number. She put the phone to her ear knowing exactly what she was going to say... "Mrs. Daniels you need to get back here I can't find Huey." Mysti was fully braced now ready for the consequences.

But she wasn't expecting what would actually happen.

Mrs. Daniels didn't pick up the phone. The line rang five times then Mysti heard Mrs. Daniels' pleasant outgoing message. Then there was a beep. Caught off guard Mysti sputtered, "Mrs. Daniels it's Mysti. You should call me back." She hung up.

Then Mysti sat down and cleared her head. All she had to do was leave on the message what she was going to say in person. Sheesh! Mysti picked up the phone again and hit redial. There was Mrs. Daniels' message, the beep and Mysti said... "Mrs. Daniels you need to get back here. I can't find Huey. I don't know how it happened but he just..." she felt tears welling up again, "He's just gone and I looked everywhere. Bye." She hung up again felt the tears stream down her face.

There she was in the baby's room again. With its bright colors and pictures of cute things everywhere, a baby's room looks very strange without the baby in it. Where could he have gone? She'd heard him crying too... just before she walked into the room.

Mysti stopped for a second. How could it be that she heard him crying right up until she walked in? Her adrenaline started racing. *He's under the crib!* she thought, getting more exciting. An infinite number of thoughts ran through her head as she got on her knees to look underneath Huey's crib. He's been under there this whole time! Boy am I going to be embarrassed and relieved when the cops get here! And is Mrs. Daniels going to be relieved when she finally calls me back!

But when Mysti looked she saw no Huey. Just a big empty almost immaculate space. That pit in her stomach that had just disappeared returned now, worse than ever. Mysti got to her feet again and was about to leave the room then she froze. Something was bothering her.

Mysti ran to the closet and, amid the diapers, baby wipes and tubes of antibacterial ointment, found a flashlight in easy grasp.

Mysti got back on her knees and shone the flashlight under the crib. In the dark corner where the wall and the floor met was a tiny glimmering spec. She grabbed the glimmering spec and held it up. It was a screw. Weird. She looked around the room unable to find anything that the screw belonged to. The rest of the floor had been freshly vacuumed too. People always clean like freaks before the babysitter comes.

A sense of dread crept across Mysti's face as she looked up. No... The vent just above the crib had been forced open.

Possessed by something she could not identify Mysti stepped up on the crib and studied the louvered vent cover. It was partially damaged. The lower left portion was torn off. And on the right side... a screw was missing. The screw Mysti was holding.

A gust of warm air suddenly blew out caressing Mysti's face. The vent cover clanked emptily from the air movement. Was something breathing on the other side of this vent cover? Like a little baby with too many arms and no head just a big mouth where its neck should be? Mysti took the bottom of the vent and, steeling herself, lifted it not knowing what to expect on the other side.

There was nothing on the other side, fortunately, or unfortunately, depending on how you look at it. At least if there was a monster on the other side she would be that much closer to finding Huey...

Only the first foot and half of the vent was visible. The rest of the metallic rectangular tube plunged into darkness. Gulping again Mysti shined the flashlight down the empty vent. About thirty feet ahead the vent took a left turn...

Mysti started to feel pretty damn stupid. Robbie had gotten to her at just the wrong time too. Mysti needed to keep her head. Logic was going to find Huey not an urban legend about some hideous monster baby! Mysti would just put the screw in then she'd get back to finding Huey and waiting for the cops to arrive. Hopefully, one thing would happen before the other. As she put the vent down she stopped and gulped. She lifted the vent cover again and looked at something that had been there the whole time.

A new kind of adrenaline took over now. Panic. Mysti's breaths were becoming shorter. Sweat had broken out on her brow.

And she couldn't think of anything to do right now other than to stare... at the tiny handprint just inside the entrance to the vent. She pointed the flashlight down the vent again and gasped in horror. Those tiny hand-prints spotted the entire length of the tube right down to the point where took a turn.

Chapter Four

Two minutes ago Sash Campbell was just hanging out in her room. An episode of "Whatever" was on but it was a rerun. So Sash was looking at her pink high-tops instead, which had been propped up on her desk. She'd been praying that one of her oh-so-busy-and-so-called "friends" would call her back so she'd have more something constructive to do. For example, gossip. But with her high-tops now planted on the floor and her phone to her ear she wished she could take that prayer back because:

A) Her best friend Mysti sounded absolutely insane and 2) she would not shut up, not even for one nanosecond.

"Hold up hold up hold up!" Sash cried into the phone silencing Mysti for that one nanosecond, "What the hell was that last part?"

"There was no blood," Mysti repeated from the other end, "All these baby handprints but no blood. You know what that means?"

Sash's brain was so gridlocked it could not even formulate the one-word response.

"It means," Mysti continued, "That Huey is still alive!"

"I'm going to hang up now," Sash finally said, "You're freaking me the hell out."

"Sasha Michelle Vernon!" hollered Mysti in a perfect and unintentional imitation of Sash's mom, "Do not hang up! I'm not joking. A baby has disappeared on my watch and I need your help. How soon can you get to Charlesgate Apartments?"

Sash mumbled something.

"What?" Mysti said more angry than insistent.

"Five minutes on my bike!" Sash yelled.

"Then stop talking and get over here!" Mysti yelled back and hung up.

"Bitch!" Sash yelled at the deadline.

Derek got excited when he saw who the text was from 0mystic1. He got even more excited when he read it. Four simple words: "come back need u". He nearly collided his mom's Lexus with a tractor-trailer as he spontaneously u-turned.   The truck's horn blared and he could see the driver flipping him off. Derek just smiled and waved back with all five fingers. If he understood Mysti's text right- and Derek Woods was rarely wrong about female behavior- tonight was about to get a whole lot better.

Mysti heard a knock at the door. Her hopes of it being the police were dashed the minute she heard Sash's yell: "Open up this hallway's dark!"

Mysti rushed to the door and opened it before Sash could yell again. And of course, the girl was listening to her old mp3 player. Probably at full blast too. Shaking her head, Mysti pulled Sash into the apartment. She put her finger to her lips and yanked Sash's earbuds out.

"Oww!" Sash hollered.

"Will you please?" Mysti said, "We've got a sleeping eight-year-old."

"Sorry, wow," Sash said rolling her eyes. She immediately went for the fridge. "They got any soda?"

"Sash," Mysti said trying to control her temper, "I lost a baby and I need to find him. No drinks. You are just here to keep an eye on Robbie. That's the eight-year-old. He is asleep let's keep it that way and when I find Huey I will buy you a 3-liter of whatever soda you want."

Amazingly Sash listened to that whole speech without interrupting or drifting her gaze to another part of the room. "So," Sash began, "No soda? What about food?"

Mysti pushed Sash into one of the seats at the table, "Why don't you catch up on your reading?"

"I don't have my books."

"Well I've got mine and you can use them," Mysti said trying to be patient, "After all we've got the same classes. Mi homework su homework. Okay,

224

I got to go. If the cops come, call me and I'll talk to them."

Sash rolled her eyes and started rifling through Mysti's backpack. "So," she said, "What am I supposed to tell this kid Robbie if he wakes up? If I tell him the truth he's probably never gonna sleep again..."

Mysti nodded. Good question. "Just tell him you're one of his momma's helpers and that his momma said he needs to get back to bed right away..."

Sash nodded.

Mysti turned the knob. In all her babysitting career she'd never left a child. But she knew Sash was better than nobody and really she had no other option at this point. Mysti opened the apartment door to head out...

"Hey Mysti?" Sash called out.

Mysti turned to Sash as the door closed.

Sash smiled, "Good luck girl."

"Thanks," Mysti said, "I'm gonna need it."

Standing at the elevator doors Mysti contemplated the system of vents in the ten-story apartment building, wondering where Huey was right now and if he was still alive. Looking around she noticed Sash was absolutely right. Even though there was plenty of lighting the D Building halls seemed so dim. It was like the darkness hid in them. Mysti punched in "were r u?" and hit send.

Derek's response was quick: "@ front door 2 sec."

"W8 thr", she typed then hit send.

Poor Derek, Mysti thought. He had no idea what he was in for. She wouldn't be surprised if he bailed on her right after she told him what was up.

Mysti pressed the call button for the elevator again. She'd been waiting a little while now and it still hadn't arrived. That's right, Mysti thought, Derek, said the elevator wasn't working. Mysti did not like the idea of walking out of a dark hallway and into an even darker stairwell, but she fought it and pushed the nearby stairwell door open.

She was relieved to find the stairwell a lot brighter than the halls thanks to an abundance of fluorescent lighting. She began heading down the stairs and stopped when she heard a familiar noise.

Scritch-scratch!

Mysti stopped, looked up and caught sight of a louvered ventilation cover. The noise had stopped.

Mysti stared at the blackness between the vent's slats. Was something looking back? A rat? A thingamabob? Nothing at all? She could not see. But she heard... breathing. Suddenly the-

-scritch-scratch!-

-noise started again making her jump.

It took all she had to unfreeze herself and move again but when she did she went twice as fast taking some of the stairs two at a time until she hit the bottom.

Outside the front door, Derek was confused. And a little creeped out. Not officially scared or anything. Concerned was the word. After all, Charlesgate was considered the tough part of town. Just for laughs, Derek tried to open the door. It wouldn't budge, not without somebody buzzing you in. He paced away from the door looking out at the parking lot. Just a bunch of crappy Fords and Chevys. And nary a Mustang nor a Camaro in sight. He paced back toward the door and flinched when he saw someone standing behind the door.

It was Mysti. She was trying to unlock the door. Derek was embarrassed and hoped Mysti hadn't seen him scared. She looked preoccupied. Very preoccupied. Uh-oh. This night was not going to go the way he'd previously thought.

Then Mysti opened the door, pulled Derek in, wrapped her arms around him and hugged him. Hey, this was going to go better than he'd previously thought!

"Thank you," she said sweetly.

Derek didn't answer just leaned in to kiss Mysti. But before he could do anything she broke away, looking at a sign on the front door.

"Uh…" Derek began. Mysti didn't let him finish.

"One more call," she said punching a phone number into her phone.

Derek looked at the sign on the door. It simply read: "Building Maintenance 24 Hour Phone Number…" followed by a local number.

"Hello?" Mysti said into her phone, "Is this maintenance? Yes, I need help… just… stay with me on this. I lost a baby… in the air duct."

Derek's expression dropped. He glared at Mysti.

"No this isn't a joke," Mysti said into the phone, "I need to know where the air duct from apartment two-ten goes because the baby I was watching got in there and disappeared." Mysti listened to the other end but she smiled weakly at Derek. "Okay, I'll meet you at the elevator."

Still smiling weakly at Derek she hung up.

"Uh…" Derek began again.

"I know," Mysti cut him off again, "I'm sorry. I don't want to be alone right now and I didn't know who else to call. Did you see a cop, any cop, drive by outside?"

Derek shook his head and shrugged.

"Where are they?" Mysti said loudly and to herself.

A rattling noise from the vent above made Mysti shriek and jump into Derek's arms again. The rattling turned out to be from the air coming on, nothing more.

"Mysti I started out confused," Derek said, "But I'm just plain wigged out now."

"So am I," Mysti said, face buried in his chest. "Please, Derek, just stay with me at least until the cops get here."

"You got it," said Derek. He rolled his eyes as he patted her shoulder.

A few minutes later they were standing at the elevator doors. Mysti had caught Derek up on Huey as they waited for the maintenance man, Mr. Cloves, to get there. He actually lived in C building so they wouldn't be waiting long.

"I just got one question," Derek said when Mysti was finished with the story, "How did a little baby get up in one of these vents?"

"I don't know," oh yes Mysti had not told Huey about Thingamabob, "Babies can get into some amazing situations..."

They heard footsteps coming from the entrance. Saved by the bell, Mysti thought.

"Hey," the man said to them as he rounded the corner. He was white, middle-aged and dressed in dirty jeans and a tee shirt. Mysti caught the stench of booze and cigarettes coming a mile away.

"Mr. Cloves?" Mysti said.

The man nodded and pressed the elevator call button and there was that hydraulic cough that Mysti had heard before. "Great," the man said, "Looks like we're taking the stairs tonight..."

The three of them were now standing outside the boiler room. Cloves jiggled the key inside the archaic padlock, loosening the ring.

"So is this-?" Mysti started.

"You wanted to know where the duct for two-ten leads," Cloves said impatiently, pulling the lock off the door. He pushed it open and there was pitch darkness on the other side. "It's a two story drop into this room." He reached into the room and flicked a switch. "Into the boiler..."

Mysti and Derek stared at the big red behemoth in the middle of the room. Looking up they saw the system of ventilation tubes branching out and up into the ceiling.

"The boiler..." Mysti said.

"Yeah," Mr. Cloves said.

Mysti felt Derek's hand on hers. He gave it a squeeze. Good man, she thought.

"Mr. Cloves, I'm like ninety-nine percent sure that baby's still alive," Mysti sighed, "And that it's somewhere in that vent between two-ten and here."

Cloves just raised his eyebrows, "How the hell are we gonna fit someone inside these vents? We're a lot bigger than a frigging..." Cloves looked up suddenly, listening.

Mysti and Derek listened now. They could hear it too. A low wailing noise. It was coming from outside the boiler room.

The three of them stepped outside the room and listened some more. The wailing noise, which could have easily been a cat as well, was coming from somewhere above them. But it was too distant to pinpoint.

"I don't believe it," Cloves said walking up to the closest vent grill, "It's coming from one of the ducts..."

"It's coming from down the hall!" Mysti said and bolted out of the door.

Cloves and Derek followed.

But as Mysti and Cloves disappeared around the corner, Derek stopped the second he heard a loud thump coming from behind him. He slowly crept back into the boiler room. He stared at the boiler's metal door. Listening closely he heard movement.

Out the hall and around the corner Mysti and Cloves stood beneath a vent cover. The wailing they'd heard before was booming now. Mysti's heart hammered in her chest.

"I still don't believe this," Cloves muttered, "How could a frigging baby get up in..."

The wailing stopped, silencing Cloves as well. Now, standing in the almost pitch darkness, Mysti and Cloves heard yet another noise coming from just behind the vent. Breathing. But not the kind a baby makes. Or anything natural. This breathing was deep and layered. Like it was coming from a bellows.

"What is up there?" Cloves echoed Mysti's thought as she thought it.

Mysti watched as he got a screwdriver out of his back pocket. As an afterthought, he took a retractable blade out and handed it to Mysti. "Hope you don't need to use this but better safe than sorry. It could be a raccoon with distemper. You never know."

Mysti couldn't even look at the knife. Her eyes were focused on the vent cover. Was there something looking at them from the darkness behind those slats? A raccoon? She had never heard raccoon breathing. But something told her this was not the what raccoon breaths sounded like.

Cloves began unscrewing the vent cover. The breathing stopped for a second then became a little faster.

Adrenaline, Mysti thought. From what though? Anger? Fear? Both? "Mr. Cloves?" she said, "We should wait until the police get here. This doesn't seem safe."

"What are you talking about?" Cloves asked incredulously, "Don't you want your baby back?"

"That might not be our baby, Mr. Cloves..." Mysti said, her voice cracking.

Cloves just went back to unscrew the vent. He was done with the first screw now and was starting on the second. Only two more to go.

"Mr. Cloves stop!" Mysti said.

Cloves turned and looked at her now.

"This is going to sound a little weird," Mysti began. "Okay really weird..." She couldn't believe she was actually going to tell Cloves about Thingamabob.

"Is this about that thing that lives in the vents?" Cloves shot out suddenly.

Mysti couldn't do anything more than give Cloves a relieved nod.

"Sheesh if I had a nickel," Cloves said and went back to unscrewing the vent cover. "Damn kids and your urban legends." He got the third screw off but it fell on the floor. As the vent cover swung on its last screw, Cloves went to pick up the one that just fell...

... not seeing the thing sitting in the shadows of the vent.

Mysti gasped in absolute horror at the twisted, faceless form behind the vent. It wriggled just up to the vent's edge and yawned from its torso-neck, revealing row upon row of razor-sharp teeth. The thing was basically a mouth with five or six multi-jointed arms. It was covered with... what, freckles? One of them blinked and Mysti realized they were eyes. Dozens of little pink hamster eyes.

Chapter Five

"Here it is," Cloves said lifting up the screw he just dropped. He gave Mysti a concerned look. "Hey kid," Cloves said gesturing to her legs, "You wet yourself?"

Mysti felt the dampness now. But she couldn't even speak. She just stared up at the thing in the vent. Those teeth were dripping with something clear and viscous. And from deep within the mouth something emerged. A finger. With a talon on its tip.

"You okay?" Cloves said. He took a step toward Mysti and behind him-

-the taloned finger whipped out and down in point two-five seconds. It was six feet long with a knuckle every four inches or so.   The talon disappeared behind Cloves' head and next second-

-Mysti heard a moist crunching noise and Cloves' eyes bulged. He gagged a little and dropped his screwdriver. Then there was an illusion... Cloves' Adam's apple seemed to grow, protruding from his neck like an extra nose. The illusion lasted only a moment then there was a pop! And Mysti found herself sprayed with blood.

What she saw next nearly made her pass out.

The taloned finger now emerged from the fresh wound in Cloves' neck. The finger had punched a hole in the back of Cloves' neck and pushed through the front.

"Oh God," was all Mysti could muster. She had long since dropped the knife and had lost the logic and motor functions needed to pick it up. She was just too damn scared.

The finger extended further out from Cloves' neck wound. The man's arms hung lifelessly by his sides. But he wasn't dead. His eyes were moving-blinking, darting this way and that... The lethal finger had caused enough nerve damage to paralyze Cloves but not to kill him. Not yet. The finger suddenly hooked up and poked Cloves between the eyes, just at the bridge of his nose. There was another sickening crunch as the finger broke through Cloves skull, pushing itself in. Cloves' face was getting more and more distorted like it was being filtered by some photo altering program. The ones that can make a face look "pinched" in the middle.

The finger seemed to tighten itself. It was now a hook burrowed though Cloves' neck and buried just below his forehead.

Mysti looked down. Cloves' legs had long since buckled. He was dangling on this horrific hook now, a puppet on a knuckled string. Then-

-Cloves was suddenly pulled up in the air-

-back toward the vent.

There was a violent clang as his shoulders hit the narrow opening. Then Cloves' body began to shudder and shake from whatever force was just inside the vent.

Mysti could not see what happened. She heard the sound of flesh ripping and bones popping. The wall below the vent began running with crimson. Mysti had never seen so much blood in her life.

I should be passed out by now, she thought. I should at least be throwing up.

No.

She should be running away. But she couldn't even do that.

Finally, the ripping and popping stopped and Cloves' body fell to the floor, where it slumped. Mysti stopped breathing.

Cloves' body no longer had a head! Just a very sloppy stump, collar bones and arteries poking out. The vent cover, which lost its last screw, now fell to the floor beside Cloves' headless body. Up in the vent was darkness again. The creature was inside the shadows again.

Now Mysti could feel everything begin to spin. She was about to pass out. Her phone rang.

A bouncing noise came from the vent now just before-

-Cloves' recently misshapen head rolled out. It plopped in his own body's lap and that is where it came to rest. The head was covered with that viscous saliva.

Mysti's phone rang again.

What a strange picture it was. The headless man cradling his own head in his lap.

On the third ring, Mysti looked at the caller ID. It was Sash.

Mysti looked up. She could no longer see anything up there. But she heard those scuffling noises again. They were moving further away.

The phone rang again.

The thing skittered further off until it could no longer be heard.

Mysti brought the phone to her ear, "Hello?"

But the call had already gone to voicemail.

"Mysti!" she heard Derek's voice.

Thank God! Mysti turned to see his silhouette turning the corner in the hallway.

She ran to him. In the glow of one of the exit signs she noticed now he was carrying something. Could it be...?

They met finally and Mysti nearly broke down and cried at the sight.

Derek had little Huey in his arms. He was moving, whimpering and most of all he was alive!

"Oh thank you, Derek!" Mysti said taking the baby. She gave Derek a kiss on the cheek. She noticed now the baby was covered in dust. And that same sticky saliva...

"Whoa, Mysti!" Derek said looking at her bloody sweatshirt, "You bleeding?"

Mysti's smile faded. "No. But we've still got a problem. A big one."

"What?" Derek asked.

"First of all", Mysti answered, "we have to steer clear of these vents."

"Why?"

Mysti stepped aside and pointed down the corridor.

Derek saw the body in the distance. He gasped when he noticed it didn't have a head. Then he double-gasped when he saw where the head was... "That's," he started, "messed up!"

"You don't know how messed up this is," Mysti said...

"So Thingamabob is real?" Derek said as they walked back up the stairs.

"You heard the legend too?" Mysti asked, "How come I never hear about these things?"

"You're too busy with your schoolwork."

"Well excuse me for caring about my future."

"Hang on a sec," Derek said stopping, "We've got the baby. There's a man-eating creature in the vents. What are we still doing in here?"

"You're right," Mysti answered, "You should get going. Try to find some cops or something..."

"What about you?"

"Sash and Robbie- Huey's big brother- they're still upstairs. I should go get them," with that Mysti started walking toward the stairwell.

"Hang on!" Derek said, "I'm not leaving your side until this is finished. Lead on."

As Mysti lead Derek up the stairs she noticed Huey was now fast asleep. Questions, questions, questions. How was Huey still alive? After what Mysti saw happen to Cloves it was hard to believe the worst hadn't happened to the baby, let alone the least. Had Thingamabob been holding the baby hostage? Did he need to have Cloves' head as an appetizer before devouring Huey?

"Derek?" Mysti asked, "How did you find Huey anyway? Was he inside the vents?"

"I heard him inside the boiler. Thank God the heat was off."

"So that was it?"

"He was all covered with that goop though, like, marinating in it..."

Like Mr. Cloves' head, Mysti thought. So that was it. Thingamabob's saliva maybe softened skin? Added a nice flavor to the meal?

They got to the second floor and headed down the dark hall toward room 210.

Mysti's phone rang. It was Sash again. Mysti put the phone to her ear. "Sorry I missed your call before, what's up?"

Sash's voice was sobbing on the other line. "Robbie's gone!"

Chapter Six

Up in Robbie's room, Sash was still crying as she and Mysti stood staring at his empty bed... just below the vent. Mysti had Derek hold Huey near the doorway, as far as possible from any of the vents.

"I went and checked on him right after you left," she said trying to maintain her composure, "Then I sat down and I swear I did not move. I could see his door the whole time so there's no way he could have gotten out. The windows are childproof and they're not broken. It's like he vanished into thin air!"

Mysti looked up at the vent again. The bottom two screws were missing and the cover was slightly bent. Then she looked down again at Huey's bed. Something was wrong.

"Why do you keep looking up at the vents, Myst?" Sash asked.

Mysti turned to Derek. He was staring at the vent too. He looked at Mysti now.

"Sash," Mysti said to Sash, "Have you ever heard of Thingamabob?"

"Depends," Sash said after a little pause, "Any relation to Whatchamacallit? Of course, I've heard of Thingamabob!"

"Well…" Mysti's voice trailed off when she noticed a small bump under Huey's blankets near the far edge of the bed. She felt the bump and uncovered it…

"What the hell…? A screwdriver?" Sash said.

Holding the Phillips head screwdriver Mysti stood back and imagined Robbie's eight-year-old frame, arms stretched as far up as they could go. He could have done it.

"He knew something was wrong," Mysti said, "That's why you didn't hear anything. If Thingamabob came for him he would have been screaming for his life. But he went up himself."

"Why?" asked Derek, incredulous.

"To save his little brother," Mysti answered.

"Time out," Sash said making the universal "T" hand gesture. "Uhh… you mean this Thingamabob stuff is real. Like, Thingamabob exists in real life?"

Mysti gave Sash the reader's digest version of the events leading up to now.

Sash suddenly moved as far away from the vent as she could.

The ensuing silence was broken by a loud knock door.

A second later Mysti was at the door, unlocking it. When she opened the door she breathed a deep sigh of relief. The police woman's badge read Velez.

"Thank God!" Mysti said then gave Officer Velez a piercing gaze, "What took you so long?"

"It's been a crazy night," Officer Velez said in her best apologetic tone, "And we're way understaffed tonight. I'm sorry. We got a report of a missing..."

"Oh the baby's fine thanks to Derek," Mysti said gesturing to Derek who was holding the baby, "But we've got another missing kid now and... a dead maintenance dude on the first floor outside the boiler room... umm. It's ugly."

At 28, Officer Lucinda Velez was still young. She hadn't seen enough to start writing people off like the older cops. So while she may not have believed the stories that the girl Mysti, her apparent boyfriend Derek (the one holding the baby), and her friend Sash (who could not put her cell phone away) told her- she believed that they believed. But she was sure by now her elder associates would have hauled the three of them downtown for drug testing. Hallucinogens, specifically.

"Please," Mysti said, "Robbie is still missing and every second counts."

"Well if there's something in the vents killing people and kidnapping children," Velez said, astounded that she could put that sentence together and actually say it, "There are only two places it could be. In the boiler room or on the roof."

"Roof?" Mysti said.

"Vents are vessels for heat and air," Velez continued, "There's probably an A.C. unit on the roof that feeds into the ventilation system as well."

Mysti looked relieved for the first time Velez entered the apartment.

"We'll find your boy, Mysti," Velez said, "But I should probably take a look at that, uh, dead maintenance dude so I can call it in."

"Let me get the baby carrier first," Mysti said taking Huey away from Derek, "There is no way I'm letting that baby out of my sight again."

"Fine with me," Derek said.

In all the excitement Mysti forgot to fill Sash in on the sordid details of Cloves' decapitation. Presently Sash was around the corner barfing.

"Unit one-eleven requesting back up," Velez said into her radio handset, staring at Cloves' body and the pattern of blood under the vent.

"What's your twenty?" came the dispatch's response.

As Velez reported her location, Mysti was surprised at Velez's ability to maintain her composure and remain business-like. Mysti had Huey slung in the baby carrier, holding him close. She kissed the baby's head and said a silent prayer for his big brother.

Derek studied Cloves' body more closely now. The tendons, the arteries, the... the... bones sticking out. What on earth could have done something like that? When Derek had heard the stories about Thingamabob, he remembered laughing at them...

"So what do we do until your backup gets here?" Derek finally asked, "The last time we heard Huey crying but..." Derek let the silence hand for a moment, "... I don't hear anything now."

"Not yet," said Velez, "But this, uh, Thingamabob will come home eventually."

"Which is where?" Derek asked.

"Either here or the roof. There are four of us..." Velez started, then winked at Huey, "and a half of course. So two head up to the roof, to the AC unit. The other two stay here in the boiler room."

"I don't know if Sash can handle it," Mysti said.

"She'll be on my team," Velez smiled, "She won't have to handle anything for long. Back up is on the way. I'm just sorry you kids had to see all this. Okay. Time to find Huey's big brother."

246

Velez walked up to Sash, "Let's go to the roof. You could use some fresh air."

Sash stood up and gave Mysti a weary look.

"It'll be okay, Sash," Mysti said.

Sash didn't look at Mysti, just shrugged and followed Velez toward the stairs. Mysti was going to have to take Sash shopping if they... when they survived this.

Crawling through the claustrophobic vents with nothing more than a little flashlight and a butter knife, eight-year-old Robbie Daniels felt like a hero from one of those late night movies. He may have been afraid of Thingamabob. But that's what bravery was. Being afraid to do something and doing it anyway. Because now it was personal. Robbie had overheard the babysitter and her friend talking about Huey. Robbie knew he was the only one who could fit in the vents. So, scared as he was, he took the initiative.

Robbie took another corner in the vent and shined the flashlight down. Nothing. Robbie kept crawling. He was going to find Thingamabob and get his brother back.

After about fifteen seconds, Robbie noticed he had been crawling in the same spot and nothing was happening. Something was preventing him from going any further.

Turning around he saw nothing in the pitch darkness behind him but he could see something wrapped around his ankle. A long finger. He shined the flashlight back there.

Thingamabob's hundred pupils all dilated at once.

Robbie wanted to scream but his mind was suddenly overloaded with something else. Thoughts that weren't his. Thingamabob was thinking to Robbie. Now Robbie knew that Huey was okay and that Thingamabob was playing hide and seek and Huey had found a really good hiding place. Thingamabob wanted to take Robbie to the inskinerator to play hide and seek also. Robbie sent the thought back to Thingamabob that he would die in such a hot place. So Thingamabob decided to take Robbie to the roof where it was cool. When they found Huey they'd bring him up there too. They could all hang out and be friends for a while. Robbie nodded as Thingamabob opened its massive mouth… and Robbie crawled backward into it until he was snug in there. Then, Thingamabob's many arms went into motion. They crawled onward then… upward.

A few minutes later Derek and Mysti stood just inside the boiler room, both keeping one eye on the incinerator's ominous metal door.

"So," Derek said walking up to Mysti, "The cop forgot the part about how we're supposed to kill it. She's got a gun what do we have?"

"Derek, I got Huey so if something happens you're the man…"

"I know," Derek said. He took her shoulders in his hands, "No pressure right?"

Huey began to whimper.

"I wish his mama would call," Mysti said bouncing a little. It quieted the baby a little. "What kind of mother would not even acknowledge that her baby was missing?"

"Maybe she was out of range?"

"Where'd they go, the Bermuda Triangle?"

"You know," Derek mused, "There's a couple of places in town where cell phones don't work."

"Like?"

"The supermarket?"

"Derek," Mysti said, "If a supermarket is your idea of a hot first date…"

"The Palace. You know that old theater downtown? My parents went there when my grandmother had her heart attack. They didn't know about it until intermission."

"Oh my God," Mysti said, "He took her to the Palace!"

"If that's the case," Derek said looking at his watch, "Mrs. Daniels won't know she got a message until quarter of ten."

Mysti rolled her eyes.

"Hey," Derek said, "This is pretty funny you know. Me, you and this baby and we haven't even been out on a date yet. Officially you know."

Mysti looked into Derek's caramel colored eyes. She started to melt. Mindful of the baby, they leaned toward each other... and kissed. It was long and slow. This boy can kiss, Mysti thought.

The beeping from Mysti's cell phone put an end to their little moment.

"Mysti..." Sash's voice was low, husky like she was whispering. Silence.

"Sash?" Mysti said putting Sash on speakerphone.

"I'm on the roof..." Sash whispered.

"Yes," Mysti said, "...and?"

"The cop lady's dead," Sash said, "Thingamabob killed her..."

Chapter Seven

Derek's eyes widened and for the second time in her life, Mysti's blood ran cold.

"Ripped her in half," Sash's voice went on, "Right in front of me!"

"This better not be a joke," Mysti said.

"He can't hear..." Sash said, "I-I think he's deaf. If I don't move he doesn't see me either so his eyes aren't so good either. I would have run a long time ago believe me."

"He's still there?" Mysti asked.

"He's just sitting inside this big vent thingie sticking up on the roof. The cop pulled the cover off and now she's in two pieces..."

"Sash do you see Robbie?"

"No..." Sash's voice was cracking badly.

"Listen," Mysti said, "See if you can get the cop's gun..."

"I can't move or he'll hear me! My phone's on silent now so just text me from now on."

Both Mysti and Derek instinctively put their phones on silent.

Mysti led Derek down the hall toward the stairs.

"Okay, okay," Mysti said, "We're coming up! Just sit tight..."

"I'm not going anywhere!"

Mysti gave Derek a hopeless glance, "Forget this I'm calling Mrs. Daniels again." Mysti dialed then-

She and Derek froze when they heard a cell phone ringing... It was behind a wall... from somewhere above them. Mysti hung up. The ringing stopped. Mysti hit redial. They heard the phone start ringing again. It was coming from the elevator.

Derek absently hit the call button and they heard the hydraulic cough. He hit the call button again. Again the hydraulic cough. One more time and...

... the elevator doors opened. The ringing was louder now.

Derek stepped into the elevator and there was a squishy noise. "Uh-oh," Derek said looking down. Mysti looked down to and gasped. There was a puddle of blood forming on the floor. Droplets were falling from a corner of... the opened vent.

On the speaker, they heard Mrs. Daniels' voice: "This is Clare Daniels. Please leave a message." Mysti hung up.

Huey started crying and Mysti started bouncing again.

Derek grabbed onto the vent and pulled himself up. Unlike most of the other vent covers, this was wide enough for a person. For a second all Mysti saw was half Derek's torso and his legs.

"Flashlight, Myst!" he waved at her.

Mysti reluctantly got the flashlight out of her sweatshirt pocket and put it in Derek's hand, which disappeared back up into the vent.

Silence and stillness that seemed to go on forever...

"Derek?" Mysti said, bouncing the increasingly fussy Huey.

Finally, Derek slid back down facing her. At first, Mysti thought he was looking at her. But he was looking through her. It was like he had seen a ghost.

"Did Mrs. Daniels have her dad with her?" Derek asked.

"No," Mysti felt disconnected from her own voice, "That was Phillip. Her date."

"Thingamabob must have pulled the two of them up through the vent," Derek said. "The old guy got- uh, taken apart. Like a doll. Looks like... he's in five or six pieces. One of the pieces is caught in the elevator pulley. That's why it's not moving."

Despite the immediate onset of nausea, Mysti kept gently bouncing Huey, who was almost asleep again.

` Derek went on: "Mrs. Daniels is in one piece though. Got a big black and blue on her head and her ears are bleeding."

"A concussion. So she might still..." Mysti stopped bouncing Huey- who began to cry, louder than ever. Mysti started bouncing again and he quieted down.

That's when Mysti and Derek heard the moaning coming from the vent. It was soft but high-pitched.

Mysti got under the vent, "Mrs. Daniels?" she shouted up, "Can you hear us?"

Silence again.

"Take him," Mysti unhooked the baby carrier put Huey in Derek's arms.

"What...?"

"Shhh..." Mysti said to Derek.

Disoriented now, Huey began to cry. The moaning came from above again.

Mysti took her flashlight back from Derek and stood under the vent. She jumped up awkwardly grabbing the vent opening, trying to hang onto the flashlight at the same time. She tried to pull herself up but couldn't. "Crap!" Mysti said.

"Here," Derek said crouching underneath her, "Stand on my shoulders."

Mysti's feet found Derek's shoulders, "Be careful…"

"Yeah, yeah," Derek said, "The baby's fine."

Once Mysti's feet were planted on his shoulders Derek slowly stood, pushing Mysti up through the vent.

A pungent smell hit Mysti's nostrils… blood. At first, the flashlight's beam found Phillip's "pieces". Limbs, a chunk of torso. Mysti avoided a distant mass correctly assuming it was Phillip's head. She didn't need to see two of those in one night, thank you. The elevator pulley was jamming on what appeared to be a shoe. With a foot in it.

She didn't want to look anymore but Mysti craned her neck shining the flashlight behind her. And there laid the twisted body of Mrs. Daniels. One of her legs rested at an impossible angle. She was facing Mysti but appeared to be unconscious. Nonetheless, she moaned when Huey's cry came from below.

Mysti felt tears coming. "Mrs. Daniels", Mysti said, "We're going to fix this…"

Derek crouched again, lowering Mysti, who finally jumped off his shoulders and faced him. She looked at Huey and shook her head.

"Maybe Officer Velez's back up will be here soon," Derek said.

"It's going to take a lot of back up don't you think?" Mysti said. She lifted her phone and texted Sash.

A second later came Sash's text, "Still here"

"What about Thingamabob?"

"Rolling around in vent," Sash texts read, "Can't see him but hear him in there"

Mysti looked up at Derek, "Get Huey out of here Derek."

"Me get the baby out?" Derek said in disbelief.

"I've got to try to save Sash," Mysti said, "She's my friend."

"She's my friend too!" Derek said, "You're the babysitter remember? You can't not sit the baby..."

Mysti took Derek's shoulder, "Every second we're in here our lives are in...", still holding the flashlight, she pointed it forward-

-and there floating in the darkness, just a few feet away, was the most insane face Mysti had ever seen!

Both she and Derek shrieked. Huey began crying again.

"What the hell's going on over here?" the face yelled. It belonged to a white woman in a bathrobe. As she approached, Mysti and Derek both recoiled at the rank smell of alcohol on the woman's breath.

"Who are you?" Mysti yelled back.

"The maintenance man's wife!" she yelled again, "Where is he?"

Mysti's phone vibrated twice and Mysti looked at the screen as Sash text came in: "Tbob stopped moving"

"What's happening?" the maintenance man's wife didn't yell now. She spoke very quietly and kept staring at Huey.

"Maybe we should just show you…" Mysti said.

A moment later they were standing in front of what was left of her husband. Mrs. Cloves let out a wail of sorrow as she looked down at the mutilation.

Mysti and Derek tried to control her but she was beside herself with despair and rage. Needless to say, Huey was awake and crying again.

"Who did this to him?!" she turned to Mysti and Derek backing them off two steps. "One of you better start talking! Is he with your friend on the roof?"

Mysti could barely nod at the woman. Derek moved in front of Mysti who instinctively clutched Huey close to her.

"Why isn't anybody doing anything?!" Mrs. Cloves shouted over the baby's crying, "Where are the cops!?"

"The first cop already came and she's dead now," Mysti said.

"There's more on the way..." Derek tried to sound reassuring.

"To hell with this!" Mrs. Cloves screamed and stormed back toward the staircase.

Mysti bounced Huey some more but it wasn't working. She looked to Derek for help. Glancing at Huey, Derek noticed something in the pocket of the baby's pajamas. He reached into the pocket and produced... a binky. Mysti sighed in relief as Derek put the binky into Huey's mouth. As soon as the baby started sucking he was quiet again. Derek gave Mysti a look that said "not bad for a dude huh?"

This little moment ended with the sound of glass shattering from the stairwell. Derek ran toward the sound with Mysti walking briskly behind. He disappeared into the stairwell entrance and by the time Mysti got to the entrance, Derek was already bounding back down the stairs to her.

He came up to Mysti and took her shoulders again and looked her dead in the eye, "Crazy white lady's got an ax."

Chapter Eight

Sash was crouched in one of the roof's corners, holding her knees to her chin. She'd been in this exact position for the past thirteen minutes, which turns out to be a long time to hold an uncomfortable position.

Officer Velez was in two pieces. Velez had lifted the cover from the AC vent and there was Thingamabob. Although the creature had no facial features (or anything that resembled a head for that matter), Sash could sense by its blood-curdling scream and the way its arms flailed that Thingamabob was scared. Then, in a second that lasted forever, Sash saw the explosion of blood and gore. She heard the tearing of flesh and the cracking of bone. It only took one second. Using two of its multi-jointed arms- which telescoped from his body in a nanosecond- Thingamabob had grabbed Velez by the shoulders and tore her in half like a telephone book... not symmetrically though.

To Sash's right was the half of Velez's body that had her head and spine, to the left was the half with just an arm and a leg. That was the side with the gun, which Sash did not dream of taking to defend herself for fear of being noticed.

When it had happened Sash panicked and stumbled backward falling to the ground. Thingamabob seemed to sense this and rose out of the vent toward her. Terrified, Sash froze and at once Thingamabob looked confused. It started moving around as if trying to see what happened to Sash. When Mysti blew up her phone the first time Sash thought she was a goner. But Thingamabob did not react to the noise. Nonetheless, Sash muted her phone.

After a few more seconds Thingamabob lowered itself letting the AC unit cover came back down to cover the vent again. Thingamabob seemed to roll around inside the vent for a few minutes, like a tiger in a cage. But there hadn't been any movement for the past two minutes.

Her phone vibrated making her flinch. Sash slowly brought the phone to her ear.

"Sash you there?" Mysti's voice said, "Talk to me."

"I haven't moved," Sash whispered, "Neither has Thingamabob. Btw, what happened to texting?"

"Listen," Mysti said, "There's a lady coming up there. The wife of the dead guy. And she's pissed and… she's got a… a break-glass-in-case-of-emergency ax."

Sash pressed push-to-talk and asked nonchalantly: "Does she have a gun too?"

"Uh, no," Mysti answered.

"Then she. Is going. To die," Sash said matter-of-factly.

"Sash you have to take a chance and hide or something," Mysti begged.

"I'm not moving and I am very mad at you for bringing this all on me tonight," Sash said, "You hear me Mysti?" No answer. Sash looked at her phone. Dead battery. Didn't matter. The hell with Mysti.

Sash looked over at Velez's dead face now. Her eyes were open and she had the same quizzical expression on her face that she did when she approached the vent. Velez never knew what hit her. Sash shuddered.

In the quiet, she heard the first thing that made her relax. The sound of police sirens in the distance. Velez's back up was finally coming.

That sound was overtaken by footsteps coming up the stairwell accompanied by isolated mumbling. The pissed off lady with the ax was coming to meet her doom. Sash decided to turn her head away so she wouldn't have to see the pissed off lady die.

Mrs. Cloves got to the rooftop door and shouldered the door open with all her might. The door banged against the wall as she stepped out onto the roof, brandishing the emergency ax.

The first thing Mrs. Cloves saw was another young black girl crouched in the far corner of the roof. The girl's head was turned away. Mrs. Cloves also saw the two halves of a policewoman. Entrails, blood, broken bones. Whatever it was that did this was badass all right. But it had never met Mary Cloves neither.

Walking past a large vent that stuck straight up from the roof Mrs. Cloves approached the young girl. "Where is he?!" Mrs. Cloves barked almost slipping on the police woman's blood, "I murdered for my husband before I got no problem with it. Now where the hell is the man who killed him?!"

The young girl was scared now. But she didn't move her head. She just pointed at the vent and said, "Wasn't any man."

Mrs. Cloves didn't have time to play games. The vent? She walked back toward the vent and awkwardly readied the ax with her right hand. With her left hand, she flipped the vent cover open. It wasn't as heavy as it looked so it flopped over to the other side no problem. Now...

.... Mrs. Cloves stared into the pitch darkness. She looked up at the young girl again. "What is this some kind of...?"

Suddenly Mrs. Cloves felt two small arms around her neck and shrieked. She pulled away from the arms and raised the ax over her head again as she looked at...

... an eight-year-old boy with an anxious look in his eyes.

The girl, presumably the boy's babysitter suddenly bolted to her feet: "Robbie!" she cried, running up to the vent and taking the boy in her arms. His Captain Spaceman pj's were covered in some gooey substance...

Mrs. Cloves then felt two sinewy arms grab her in a bear hug from behind causing her to drop her ax.

"All right," a calm voice said. It belonged to the young man downstairs. Derek, "We all need to calm down here."

What the hell is going on? Mrs. Cloves thought as she looked up.

As if he read her mind the boy Robbie stared straight at Mrs. Cloves and pointed at her. "He wants to see you down in the inskinerator..." was all he said.

Derek let go of Mrs. Cloves and took out his phone out when Mrs. Cloves suddenly knocked the phone out of Derek's hand. Derek watched the phone bounce off the roof as Mrs. Cloves scooped the ax up again and rushed out the doorway.

By the time Derek sprang after her Mrs. Cloves was already down the first flight.

Neither Sash nor Derek had responded to Mysti's calls.

The sirens were getting closer now. Just a few more minutes. But did they have a few more minutes?

Still carrying Huey, she got to the boiler room's entrance and immediately realized she had nothing to defend herself and the baby. An explosion of hot air from the boiler room made Mysti scream out loud. Huey started crying too again.

Mysti walked down the hall and around the corner to Mr. Cloves' remains. Trying to hold herself together she pulled the screwdriver out of Cloves' dead hand. It wasn't much but it would do.

She started walking back to the boiler room, never once noticing the rash on Cloves' decapitated head. Under Thingamabob's gooey residue hundreds of little freckles were forming. Only they weren't freckles at all...

Mysti got to the entrance to the boiler room. Another hot air gust came from just on the other side of the door making her flinch.

"Okay Mysti," she said out loud, "Let's just do this."

The sound of Huey sucking on his binky gave the moment a comedic twist it probably didn't need. Mysti gave Huey a kiss on his head and pushed the door open. It did not creak like in the scary movies. But beyond the door, it was just as dark. The sparse lighting from the hallway did no good here.

There was another gust from the boiler's incinerator and now Mysti saw a burst of flame from behind its metal grill.

Mysti slowly reached in and flicked the light switch.

The boiler stood directly in front of her. The incinerator door was at eye level.

"Time to get this over with Thingamabob," Mysti said holding out the screwdriver which would be no match for whatever was on the other side of that incinerator door.

The incinerator answered her with another burst of flame. Almost like a dare.

Mysti said a little prayer for Huey now but figured it was fate that Huey be here with Mysti and that thing behind the metal door.

She reached out for the door's handle. It was a thick heavy mechanism that also unlatched the door. She grabbed the ancient handle, lifted and pulled. Mysti learned the hard way that doors like this were designed back in the day when the workers wore safety gloves. Because Mysti's hand began to burn, so badly it brought tears to her eyes. She resisted crying out. Not upsetting Huey had become job number two here.

She shook her searing hand by her side. The air wasn't cooling her hand very well but Mysti's focus was on the darkness inside the incinerator. As soon as that next burst of fire came it would illuminate him. He had to be in there somewhere.

"Come on Thingamabob," Mysti said, "Come out and..."

The feeling on the back of her neck stopped her from finishing the sentence. At first, it felt like it could have been a bug. But it was definitely a fingertip with a long nail growing from it. Mysti did not move. For a moment her burnt hand didn't even bother her. The nail scraped along the back of her neck, then the back of her head, running over her hair. Beads of sweat broke out on Mysti's forehead. Her heart started hammering in her chest and her breaths got shorter and shorter. Pressing Huey closer to her she closed her eyes feeling hot tears welling and out. When the fingertip reached the top of Mysti's head Mysti decided to open her eyes. Keeping her head perfectly still she looked up.

A ventilation tube passed directly overhead and she was standing directly below a louvered vent cover... from which the multi-jointed finger dangled. It cascaded over Mysti's head down onto her face. It caressed her nose, her lips, her chin. It kept heading down until it found Huey's head. Mysti's mouth went dry as she saw the fingernail move gently back and forth across the fontanel.

Then the finger stopped abruptly and began reeling back into the vent cover.

Mysti now craned her neck up to get a better look. In between the slats, all she could make out was darkness. It was in there staring back at her she knew it. The finger disappeared into one of the slats.

Mysti realized she had stopped moving. She had stopped breathing. It was like she was in some kind of trance. The voice behind Mysti nearly made her jump out of her own skin.

"Where is he?!" Mrs. Cloves hollered, standing at the door, ax in hand. Tears were pouring from her darting eyes.

As if to answer her question there was a clatter from the ventilation tube above them. Thingamabob was crawling toward the incinerator.

Mysti instinctively stepped back as Mrs. Cloves closed in on the incinerator now.

The fire in the incinerator flared again, Mysti had seen Thingamabob before but she still gasped. In the brief glow, she could see just how misshapen, how disfigured, how wrongly born Thingamabob was.

Mysti clenched her burned hand.

And yet Thingamabob was sitting inside a container that reached temperatures up to twelve hundred degrees Fahrenheit.

Mrs. Cloves raised the ax and pivoted herself for maximum leverage, aiming for the thing Mysti had just seen in the glow of the ember.

"You've been nothing but trouble since the day you were..." Mrs. Cloves started bringing the ax down, intending to punctuate her sentence with the crunch of a deathblow. But the sentence went unfinished along with her swing. The ax fell to the floor and Mrs. Cloves gasped.

Mysti couldn't tell at first what happened but took a good guess. Her guess was confirmed when she saw a spot of blood on Mrs. Cloves' back. Then from that spot of blood emerged the fingernail, then the fingertip, then... the rest of the finger.

"No," Mrs. Cloves whispered, then shouted, "No!"

Mrs. Cloves fought a good fight. She struggled every second but was not even remotely a match for the thing in the incinerator. The multi-jointed finger coiled up around Mrs. Cloves' hips. Then circled around her shoulders and her neck like a harness. And there was nothing she could do to stop it.

"Oh God!" she screamed, "Oh God please help me!"

Mrs. Cloves was then hoisted into the air and, kicking and screaming, pulled slowly into the incinerator door. Of course, Mrs. Cloves was a little too wide to fit. So Thingamabob made her fit.

To Mysti's horror, the finger tightened its grip on Mrs. Cloves' shoulders, breaking them along with her collar bones. It was compressing her body so Mrs. Cloves became narrow enough for the incinerator's small doorway. Mysti heard three loud snaps altogether. Mrs. Cloves' body finally, mercifully went limp on the third snap.

Thingamabob repeated the "compression" move on the woman's hips as it pulled the rest of her into the incinerator.

Mysti waited until she saw Mrs. Cloves feet disappear inside. Then... she slowly moved toward the incinerator again.

Mysti would always wonder what made her see the dial protruding from the boiler. She didn't know what part of her brain recognized it as a thermostat. Nonetheless, she reached up with her already burned hand and turned the thermostat up until the dial could not move anymore. This caused the incinerator to light up again. Only now it continued to burn. Mrs. Cloves' body and clothing were eaten by flame.

Careful of the baby, Mysti moved closer to the incinerator and made sure... She had to see. It was a gut-wrenching experience watching the woman's body disintegrate in the heat. And behind Mrs. Cloves she could see Thingamabob at the rear of the incinerator. It was still intact. But Mysti saw a slight movement. Thingamabob slumped.

He and his mother were together again. The crawler could finally rest.

It was the last movement Thingamabob made before he began to burn as well. Like he had willed himself to perish in the fire now. Skin peeled off the incomplete torso, limbs and that gaping mouth where neck and head should have been. Then the flesh began to blacken, revealing bone and sinew. And now even that began to bake into brittle, crumbling dust.

With her burned hand Mysti shut the metal door and relatched it.

She looked down at Huey who had not awoken the whole time they were in there. He was such a good baby.

"I hope my babies are as good as you," Mysti said to him as she walked back out of the boiler room.

Ninety seconds later there two police cars, three ambulances and two fire engines parked outside D Building. Other tenants began to gather round.

Mrs. Daniels had her own ambulance.

Mr. Cloves, Philip and Officer Velez were loaded in many garbage bags into a car simply marked 'morgue'.

The police were already curious about Mrs. Cloves. Mysti directed them to the boiler room and already told them they would find nothing but dust.

About a half hour later Mrs. Daniels' sister got there and took Huey and Robbie. Robbie wanted to stay and tell the police all about how Thingamabob got scared, that was why he killed the cop lady. But Robbie'd had a long night and should get some sleep.

Mysti, her hand bandaged now, answered the questions as best they could and the police seemed satisfied at the end of the night. They were already talking about an animal, like a mountain cat that could have gotten stuck up in the vents.

Sometimes the truth is so much stranger than fiction, people just stick with fiction because the fiction feels safer.

Whatever. It was almost eleven. Sash hugged Mysti and Derek goodnight and decided to get a ride home from the police, one of whom Sash noted was "real hottie". Mysti rolled her eyes and smiled.

Derek and Mysti faced each other. Mysti looked into those light brown eyes. She could just lose herself in them. Not quite yet though. Derek put his arms around Mysti and hugged her close.

"You are one hell of a first date," Derek said.

She pushed him away laughing. "That was not a date…"

"We already married?" Derek said with a wink. He couldn't help himself. He moved in again, lips on a collision course with Mysti. A car horn suddenly broke his concentration. Mysti and Derek turned to see…

Mr. Hayes… Mysti's dad. He taught night school so he always picked Mysti up after he was done teaching. As Mysti ran to her father's car Mr. Hayes waved to Derek, who waved back politely.

Just before she got into the car Mysti turned to Derek and said: "I already decided I'm never marrying you, Derek."

"Why not?" Derek looked completely offended.

"Because then my name would be Mysti Woods," Mysti said, "No thanks!"

When Mysti got in the car her father was still staring at all the emergency vehicle.

"Oh my God," Mr. Hayes said looking at Mysti's hand, "What the hell...?"

"Dad I just figured out the perfect birthday present for you."

Mr. Hayes looked at Mysti.

"A cellphone."

A minute after the Hayes car drove away two things happened.

One. An EMT bringing out the remains of Mr. Cloves noticed something very disturbing about the severed head. It had grown hundreds of little eyes. Pink ones. Like a rabbit.

Two. While holding Huey, Mrs. Daniels' sister thought Huey felt strange. Like there was too much of him. Tomorrow she would notice the extra arm growing from his back.

END

Made in the USA
Middletown, DE
01 December 2020